CORALEE TAYLOR

I Choose You, Charlotte

Ties That Bind Series- Book Three

First edition

ISBN: 979-8-9914100-1-4

Cover art by Coralee Taylor
Illustration by Coralee Taylor
Illustration by Canva

This book was professionally typeset on Reedsy.
Find out more at reedsy.com

To everyone brave enough to give a second chance. Sometimes, it can be the best decision of your life.
And if it's not... you can always buy a baseball bat.

To my forever, none of this would've been possible without your love and support.
I've loved you since I was 16, and I'll continue loving you for as long as the stars shine in the sky.

BCM4Ever

PS– Thank you for chasing me after the whole movie theater debacle.
Who would've thought that night would be the start of our story?

Contents

Content/Trigger Warning

This book contains scenes that may be triggering. Please refer to the content warnings below. This list may not be all-inclusive. Your mental health and safety is important. If you feel that any of the below items would harm you in any way, this is not the book for you. Read on safely, my friends.

Triggers may include:
 Drug Use
 Self-harm, Suicide, or Suicidal
 Thoughts
 SA/SV/Dub-Con/Non-Con
 Abuse
 Death/Death of a Parent
 Mental Health
 OWD/OMD
 Miscommunication
 Hospitalization
 Forced Medication/Drug Use
 Stalking
 Murder
 Kidnapping
 Fertility Issues
 Overseas Conflict
 Deployment (Contractor)

Medical Trauma
Violence
Eye Stabbing
Minor SA (mentioned, not described)
Alcohol Abuse
Profanity (A LOT of it)

Prologue

November 2005

Jason

"I told you she was bad news, Jay." Jade says as she pats my knee, her words dripping with condescension. Her fake concern pisses me off even more than usual. I roll my neck from side to side. The crushing tension is suffocating me.

I abruptly move to a standing position and let the photographs fall off of my lap and land on the floor of the RV. The black-and-white memories scatter like the ashes from a dying fire.

My beautiful girl. The sweet, sad girl who gave her body and heart to me. The girl who I could envision beside me for the rest of our days... and she fucking betrayed me.

I stare down at the fallen snapshots. Charlotte looks radiant. Her eyes are bright and alight with laughter, and a sly smile plays across her luscious, pouty lips.

She gazes down at the hand resting on her thigh in reverence. He stares at her like she hung the fucking stars in his sky.

I know that look. I have that look. He's in love with her.

They seem cozy together on the loveseat. Arms embracing one another as she nuzzles into his neck.

Their lips are nearly touching as their eyes are firmly locked on each other. Giving no thought to the bustling environment of The Coffee Hut around them.

His other hand rests delicately against her cheek, and his eyes pierce into her, telling her everything he feels for her without words.

This is how she chooses to punish me? The moment things don't go her way, she jumps into the waiting arms of that douchefuck from the movie theater? Hell no. I thought she put that fucker to rest eight months ago. She chose me. Didn't she? Has she been playing me this whole time?

I took Jade's words with the hefty grain of salt that they deserved. The ramblings of a jealous ex-girlfriend. But how can I ignore the photographic evidence she thrust into my lap?

Loyalty is everything to me.

I didn't think she'd go to this extent to show me how pissed she was that I went on this trip. I didn't have a fucking choice. Why couldn't she understand that? This is an annual tradition. It's not like I wanted to go on a cozy, romantic vacation with my ex.

These fucking pictures.

I kick the pile and walk to the RV's attached bathroom. Jade says something to my back as I walk away, but I can't deal with her right now. She just imploded my universe, and though she's trying to act concerned, there is definitely a smug air about her.

She's told me over and over that Charlotte was bad news. That the pretty popular girl doesn't go for the grungy outcast.

Our story was never meant for a happily ever after.

vii

* * *

I'm tired, and I'm fucking sore. A whole week is too fucking much to be camping, hiking, fishing, cutting wood, and all the other lumberjacky shit my family had me doing over the last seven days.

"Son, I'll finish putting the camping gear away. You need to go in and get presentable. We have company coming over at six." Dad says as he reaches forward to take the handle of the foldable chair from me. I hold on to the strap tightly as I look over at him and tug it closer to my body. "I am very much over company, Dad. I just want to put this shit away, grab a shower, smash my way through a can of SpaghettiOs and sleep for three days. So if you'll–" my words drift off as I yank the strap out of his hand and blow past him to put the chair with the rest of them in the garage.

"Hang it a little higher to the left." I hear my mom say as I round the corner into the kitchen. A giant banner spelling out *CONGRATULATIONS JASON AND JADE* in alternating red and gold letters hangs crookedly against the wall.

"Uh–" I sputter out.

"I said to the left, Nic!" Mom shouts at Jade's mom, Nicola. She completely ignores my presence and continues to dictate directions to Nicola.

"Mom!" I shout, and finally, she turns to face me. Her face crinkles in annoyance at the interruption, and she huffs out a breath. "What is it, Jason?"

I gesture to the shit on the walls, "What the hell is this?" On the left side of the banner, a bundle of red and gold balloons hangs just a tad too close to the "C". My mom is just enough of an organizational psycho not to leave it like that.

"Jesus Christ, Nic, move it up like just a pinch and to the right just a tad."

Nicola laughs at her friend's bossiness. "Are those specific measurements you're providing, Nora?"

"Nic!"

"Okay, okay. How's this?" Nicola asks as she follows Mom's instructions to the best of her ability.

"Yeah, I guess that'll do. Where is the bag with the other items for the table?"

My mom and Jade's mom continue to ignore my presence as they lay out decorations on a tabletop and busy themselves with trays of snacks.

Walking over to the table, I pick up a red and gold lanyard. *ASU Sun Devils.* Does that mean—?

My dad walks by and claps me on the back while holding a thick, already-opened envelope. "Congrats, son; you're a Sun Devil now."

I'm a quarter of the way through a bottle of whiskey when a knock sounds at my bedroom door. I ignore it and take another swig. I can't believe that asshole not only applied to ASU for me but then had the balls to open my fucking acceptance letter. The only reason I'm entertaining this bullshit is so he pays the bill. That's the trade-off. He foots all four years, and I attend his alma mater. He must've pulled some serious strings to get results this fast. I haven't even gotten a chance to talk to Charlie about it. I thought I had time.

Another knock sounds at the door. I ignore it once more.

The door slowly creaks open, and Jade's face appears in the crack. I'm about to tell her to fuck off when I see heavy streaks of black lining her cheeks.

"J-jay? Can I come in, please?" she stutters out between

gasps of air. Her voice is thickly laden with tears. She doesn't wait for my response before she pads into my room and sits beside me on my bed. Her head tips over onto my shoulder as she begins sobbing.

A heavy sigh breathes out into the space between us as I lift my arm around her shoulder. She immediately tucks into my chest, and I rest my cheek on top of her head. I wait in silence for her tears to slow so I can find out what the hell is going on.

"I texted and called you..." she softly informs me. I tip my head back against the headboard and huff a humorless chuckle. "Sorry. Seems I've lost my fucking phone, hopefully not in the middle of the woods. When we were packing up the campground, it was the last time I remembered putting it in my back pocket."

"Oh."

The silence between us fills the room. A soft rendition of an old Metallica song plays on my stereo, and I wait for her to speak.

"My grammy, Jay. She...she's gone." She whispers to me. *Oh no.* Her grammy is everything to Jade. The only member of her family who treats her like a human and not some prized trophy to be auctioned off to the highest bidder. I've always wondered if my family's money ever had anything to do with her parents always trying to push us together.

I tighten my grip on her shoulder, giving it a gentle squeeze in comfort. "I'm so sorry, Jade. What happened?"

"Heart attack. Smoking two packs a day for fifty years finally caught up with her. I don't know what to do, Jay. I feel so lost. How do I go on in a world without Grammy? My aunt didn't even tell my parents. She knew they wouldn't care."

I've never been great at death and emotions. I never know

what to say, and I just feel awkward. So, I offer the thing I know would make *me* feel better.

* * *

A sharp noise stirs me from my drunken slumber. My eyes are drier than a dusty chalkboard, and the Jack that went down so smoothly last night is now sitting heavily in my stomach. Acid burns in my throat when I take a deep breath. Fuck.

The heaviness against my chest and stomach is too much to bear as my stomach contents threaten to make a reappearance. The warm body against me gives me pause for a moment. *Jade's Grammy.* As I look down at her sleeping form, I want to jerk away from the girl who should definitely not be in my bed, but I feel so bad for her.

Slowly, I remove myself from her grip and pull the sheet up to cover her. Once my limbs are free, I lay back and close my eyes, taking a moment to try to figure out what happened after we started sharing the bottle back and forth. I know there were a lot of tears from Jade. A lot of swearing from me as we had yet another discussion about Charlotte stepping out on me.

I move to sit on the edge of my bed while a merry Polka band performs loudly against my frontal cortex. I definitely wasn't thinking about the hangover that would accompany downing almost half a bottle of whiskey. Shaking my head slightly, I try to dispel the ache inside, but it only makes it worse. I need a piss, a whole pot of coffee, and a hot ass shower, in that order.

My knee cracks loudly as I move to a standing position. My entire fucking body is sore from all the moving of equipment and apparently sleeping in the same position all night. I take a small step before my foot gets tangled in a pile of clothes. *Damn, did I not put anything away last night?* I kick them off to the side, and as my gaze traces back up toward my bedroom door, the world freezes on its axis.

My girlfriend stands wide-eyed with a top-less McKinley Gulp clenched tightly in her hand.

Oh, fuck. *Jade.* I snap my gaze back to the bare-backed girl who doesn't belong in my bed before frantically coming back to Charlotte. *Fuck.* How do I explain this? I reach my hand out to her, wanting to pull her into me and keep her from getting the wrong idea. *Is it the wrong idea? I can't fucking think with these Polka fucks bashing around in my head. What happened last night?*

Her head shakes frantically, and she darts out of the room. I immediately chase after her, "Charlotte!" I scream. The sound is another cymbal beat against my hungover brain. She continues to run right out the front door. I have no shoes on but fuck it, I can't let her leave like this.

I catch up to her at the end of our gravel driveway. She bends down to grab the keys that fell, and I reach out to her, gently touching her shoulder to turn her around. A lump forms in my throat as I try to form words. "Baby, please," I beg, though I'm not really sure what I'm begging for.

Her normally angelic, soft features harden with anger. Her nostrils flare as she opens her mouth. I know nothing good is about to happen. "Please, what, Jason? Are you about to spin me some bullshit like there's any possible fucking reason for you to be half naked, tangled in bed with someone who is not your goddamn girlfriend? Do you think I'm that fucking dumb?"

Charlotte walks closer to me, tipping her chin up to pierce

me with a glare. I hold back the tears that want to roll down. "Go on, *baby*, tell me those sweet lies. Explain this away."

What can I say? I know it looks bad. What fucking happened last night? I need a moment. I need the fog in my brain to clear so I can string two fucking thoughts together to figure things out.

My eyes squeeze shut as I try like hell to fight through the haze of my memory. The pain in my head is damn near crippling at this point. I open my eyes to look at her, and a tear leaks down. I guess I'll start with what I know. "Jade's grandma died a few days ago. She was upset and crying, and she asked me if I would comfort her by holding her," Fuck, it does sound bad.

Is there any way I can phrase this better? Jesus. It all looks bad. If she weren't an ex, it would be more acceptable. But because they already have bad blood, this is really not good optics. I've been taking too long to answer because Charlotte gestures for me to get on with it. I reach out to take her hand, and she jerks away from me. "Don't fucking touch me. Keep going."

Okay, think. What happened? "She laid in bed with me, and I held her while she cried. We had both been drinking..."

"Tell me nothing happened, Jason." She demands. *Fuck. Think. What happened? Bed. Bottle. Music. Anger. Tears. Laughter.*

"Jason. Tell me. Nothing happened, right?" she urges.

Why can't I fucking think? My heart feels like it is going to burst out of my chest. The tears freely flow down my face against my will as I search my brain high and low for the information she's asking of me.

"Tell me!" She screams.

Tell her, man. Fuck. What happened? Nothing, right? Right? Bed. Bottle. Music. Anger. Tears. Laughter... and? Fucking blank. Nothing.

The words feel like ash as they softly come out. "I can't." I can't in good conscience tell her something I don't fucking know for a fact right now.

The hurt and betrayal marring her beautifully freckled face is another stab to the heart. I search my mind for something to say, anything to make this better. All thought leaves me when I see her lift the McKinley cup. I have no time to speak or move before she lunges forward and empties its contents in my face.

My body is frozen in place momentarily. What the hell just happened? She takes off running to her car. "Charlotte!" I scream after her. I don't know what to say; all I know is that if I let her leave, this is the end.

The car door slams as she gets inside, and I don't even think. I just run. I slam my hands against the driver-side window. Her body jerks with the sound, but she doesn't look at me. *Come on, baby, don't give up on us. Come on, look at me.*

Her body shakes with the force of the tears, and it guts me. All I want to do is take her out of this car and into my arms. The car finally starts, and without looking back at me, she slams her foot against the gas pedal and flies down the street.

I stand like an asshole staring after her car in the middle of the street, not giving a fuck who's around.

My tongue snakes out across my lips and gathers some of the liquid dripping down my face. Blue-motherfucking-raspberry.

* * *

The Day Before Thanksgiving 2005

I call Charlotte for the eighth time. She doesn't pick up yet again. It's been four days since slush-geddon, and she still refuses to speak to me.

When I returned to my house, I showered the sticky slush off of me and downed several cups of coffee. Then, I made my way back to my room to speak to Jade.

When she removed my sheet off her body, and I saw her clothes or lack thereof that she was wearing, I was fucking pissed. She had no business being dressed in such little clothing in my bed. When I lifted her pants from the floor to throw at her, my phone miraculously made an appearance. Right out of her fucking pocket.

I sat her down and made her walk me through the last night's events. We didn't fuck. Thank God. She says I kissed her. I think she's full of shit. But since I have no recollection, I have to assume that no matter whose fault, we must have lip locked in some capacity. Fuck!

I kicked her out. My dad drove her home and glared me down the whole time he walked her out of the house. He's a bit too protective over her. It's weird.

Shaking off the lingering anger I feel toward Jade, I open up the text thread with Charlotte and send her a message.

Me: We need 2 talk.

Though I didn't fuck Jade like I'm certain she thinks, I did cross a line, and I need to own up to that. I also need to ask her where the fuck she gets off having that kind of reaction and won't speak to me when I have evidence that she was sleazing around.

No answer.

In fact, she never answered me again. She pretended I didn't exist. Jade clung to me like a bad smell, and I know rumors went around that we were a thing again; we weren't. But I like to think it bothered Charlotte to hear that, and I'm a little fucking angry at her right now, so maybe she deserves a little hurt and jealousy. I've had to watch that fucking football douche pine after her for the last few weeks. It's taken everything in me not to get him in a dark corner and beat the living shit out of him.

I may not have a claim on Charlotte anymore, but I damn sure don't want to see another guy's hands on her. Or think about her fucking someone else. Just the mere thought fills me with rage.

* * *

January 2006

It's my last day at RHS. I can't stand to walk the same halls as Charlie and not be able to speak to her or touch her. She's getting closer to that blond-headed prick, and she's been spotted with Poole. He's bad fucking news, and I don't know what possessed her to befriend that shithead.

The rumors going on about the two of them set my blood on fire. They can't be true. There's no way the girl who lost her virginity to me only months ago is giving it away to any fucker who looks in her direction. There's no fucking way she's blowing him in the parking lot. Part of me thinks Jade may be the cause of some of these rumors, but I can't prove it.

I tried to distance myself from Jade, but my dad threatened to pull funding for college. I don't know why the hell he cares so much. It's like he wants her close or something.

I've worked my ass off to have enough credits to graduate a year early, while I'm pretty sure Jade's been buying her grades so she can as well. I broke down and begged my mom to convince my dad to let me finish out the school year at home.

I gave her some bullshit about wanting to get prepped for college and spend time with her before I take off. She, of course, bought it, and I don't know what she said to Dad to get him to agree, but I don't really give a shit. They agreed, and that's what matters.

The truth is, my fucking heart is broken. I've held on to my anger over these last couple of months since the breakup, if you can even call it that. But I fucking love Charlotte. I never got a chance to tell her. And now, I never will.

I don't feel like attending the rest of the classes for the day, so I make my way to my locker. Might as well clear it out and turn my books in.

I rummage through my locker and throw most of the shit away. I have no need for it anymore. Once everything is cleared, I stare at the now empty vessel. *Where the fuck is my hoodie?*

Slamming the metal door, I spin around and start down the hallway when a door ahead flies open so hard it slams against the wall behind it.

A very angry and homely-looking Charlie storms out of Mr. Vale's classroom and stomps down the hallway. I watch her for a moment, frozen with indecision. This could be my last chance to talk to her. Maybe we could hash everything out. I can explain what did and didn't happen with Jade, and she can tell me why the fuck she was cozied up with her ex.

She stops at her locker and drops her bag and books. She

starts to walk away before I gather the courage to call out to her. "Charlotte?" I ask, hoping I don't sound as timid as I feel.

Her shoulders bunch up, and her spine snaps straight at my voice. She doesn't turn to face me. Instead, she thrusts her right hand in the air and flips me the middle finger. "Nope, not today, Satan. Go fuck yourself!"

I heave a breath as I watch her walk away. My head shakes as the anger begins to creep in again. Fuck her. She can't even spare a goddamn minute for me? Fine.

* * *

June 2006

It's hotter than the devil's nutsack in Arizona. I was fucking chased by a scorpion. *Chased.* That's right. Lucifer's pet came after me on a goddamn sidewalk. I hate this place already. Dad got an off-campus apartment for what I thought was just me, but surprise, the brown-noser was moving in, too. Why is she fucking everywhere in my life?

I'm thinking about getting a summer job at the Fast Lube down the street. I cannot be locked in that apartment twenty-four-seven with Jade, or I will lose what's left of my sanity.

On the plus side, I made a little collage out of the pictures of Charlotte and the ex. I may have carved out his eyes and given him devil horns in each one, but it gives a certain demonic essence to the death of my relationship. I thought it was only fair to immortalize it.

I couldn't stand to see Charlotte's glowing face, so I scratched hers out. I no longer have any photos to remember her by. Who am I kidding? Her likeness is burned in my memory. And, should that ever fail me, I have page upon page upon motherfucking page of sketches of her. Some, she's simply staring off into space. Losing herself in her mind. Her mask slips a bit, and I capture it. And in others, she is lost in the throws of passion as she rides my cock.

Those are my favorites. Not for the reasons one might expect. Though, yes, Charlie is objectively attractive and makes the sexiest orgasm faces, but that's not what draws me to them. It's the freedom. For those moments, she is completely herself. No mask. No shield. No lies. All raw, open, honest.

* * *

December 2007

"I fucking said no, Jade. What don't you get? For one thing, I'm casually seeing somebody. For another, I told you when we moved here almost two years ago, and each time you've tried to crawl into my bed since, it's never going to happen." She really thought walking into my room wearing a push-up bra and red lace panties was going to change my stance. This girl doesn't ever fucking learn.

"Get out, Jade."

"But Jay, come on. I'm horny, and I just need you. It doesn't have to mean anything. Please?" she whines as she begs for my dick.

"There's a store downtown that has everything you could need to get yourself off. It's not going to be my cock. Not now, not ever."

I'm harsh on her because I have to be. If I give her an inch, she will take ten miles. The tactics she's tried have been ridiculous. It's always something. She's sad. She's angry. She's celebrating. She got dumped. She got a bad grade. She got a good grade. She's simply horny. Always something.

She swings her hips exaggeratedly as she strolls to my bed. She crawls on all fours and makes it halfway up my body before I press my palm firmly against her chest, stopping her movements. She leans into the touch and glides her fingers across my very flaccid dick. I grab her hand and squeeze hard enough to capture her full attention. "I said no." I growl at her and give her a small shove backward.

"What will it take, Jason? I bet if I dyed my hair blonde and acted like a junkie slut you'd fuck me, huh?" she fumes as she scurries backward to get off my bed. Junkie slut? What the hell is she talking about? I open my mouth to ask her as much, but before I can, she storms out of my room and slams the door behind her.

* * *

January 2008

"Did you know, Jason?" My mom demands. She showed up at my apartment moments ago and looked like she wanted to punch me when I opened the door.

"Did I know what?" I ask flippantly. *Always with the dramatics.* I take a sip of my water as I wait for her to answer.

She narrows her eyes at me and folds her arms across her chest. "Did you know that your father has been sticking his dick in that precious little girlfriend of yours?"

I inhale a shocked breath that collides with the water in my throat, temporarily choking the shit out of me. When I can breathe again and make words come out, I ask, "Do what? What are you talking about?"

"Yeah. He thought he was slick. But I know, Jason. I went through his office, and I found a long history between them."

I wouldn't call Selena my girlfriend. She's a casual fuck at best. We've both agreed on no strings.

"You!" Mom cries as she shoves past me into my apartment. When the shock wears off, it occurs to me that she currently has a fist full of *Jade's* hair, not Selena's. What the hell?

Before I can make my way over to separate them, my dad comes flying in through the front door and launches himself between them.

"Don't!" Jade shouts as my mom fights past my dad to attack her. Mom is acting like a rabid animal, and I'd be a little scared if I were Jade.

"I'm pregnant!" She shouts through tears at the top of her lungs. Those words pause everyone's movements.

My dad snaps his head back to look at me and glares. "You knocked her up?" he seethes.

I laugh, and his face turns a brilliant shade of crimson. I need to try to replicate that in a sketch later. "I'm not the baby daddy. No way."

"Contraceptive isn't always one hundred percent effective, son. You need to step up and accept responsibility."

I shake my head back and forth, a small smile that I can't help on my lips. "Ain't possible. I haven't fucked Jade. Ever. So no, I don't need to accept shit."

His head swings back over to Jade, his rage now pointed in her direction. "I thought you were going to sleep with him weeks ago? You stupid, stupid girl. Can't you do anything right?"

Jade's cries fill the air as my mom and I watch on in stunned silence. We both try to piece together what's going on here.

"I t-tried! He wouldn't go for it." Jade blubbers.

It was an enlightening meeting. We learned that my dad had been fucking Jade since well before she was eighteen. He, in fact, knocked her up, and when she told him, he came up with the brilliant plan for her to seduce me and pass the kid off as mine.

But the kink in that plan is I wouldn't touch her, which I guess was a little tidbit she forgot to mention to him.

There was a lot of shouting and crying between all three of them. I was pretty apathetic to the whole display. The thing that got me was when Jade threw in his face that she had driven a wedge between me and Charlie like he'd asked her to do.

Turns out, Charlotte wasn't fucking her ex. She was simply having a conversation, and Jade purposefully took photos that made it look more than it was.

My dad then spit some truth about Jade purposely getting me blackout drunk. While she merely sipped on the booze. I was too fucked up and in my head to notice. They fucked in his office, and he sent her to my bed in her underwear. I was already passed out when she climbed in and laid against me. We did have a kiss that she initiated. While I was sleeping. When I couldn't reciprocate, she gave up and went to sleep.

Cops were called. My dad was arrested. He'll be extradited to Alaska to answer for his crimes of statutory rape. Mom will be filing for divorce, seeking full custody of Alex, and making it as painful as humanly possible. Thank God Alex was able to stay in Alaska at his friend's house. He may be fifteen now and probably has an idea of how fucked up our parents are, but this is overkill.

I kicked Jade out and withdrew from school. I took a solo road trip and ended up in Mississippi. I've let my facial hair grow out over the last couple of years, so I easily pass in bars. I hopped from one to another before I met Randall Jacobs.

Randall works for a private contracting firm that operates in undisclosed locations overseas. Always on the move. Often in danger. Making a shit ton of money. Hell fucking yes I agreed when he offered to hook me up with a position.

* * *

March 2008

"Donovan, we're doing shots. Bring your ass over here!" Jacobs shouts in a slur at me. I turn from the blissful currents of the ocean and look at him. He's joined a party of co-eds that are having a bonfire on the beach.

I inhale another deep breath of the calming sea air before turning back to join him. He tosses over a beer and shoves a breasty blonde at me. I catch her and straighten her up before she falls. She giggles, and I introduce myself. She smiles wide at me, licking her lips as if she can already taste my cum running off of them, "I'm Natasha."

So I fuck Natasha on the beach. Then take her back to our hotel and fuck her again. She gives me her number, and since I'm leaving in a little over a week, I say fuck it. She can be my bang buddy until we ship out. Saves me the hassle of trying to find it elsewhere.

The next day, I showed up at her dorm a little earlier than expected. I knock on the door, with my arm resting on the door frame, ready to devour her whole and then get the fuck out of here.

But instead of the busty blonde, I am greeted by a very angry, tall, curly-headed woman I never thought I'd see again. "Savannah?"

She punched me in the fucking mouth. When the shock wore off, she dragged me into her dorm, helped me clean the blood off, and handed me some ice.

I explained everything to her. I held nothing back. When I got to the part about fucking Natasha, she punched me again. The first one was free and deserved. Now she's pissing me off.

She didn't want her roommate, who happens to be the busty blonde, to come and interrupt us, so we took a walk around campus. To be honest, after being punched in the face *twice* and rehashing the shitshow of my last two years, my dick wouldn't stand at attention with all the blue pills in the world.

Several hours and tears later, Savvy stares at me. She inspects me for way too long before asking, "Did you love her?"

"I still do." I respond with heavy regret and longing.

She stares at me some more before nodding. There is a conversation going on in her head, but she seems to have come to a decision.

"Don't make me fucking regret this, Gothic Boy." She warns as she puts the phone to her ear.

I

Part One

Chapter 1

March 2008

Jason

Why are my hands sweating so fucking much? I really should have practiced what I was going to say.

The shaggy rainbow rug beneath my feet bears the pattern of my shoes from pacing back and forth.

Thank fuck, the roommate is out of town. I don't even have the bandwidth to deal with that nightmare. Even though I'm very single and didn't do anything wrong, something just feels wack about trying to beg the girl of my dreams to forgive me and take me back while the last chick I got my dick wet in is standing across the room. Could just be me.

I don't even know how to thank Savannah. Even if Charlotte gives me the third punch in the face and bails, at least Savvy gave us a chance. No one's opinion means more to Charlotte than hers.

The last week has been fucking torture. I've spent ninety-nine percent of my time thinking about this moment. Under normal circumstances, I'm not one to back down from confrontation or speak my piece. But this is no normal circumstance.   This fucking terrifies me.   More so than thinking about what awaits me on my impending deployment. I will have one shot.

One shot to clear the air.

One shot to plead my case.

One shot to get her to listen.

One shot to change our lives.

I run my sweaty palms over my black cargo pants. A smile curls up my lips as I remember dancing in the wind with Charlie on top of Sky Ridge. The wind would fill the legs of my rave pants, and she would beam the most mesmerizing smile at me. I loved to make her laugh. In those moments, the real Charlotte peeked out.

"Yes. Savs. Why are you being so weird? You're the only person in this world I can trust wholeheartedly. I know you would never do something to hurt me." It may have been two years since I've heard the melodic tone of my first love's voice, but I'll never forget it. My heart instantly picks up pace at the sound of Charlotte on the other side of the door. *Fuck, please don't let her punch me.* I instinctively bring my hand up to the bump on the bridge of my nose.

As the door knob begins to turn, the world slows down. I'm sure if I could take my eyes off the shiny metal, birds would be suspended in flight outside the window. Co-eds would be frozen in mid-stride as they make their way across campus. "I'm so glad you put it like that, Charls. Keep that in mind."

A short-haired Charlie is shoved through the door frame. Savvy winks at me before slamming the door shut in her face. Charlie clumsily stumbles to gain her footing and takes a deep breath. As her hand reaches for the knob, I clear my throat. Her movements come to a stuttering halt.

4

It's now or never, Jay. Let's get our girl. "Hey, Sweets." I greet her with more shyness than I intended.

Her body slowly turns in my direction. There's a split second before our eyes meet that I think maybe she will be so happy to see me that she'll leap into my arms. We'll share a tight embrace, admit our still-present love for each other, and skip off into the sunset.

A split second before the absolute horror across her face tells me that scenario is the furthest thing from her mind.

Disappointment washes over me as I watch the mask that I fucking hate slide into place. Some things never change. Always trying to hide herself. *Doesn't work with me, sweet girl. I see you.*

Her shoulders stiffen as her back snaps straight. Ever the proper vision of an acceptable young lady. The short hair whips out of her face with a tight shake of her head. The strands fall in line, just as she's trained them to. Everything in its place.

The nerves running through my body find an outlet in my hands. They flap perpetually against my thigh without permission. She is the only person who brings out my stims. Sometimes, if I get really stressed or angry, it happens, but never with just the presence of a person—not until her.

"No." She quickly snaps with a hand held up between us in a *stop* motion.

Before I can utter any words, she spins back around and begins pulling on the door knob. Her concentrated effort, while futile, is also fucking adorable.

"Savannah. Open this fucking door. Now." Charlie seethes at her best friend through the closed door.

A snicker from the other side and the lack of turning of

the knob tells me that Savvy is definitely on the other side of that door holding the knob and putting all those years of competitive cheerleading to use. Charlie doesn't stand a chance at out-muscling Savvy.

"Remember all those sweet things I just said to you? I take them back. All of them, Savs! You're Lilith, and you've locked me in here with the fucking Devil!"

I suck in a faux-offended breath between my teeth, "Ouch."

Charlotte snaps her rage-filled, spicy chocolate eyes at me, and I can't help the smile that takes over my lips. I clutch my chest so she can see the faux offense is coupled with a faux stab to the heart.

I probably shouldn't have smoked that bowl earlier. It may have calmed the nerves too much.

After several more futile attempts at out-smarting Savvy with a ruse of leaving the doorway only to pull as hard as she could when she thought Savvy let go, she finally seems to wave the proverbial white flag. In the form of a huff and a double middle finger to the door while mouthing "fuck you".

Charlotte storms past me and unceremoniously plops herself down on the bed on the noticeably tidier side of the room. I assume it belongs to Savvy, but it's not like Natalie and I did much talking. Natalie? Is that right? Nadine? Nephernie? What the fuck kind of name is Nephernie? No, it was definitely Natalie.

I dismiss the unimportant blonde's name and soak up being surrounded by the scent of vanilla and sugar. Fuck. The smell goes straight to the core of my being. Warmth settles throughout my body. It's not sexual. Though, she still gets my dick hard. The last couple of years have been hella good on her physique. But no, it's more than that. It's a familiarity.

6

It's a comfort. It's *home*.

"So." I nervously whisper to the space between us. All words have seemingly left my fucking brain.

She doesn't acknowledge me in the slightest. A ping sounds out from her ass. Charlie pulls out her cell and scowls at the message on the screen before picking up a large, veiny, hot pink, stuffed dick at the door and shouts, "You're dead to me!"

I try–and fail– to get a peek at the screen before she locks it and throws it behind her. "Was that a–?" I don't even get the full question out before Charlie scoffs and cuts me off. "A big fucking cock? Wow. Look at you, fucking detective of the year." She sarcastically claps while ripping on me. I'm just happy to hear her speak. The sass doesn't bother me a bit.

"Oh, you poor, fragile man. Is it hurting your feelings? Do you want me to hide it under some blankets? I'm sure it's embarrassing for a guy to see what a huge cock looks like." She asks, her voice dripping with snark. I know she thinks she's taking jabs, but all it does is make me want to bend her over my knee and watch that pert ass of hers turn a delicious shade of scarlet.

Before I can stop myself, I lean in close enough that my breath causes goosebumps to erupt over the skin of her neck. "You know damn good and well I have nothing to be jealous over. You have close, *personal* experience, remember?"

She fights to appear unaffected and leans close to my face. Our lips nearly touch as we breathe each other's breaths in and out. Her tongue traces a path over her bottom lip, and her lips part, "Oh, I remember. I also remember that I'm not the only one with close, *personal* experience."

Her arm pulls back, and I instinctively flinch and shut my eyes tight. When a third punch doesn't land, I peek open one eye to find Charlotte giving me a very judgy side-eye.

"Did you think I was going to hit you?" she questions with a snort.

Hell yes, I did. "Nah, I was just fighting back a sneeze." I feign nonchalantly as I fold my arms tightly across my chest.

"Sure you were. Why the fuck would I hit you? From the healing bruising around your nose and eye, it looks like someone beat me to it."

Tread lightly here, Jay. Let's hit her with some humor to diffuse the tension. "Well," I clear my throat and force my arms to relax their grip on each other. "The last time we spoke, you hurled a giant slushy in my face. Excuse me if I'm a little gun-shy with your sudden movements."

An immediate sneer takes over her once indifferent face. *Fuck. Abort, abort, abort!* Charlotte springs to her feet and fists her hands at her hips. "I feel like a slushy to the face was the nicest thing I could do to you after finding out you cheated on me—" She stomps over and picks up the stuffed dick. "And you're wrong. That wasn't the last time we spoke, but I'll tell you the same thing now that I told you that day."

The stuffed penis catches me off-guard and slaps its swollen mushroom tip against my mouth. Damn, that girl has got a good arm on her.

"Not today, Satan!" She shouts as she storms towards the door again. This time it opens. Before she fully crosses the threshold, she turns back to me, "And Jason? You should be jealous. I bet that stuffed peen could get me off better than you ever did. I hope you have the life you deserve."

She slams the door shut behind her. Leaving my jaw practically on the floor. Damn, sick burn.

8

Charlotte

How fucking dare he! My blood boils as I stomp down the asymmetrically patterned carpet toward the elevators. The flowy laughter of my best friend makes my feet move double-time in her direction.

Savvy remains completely unbothered as I get in between her and the nerdy dude she was chatting with. With my body blocking him entirely, she leans past me to dismiss him. "Clearly, my *rude* best friend needs me right now. I'll text you later, and we can work on that... thing."

The guy skitters away without a second glance, and I seethe while Savs smiles brightly in my face.

"So... how'd it go?" she gushes with excitement.

"*How did it go*? Are you for fucking real right now, Savannah? Never mind why the fuck Jason just happens to be in Florida and in your goddamn room, but you honestly thought I'd want to speak to the first man who broke me?" I'm trying as hard as I can to remain strong and let anger rule my reaction, but I feel the stuttering in my chest and the burning of the tears behind my lids.

Savvy cocks her head at me, "Uh, did you guys not talk?" she asks, seemingly puzzled.

I shake my head at her and pull away in disgust. "Why the hell would I want to talk to him? You know what?" I make an about-face and storm over to the bank of elevators. Savvy hollers at my back as I jab my finger against the call button repeatedly. "I thought you trusted me." Genuine hurt laces her words, and they're so confusing that they slap me right in the gut.

My best friend walks up behind me and gently pulls my

9

finger away from the button, turning me to face her. Smirk long gone, she bends down slightly to put us eye to eye. "Charls, I wouldn't have put you in that room if I didn't have a good reason. Do you or don't you trust me?"

My shoulders sag as I peer into her distressed eyes. "I do." I whisper, resolute in my answer but worried about the panic rising to the surface.

Savvy turns us back toward her room and cups my shoulder as we walk. We stop in front of her door once again, and she leans down to press our foreheads together. "Talk to him, Charlie. You both need it."

Putting every bit of faith and trust into my best friend, I take a deep breath and nod. "Okay. I'll talk to him. But before I go in, I just need to know one thing..."

She nods softly at me, urging me to ask the burning question on my mind. I jerk my head toward the door and point my thumb at it. "Was that bruise your handiwork?"

A sly smile forms across her mouth, she straightens back up, and a cocky aura falls around her as she answers. "No one hurts my best friend."

I giggle and throw my arms around her, embracing her tightly. "I fucking love you, Savs."

She pats my butt and pushes me toward the door, gently this time. She bends to my ear as she turns the knob and whispers, "And I hit the prick twice for good measure."

Chapter 2

Charlotte

When I walk back through the door, this time of my own volition, the sight of Jason slumped over with his head in his hands itches at that hole that used to contain my heart. As quickly as the concern hit, the memory of Jade's tight ass in his bed shows up, and now I kinda want to hit him a third time.

His head snaps up when I clear my throat. His eyes are glazed and red. Was he crying? I scoff, "Jesus. No need to cry over your jealousy of Richard Head."

Jason narrows his eyes and purses his lips together before he asks, "Who the fuck is Richard Head?"

I tip my chin in the direction of the edge of the bed. He follows the path and barks out a loud laugh. One that clearly caught himself off-guard. "Ah, Richard. Also known as Dick. I get it."

I shrug and give him a smirk. His eyes lock onto mine as I make my way toward him. I stop when we are toe-to-toe. "So. Whatever witchery you've done on my best friend seems to be working in your favor. She wants us to talk. So, talk."

A slight vulnerability crosses his sharp, handsome features. "And you? What do you want?"

I move to sit beside him, close enough that our thighs almost touch. I sigh, "I kinda want to get a swing in. I'm not gonna lie; I'm having a bit of FOMO."

"FOMO?" he asks.

"Fear of missing out." I respond and bump my shoulder against his. He leans into it and bumps me back. "Well, if anyone is deserving of a swing..." he responds with the tiredness of a man who bears a heavy weight on his shoulders.

I pat his thigh, trying my best to avoid the warm tingles that shoot through my fingers at the touch. "Don't worry. I prefer to inflict violence with my mouth, not my fists."

He splutters for a moment and chuckles to himself.

"How hard is it for you not to make a dick joke right now?" I ask.

"So hard. So very hard." He answers with a playfully pained tone. He opens his mouth to continue his response when my stomach lets out a very loud and embarrassing grumble. I latch my arm around the noisy organ in hopes he somehow didn't hear it.

"Hungry?" Well, clearly, he heard it. I nod. "I haven't eaten since last night." His brows knit together in concern. Can't have him thinking on top of all my other problems that I've also developed an eating disorder. "I'm a nervous flyer. It's best to keep all solids out of my tummy before getting on the tin can of death."

He nods his head slowly, his eyes making a slow perusal around my face. A slight smile ticks up on the side of his mouth. "What?" I ask, feeling exposed and uncomfortable with the way his gaze always seems to pierce through my armor.

"Can I take you to dinner? We can calm the tummy monster and talk. Two birds. One stone."

I debate his question internally for several seconds, he doesn't rush or push me. He has to know how fucking difficult this is for me. My stomach lets loose another growl, making the choice for me.

"No fucking seafood." I stand and glare down at him when he laughs at my demand.

"Sweets, I know you hate seafood. I hadn't imagined that changed. How about some Italian? I passed this amazing-smelling restaurant on my way over here."

I shrug my shoulder, pretending I'm not chomping at the bit to have my favorite cuisine and quell the raging beast in my stomach at the same time. "Yeah, I guess that's okay."

Jason smirks because he fucking knows I love Italian and would do dirty things for it. We make our way to the hallway, and Savvy is nowhere to be found, so I shoot her a quick text letting her know our plans. She sends me back a thumbs up, an eggplant, and a peach. Is she hungry, too? Seems like weird food to eat together, but I send back a thumbs up as well.

We stop in front of a blacked-out coupe, and I raise my eyebrow at him when he pulls the passenger door open for me. "It's a rental." he answers the question I didn't ask aloud. I nod as I slide onto the silky leather seat.

Muted curses bring my attention to the driver-side window. Jason is frantically patting around his body. I lean over and pop the door, startling him when it bumps against his ass. "Problem?" I ask.

His head falls back as he lets out a big huff. "I left my wallet at the hotel." he says. I reach back and feel for my important cards. I never carry a wallet—it's too bulky. I always just grab my ID, debit card, and Cold Cream punch card, and I'm set.

"Not a fucking chance," Jason growls as he slides into his

seat and starts the engine. "We'll make a real quick pit stop so I can grab it."

If I'm honest, I don't want to argue or spend the money. I simply nod and buckle up.

The beach-front hotel is nice enough. Not too fancy, which definitely isn't Jason's style. But the views are to die for. The sea air flows through my short locks. I'm still trying to get used to having a lob or long-bob. My hair hasn't been this short since I was in first grade.

Jason gently puts his hand in mine to lead me inside. Memories of the last time a guy led me into a hotel flash in my brain. My teeth grind against each other as I follow beside him. Fucking Zach. The irony isn't lost on me that the last time I was cursing Jason, I was with Zach. And now, it's happening in reverse.

Music thumps and echoes down the hallway as we walk toward Jason's room. "Someone's having a good time." I snort.

Jason gives me a nervous look as we stop in front of the noisy door. His hand hesitates over the card reader. I laugh and reach over, covering his hand with mine, and tap the card against it. The light turns green, and I push the door in.

The strobing lights are immediately disorienting, and I lose Jason in the room as I spin for bearings. "Jason?" I call out, but the deafening sounds of heavy metal fill the space. Blinking my eyes hard, I narrow them to try to make out the elements in the room. My back presses against a hard surface. I run my hands along the wall until I find what I'm looking for.

As light floods the room, my eyes have a hard time picking what to latch onto first. To the topless girl snorting a line on the glass table by the window. To the two girls sixty-nineing at the foot of the bed. To the guy fucking the girl doggy style while shoving her face into the pillow. Could go to any of those. But not my eyes. No, the traitorous orbs go straight to the fully naked girl on her knees with her hands desperately clawing at Jason's dick through his exposed boxers.

Is this why he brought me here? Some sick, twisted form of torture?

He doesn't get to do this to me again. I'm not the same girl I was two years ago. Time has hardened my heart. My faith in men is non-existent. I shake my head and make my way back to the door. I'll walk back to campus if I have to.

I make three steps out of the room when I'm jerked backward. A frantic Jason is tucking himself away and righting his pants. "Charlie, please believe me. I had no fucking idea we would be walking into that."

I shrug my shoulder and roll my eyes, "You don't have to explain yourself, Jason. Go back to your party. I'm going to head out." I turn to walk away, and Jason catches my hand, halting my movements. My eyes close as I take a calming breath before turning to face him. *In for four, out for eight.*

I eye him questioningly, waiting for whatever bullshit is about to come out of his mouth. "I know I don't have to explain myself. But I want to. I want us to start at a place of honesty. I didn't know this was happening. But I'm also not surprised. I haven't been chaste these past couple of years, far from."

I scoff at his brag and move to walk away again. "Yeah, and I'm sure you've been living like Mother Teresa." His words raise my hackles instantly, and before I can think better of myself, my hand reaches out and cracks him across the cheek.

Jason stares back at me, dumbfounded by my slap. I walk straight up to him, our heaving chests fighting each other for

15

dominance, and jab my finger into his rapidly moving pec. "If you only fucking knew."

His brows slam down as he processes my words. "Wait. Can we just back up for a second? This isn't going how I pictured it. Let's try this again." He takes a deep breath and steps back a few inches, enough to put some space between us but still close enough to be in each other's bubble. "I'm sorry. I'm mortified and desperate for you to hear me out, so I lashed out. I truly didn't know what we would be walking into. I apologize for my dickhead friend having an impromptu orgy."

I don't even know what I'm so worked up about. I'm no stranger to sex parties and the sights and sounds in that room. So, why? Why is my heart pounding against my chest with so much force that it echoes in my ears? Why is the breath I'm trying to catch sprinting a 5k in the opposite direction? Why did the sight of a woman on her knees for my ex feel like she personally reached her claws into my chest cavity and ripped the abnormally beating organ to minced meat?

Mask in place, I give him a small smile. "Okay. I believe you."

"Don't do that."

"Do what?" I ask.

"Don't hide from me. You don't need to pretend to be anyone else, Sweets. I want your honesty as much as you want mine." His eyes beg me as much as his words do. But I can't give him what he asks. To not hide, there needs to be trust. And he has none of mine.

"Jason, maybe this wasn't a good idea. I think I better just head back to Savvy's dorm." He doesn't seem convinced, but his shoulders slump in defeat as he nods. "Okay. But can I please drive you back and maybe hit a drive-thru on the way?"

* * *

Slurping noises fill the car as I suck down the last of the chocolate-frosted drink from Jimmy's Burgers. The end of the cup always has a concentration of salt from the many fries that took a dip.

Jason pulls into a parking spot in the campus lot. Darkness has settled across the complex, and lantern lights line the pathways, giving off a soft glow.

Jason heaves a heavy sigh in the quiet interior. "I know at this point my word is probably shit to you. But I need to say this anyway,"

Rubbing my salt-laden fingertips against my jeans and swallowing the rest of my frosted drink, I turn to give him my attention. Let him say what he thinks needs to be said so I can get out of here.

"I was in love with you. I know we weren't in a great place when I left for that camping trip. I also know that trip was the beginning of the end for us. If I could do it all over, I would've told my parents to get fucked and spent that week curled up in your bed. I can't tell you how many times I've wished I could rewrite history over the last couple of years. Even when I thought you betrayed me—"

My head jerks back as if he struck me. "Betrayed *you*?" I ask incredulously. He holds his hand up to stop my obvious descent into rage.

"I know now that you didn't, but... Jesus, Charlie, there's so much shit we need to hash out. I don't even know where to begin."

"Why don't you start with whatever's most important to you." I gently offer. Feeling more insecure than I want to. My

17

fingers fidget against the hole in my jeans as I wait for him to continue.

"The most important thing I want to say? Things weren't what they seemed, Charlie." What does that mean? Do I want to know what that means? Who am I kidding? Of course, I want to know. Strike that, I *need* to know.

"That day it all ended... with Jade," he starts.

Just hearing her name has my lip curling to a snarl. Fucking Jade. I bet she gloated so fucking hard when we fell apart. Her dream come true. Cunt.

"I didn't do it." He states firmly.

"Didn't do what?" I ask, confused.

"I didn't sleep with Jade. Nothing happened." I search his eyes for the lie. He has to be lying. He couldn't tell me nothing happened when I asked him two years ago. Every time I saw him after that, she was attached to him like a fifth slutty limb.

Jason places both hands on my biceps and brings his face right up to mine, "Nothing. Happened. I didn't cheat on you."

My mind races through the memories of the day I've tried hopelessly to forget. I didn't imagine her in his bed. She was mostly naked. He was cuddled up with her, and he was half naked. He couldn't fucking tell me nothing happened.

"You couldn't tell me nothing happened when I asked you. Why are you doing this, Jason? What do you want from me?" The tears I've tried so feverishly to keep at bay begin to fall.

He cups my cheeks and thumbs away the tears. "I was so fucking hungover that I didn't know my ass from my elbow. I didn't want to lie to you, and at that moment, I couldn't remember a damn thing that had happened the night before."

"I don't understand. I saw you. I saw her. How can you stand here and say you didn't fuck around on me?" I ask through

18

sobs.

"Charlotte, I'm not going to say it looked good. It definitely did not. It was hella inapprops and never should have happened. The moment I got back in the house, I kicked her the fuck out. She had even stolen my phone the night before. There's so much you don't know, Charlie."

That's why he didn't answer my texts or calls? This doesn't make sense. But he has no reason to lie. Not after all this time. Why would he do this if it wasn't true?

"Then I think it's time you fill me in."

Chapter 3

Jason

I wanted to tell her everything— *everything*, everything. But now is not the time, and that's a lot of shit to take in. She needs time to process if I'm going to do this correctly. I told her exactly what had gone down between Jade and me that night. I also told her Jade and I were never together like she thought. She cursed and punched me in the arm for being petty enough to let everyone—including her—believe we were together just to get under her skin.

"Okay... so, you're a dick, and Jade's a fucking succubus. I already knew that. But what did you mean when you said you thought I betrayed you?" I was kinda hoping she'd forget about that part. I've done a lot of things I'm not proud of, and taking Jade's words and "evidence" at face value is right there at the tip-top of my fuck up list.

I shudder to think where we could be by this point had I just fucking *talked* to her. Or rather, made her talk to me. We were younger, yes, but I'd like to think we both had better sense than that.

I vow right fucking now not to let us have any more goddamn miscommunications. If something seems fucky, we talk it out.

If one of us doesn't want to talk, the other gets to have a slushy on standby.

Suddenly embarrassed by my naivety, my head hangs as I rub the back of my neck. Charlotte clears her throat, urging me to get on with it. "So when I was on that camping trip, Jade was spouting her usual BS about you. I tuned her out as I normally did, but when she threw a white envelope on my lap..."

I chance a look over at her to find no expression on her face. Her mask has been slipped firmly in place... again. Like she knows this part is going to hurt. Not because it was real. But because I was dumb enough to believe it was and never ask for an explanation.

"What earth-shattering information was in the envelope, Jason?" she asks with a heavy dose of condescension.

My head falls back against the headrest, and I gaze at the dimly lit campus. I let out a large breath, "Pictures."

"Pictures? Of what?" she asks.

"You." I answer.

Startled, her face finally shows some emotion. Disbelief and a little fear. "Not *those* kinds of pictures, Sweets." I offer to quell the panic forming in her mind that somehow Jade had intimate photos of her. And while she did produce "intimate" images, they were very much fully clothed.

"Me...?" she repeats in perplexity.

"Yeah. You and that preppy dick-face from the movie theater."

Her face scrunches up as her eyes bounce back and forth, searching her memory for what event this could be.

"Dean?" she finally asks.

"Yeah, whatever his fucking name is. The d-bag who ran

21

away instead of backing you up when Chad was being an ass-wad." I scoff and fold my arms over my chest. This girl really does not have good taste in guys. Yes, I'm aware I fall into that category as well. But I did break her fucking heart, so I guess I belong in that shitty taste column too.

"I don't understand." She responds, her tone taking on an edge of defensiveness.

"She had pictures of you and Dan–"

"Dean." She corrects with an eye roll.

"Whatever. Dean. You were at The Coffee Hut and were all cozied up on one of the couches in the back."

"The Coffee Hut? When..." she begins, puzzled.

A loud gasp fills the interior of the vehicle as Charlie slaps her hand over her mouth and stares at me wide-eyed.

"*That's* what those flashes were?" she asks quietly. Clearly, the question was meant for herself and not for me to answer.

Before I can interject, she shakes her head solemnly and meets my gaze. Even in the darkened car, I can tell her eyes have taken on a misty quality.

"Jason. I remember that day. I bumped into Dean at The Coffee Hut. I hadn't seen him since I blew him off... for you. He was really angry, and we have a lot of history. But beyond that, we'd always been friends. I convinced him to hear me out. I told him about you, and he could tell how happy I was. He forgave me and wished me well. We hugged a couple of times, but that's it. I remember some flashes as my eyes closed. That must've been when she took the pictures."

Her fists clench on her thighs as she recalls the instance.

"Fucking skank!" She hisses. "I can only imagine how those pictures could appear out of context. But... why didn't you just ask me?"

I return her furrowed brow look and offer a sad smirk. "You were a little busy throwing frozen treats in my face and never speaking to me again. And to be honest... my pride was a little bruised, and I wasn't in a great headspace to be very mature about things."

She nods in agreeance. It's only been a couple of years, but I think I've grown a bit in the emotional maturity department. Don't get it twisted, though, I'm still an immature dickbag sometimes, but I've definitely improved since then. My blood boils whenever I've allowed myself to think of what could have been. How different our lives could be if we had simply talked shit out.

"Well, as long as we are admitting wrongdoings, I know I didn't make it any easier to seek me out, and the one time you even tried, I shut you down immediately without a second glance... I—" The words catch in her throat. Her eyes look away from mine like she can't stand the connection while she speaks.

"I owe you an apology. Well, an amends really..."

Amends? Uh... what?

She continues before I can question what the hell that means.

"I kinda did betray you... like a little tiny bit." She whispers and holds her forefinger and thumb a small amount apart. She at least has the good sense to look remorseful while I fight to keep my face stoic. *What the hell does that mean?* Because I can't trust my words right now, I simply cock a questioning brow at her.

Charlie fidgets uncomfortably in her seat, wringing her hands together while she gathers the courage to explain herself. "Right before I came to see you that day... I was at Sky

23

Ridge."

"Okay..." I softly respond through slightly clenched teeth.

"I was having a really shitty day, and you know I like to go up there to clear my head. So that's what I was doing. Only it turns out I wasn't alone up there..."

This can play out a multitude of ways, and my imagination is having a field day trying to decipher her cryptic words.

"You fucked a rando at Sky Ridge?" *Goddammit Jason. What happened to reining in the sassery?*

"I'll give you a pass for that shitty comment. Just fucking one, Jason. No, I didn't fuck a rando at Sky Ridge. But I did kiss someone. I immediately felt awful and pulled away. I came to your place directly afterward with the full intention of explaining to you what happened. But then..."

"Yeah, I know what happened then." I cut in, not wanting to rehash that event yet again tonight. Something's gnawing at my brain, though. "Who was it?" I question with a touch more harshness than intended.

"It doesn't matter. Especially not now."

"Humor me."

She sighs, "Zach."

Zach. Zach. Who the fuck is Zach?

"He was new to River View that year. We bonded–"

"Yeah, while I was busy falling in love with you, you were busy bonding with some other dude. Awesome." *Okay, maybe not as emotionally mature as I claimed to be.*

Charlotte

God grant me the serenity... not to punch his stupid ass in his stupid fucking mouth.

24

Hurt people, hurt people. Repeat it, Charlie!

Hurt people, hurt people.

Deep breath. "Let's put a pin in the whole 'in love' situation, but we are definitely going to circle back to that—" I try to ignore the phantom knife to the heart thinking about Zach. I want to hate the bastard. Just like I wanted to hate Jason. But goddammit, I fucking love them both. I love them both? Still? *Jesus Christ.*

I can't keep feeling this way. I can't continue to fight my way forward while being weighed down with regrets of my past. I've kind of taken the steps a bit out of order, but I'm ready for step eight with Jason. Amends.

"I'm sorry. Truly. We both had a part to play in the downfall of our relationship. I'm owning mine right now. I apologize for hurting you. I was angry... and to tell you the truth, I'm still angry."

His stupid, handsome face scrunches up with a puzzled expression. I know it's hard to follow. This shit is in my head, and I can't keep things straight half the time. But sometimes, you just gotta let the crazy loose and see what shakes out.

"I know you just told me that nothing actually happened with Jade. Logically, I know that. But—" I press my palm against my racing heart, "in here, is imprinted with two years of believing the worst of you. Trauma like that doesn't just float away. God, Jason. You have no idea the things that event set in motion for me..."

Those stormy eyes pierce into me like they always have. Searching. Investigating. Easily side-stepping the wall that I've so carefully crafted around myself.

My words catch in my throat. Trapping the horrific truths within its fleshy prison. It's not his fault. I made my choices.

"I–I'm just sorry."

His head cocks to the side as he continues to study me. After what feels like hours, he finally speaks. "I had a whole speech planned. A lot of excuses and blame have rattled around in my brain for the last couple of years. So, I'm sorry too, Sweets. I'm so sorry I hurt you. I'm sorry for whatever caused this broken shell to embed itself into your very being. I'm sorry I let my pride get in the way of what could have been a simple conversation. I'm sorry," his brows lower, almost as if he's feeling physical pain. His large, warm hand intertwines with mine. Our fingers interlock like two jagged pieces of the same puzzle.

"But the thing I'm most sorry for? I'm so fucking sorry that you've walked through whatever caused this haunted look in your eyes, not knowing how fucking much you were loved. How much I love you. I don't even give a damn if you're seeing someone now. I won't let you go one more second without knowing that this still and has always belonged to you." He declares with a slam of his fist to his chest.

"I loved you, too." I whisper, not knowing if my words made it to his side of the car. Silence fills the space between us for so long that I think he probably didn't hear me.

"Past tense?" he asks.

My head lolls back against the headrest. This seems like a lot for our first real conversation since high school. It's long overdue, but damn, I'm having a hard time sorting through my brain garbage.

On one hand, he's my first... everything. I think a part of me will always love him. On the other hand, I just got out of a fucked up situation, and my emotions are all over the place. Do I love him? The simple answer is yes. Am I in love with him? I don't think I'm capable of the emotional depth and vulnerability that calls for. I'm not the same person I was back then.

Would he still love me if he knew what I've done...? What's been done to me...

Chapter 4

Jason

"Past tense?" I ask, not knowing whether I'm actually ready for the answer or not. The utter silence between us suspends me in animation. I'm but a frozen entity floating about the endless abyss of space, waiting for a sign that it's safe to come back down.

Charlotte seems to be mulling over the question during her intermission from our conversation. It shouldn't be a thought piece... it's a pretty straightforward question. Does she love me or not? My hands grip the leather of the seat below me to keep from flapping. A surefire sign that my anxiety is ramping up, and there's not a damn thing I can do about it right now.

"Yes."

Fuck!

"And, no."

Huh?

Taken aback by the completely indecisive non-answer and still thoroughly confused, I ask, "What does that mean? Dumb it down for me."

She lets out a huff of air before finally turning to face me. "It means I love you." The immense change in the cadence of

28

my sinus rhythm at her words has me about to float right out of this damn car. She loves me. Holy fucking shit. She *loves* me. She loves *me*.

The wind gets knocked out of my sails immediately as she continues to speak. "It also means I can't love you. I'm having a hard time trying to love myself right now. I can't even begin to include anyone else in that." Tears sit heavy on the back end of her words. I can tell how hard she's trying to keep this vulnerability inside.

"I- fuck. I just can't, Jason. I can't—" The panic taking over her is evident. I place my hand gently on her thigh and rub my thumb back and forth.

"Shh, it's okay. You don't have to do anything right now. Just breathe."

She takes a couple of stuttered breaths before asking, "What do you want from me?"

That's a loaded question. The basic answer? Fucking everything. But I can't go balls deep on night one, so I say, "I want us to be friends."

"Friends?" she asks with a heavy dose of disbelief.

"Yeah, Sweets. Friends. Is that okay with you?"

Charlie nods her head slowly as my words penetrate through the fog of hysteria. "Friends. I haven't had too many of those lately, so I suppose there's a hole you could fill."

Don't make a fucking dick joke right now about filling her hole.

That sly smirk that I love glides across her lips. "Nothing? I'm lobbing you softballs here, and you're letting me down, Donovan."

"Friends don't make lewd innuendos to other friends, Charlie." I sarcastically respond with a slight boop to her nose that she immediately swats away.

29

"If I approve your application for the friend zone, I will accept nothing less than your most authentic self. Penis jokes and all." She laughs, but there's a hint of sadness to it. "There's only one rule."

"And what's that rule, Sweets?"

"No secrets. I want nothing but one hundred percent unfiltered honesty. Even if it hurts. And I'll do the same in return. Fair?"

I would agree to any fucking rule she implemented... unless it's butt stuff. Mine, not hers.

I hold my hand out for her to shake. "Agreed."

The soft melody of an alt-rock song filters through the speakers. Something about if a great wave should fall upon us all, then he hopes there's someone out there who can bring him back to her.

Funny enough, the song fits. I will absolutely go wherever she goes. Up high. Down low. Anywhere. I want to be the one to guide her through the darkest of her days. She doesn't need a savior. She needs to be her own savior.

Charlie bops her foot softly to the beat while slyly eyeing the last of my fries. She devoured her burger and then proceeded to dip a fistful of fries into her chocolate drink repeatedly. Watching her tongue dart out to taste the remnants of the salted wedge makes my dick twitch.

"Ahem," I get her attention with a shake of my fry container in her direction. She doesn't even pretend not to want them as she snatches them with the quickness of a feral bear. I've always loved that about Charlie. A lot of chicks want us to believe they are dainty little creatures who get by on a pinch of lettuce, a sip of cucumber water, and a bite of bland ass chicken. Not my Sweets, though. She won't hesitate to stab a

30

motherfucker who gets between her and her food. And heaven help you if you take a swig of her chocolate milk.

I trace the four faint tine marks on the top of my left hand. My souvenir from a time in high school when I took a drink of her milk, and she instinctively stabbed her fork at me. Whether she actually meant to break skin or not remains a mystery. Nevertheless, I have a permanent reminder to stay the fuck away from her dairy products.

Her fry-stuffed voice pulls me out of that fond memory. "So. Are we going to talk about you and Savannah being sneaky fucks? Like, how are you even in touch with her? Do you live in this swampy hell-mouth?"

My lip finds its way between my teeth as I debate how to answer her question. I want to be honest, but this is a delicate line we are dancing on. Our newfound friendship is walking on a razor wire, dangling across shark-infested waters. One small burst of air in the wrong direction, and we are fish food.

I don't need to tell her every single detail to be truthful. "I'm a bit of a Nomad right now. No, I don't live here. This is just where I'm shipping out from."

Charlotte's head jerks forward, and she fights to swallow the mouthful of fries. Eyes wide at me, she finally clears the food from her mouth. "You joined the military?" she asks incredulously. I'm a little offended at how much in disbelief she is by the possibility. I may not have joined the service, but I fucking could have.

I shake my head, "No, I didn't join the military. I have a new job as a..." My words pause as I think of the best way I can describe my employment without breaking my NDA. A very long NDA that I was forced to sign before being accepted as a member of The Ravenwood Collective. We are a small team of, let's call it, "security". Hired to attend events and locales around the world. Protecting *or* acquiring assets. Whether they be inanimate or of the human variety.

Not even Jacobs could tell me about some of his past deployments. As I've gathered, sometimes our methods are not exactly on the up and up. But whatever it takes, right? That's what I've signed up for.

"... traveling independent contractor." I settle on the most vague term I can think of while still holding truth.

Charlie's eyes narrow as she absorbs my words. "Okay... that's not fucking weird or anything," her brow quirks to let me know that, yeah, she definitely finds it weird. "But how did you run into Savs, and how in the hell did you convince her to get me here?"

After the free immersive porn we were treated to earlier, I'm not super eager to rehash how exactly I ran into Savvy. But I promised honesty, and I'm sure Savannah will tell her eventually. So, I give her a watered-down version. One without *all* the filthy sex details.

"Ew. You banged Cuntasaurus Rex? I can't even look at you right now."

"I said we chilled." I rebut with a reiteration of the words I actually used.

"Yeah, that's guy-code for penetration." She scoffs like it's the most commonly known fact in the world. "You did fuck her, correct?" she asks.

And fuck, well, I can't not answer a straight-out question. "My dick had an unfortunate meeting with her lady box, yes."

She snorts and dusts off the salt grains that have embedded in her thighs. Not wanting to talk about Naomi anymore, I change the subject. "I can't believe I'm sitting here with you.

Of all the things on my 2008 bingo card, this was not even close to on the list of things I thought possible."

Charlie scoffs in agreeance, "You're telling me. I never thought I'd see you again. Never wanted to either." She jokes and elbows me in the rib. Both the jab and the words hurt more than they should.

"Do you still want to call it a night?" I ask.

She chews on that pouty bottom lip while mulling the question over before smirking at me. "Can you promise the only tits I'm going to see again tonight will be my own?"

A bark of laughter pours out of me, "I can't control the populous, Sweets. There are junkies everywhere, even in the great Sunshine State. God knows those people are the bottom of the barrel, so you never know what they're capable of."

The smirk slides off her face, and she turns away from me to gaze out of the window. Did I say something wrong?

"Can we go somewhere out of the city? I want to look at the stars." She questions with an icy demeanor that wasn't present moments ago.

"Sure. I can't think of a better way to spend our only night together."

Without breaking her gaze from the passenger window, she asks, "Only night? When do you leave?"

"Tomorrow."

"Well, we better make it count then. Take me to the stars, Jace."

Chapter 5

Charlotte

"What the fuck was that?" I ask with a gasp and grab onto Jason's sleeve as I peer around the darkness.

A park at a lake in the middle of the night in fucking Florida was not the move. There's probably a goddamn gator staring at us right now. Its beady eyes peeping along the top of the murky water. Licking his chops, thinking he's in the mood for fast food. I know for damn sure Jason could outrun my sedentary ass.

I instinctively peek at his choice of footwear and internally cheer when I see his loosened black combat boots, which would give me a slight advantage if we had to run. As the old adage states, "I don't have to outrun the gator. I just have to outrun the ex who tricked me into seeing him for the first time in years and clearly still has some feels." Or, you know, something like that.

Jason chuckles and settles his arm around my shoulder, gently tugging me back into our lying position in the grass. "Don't you worry your pretty little head; I'll protect you." He says with the sweetest drip of condescension. Yeah, he fucking will protect me... by falling on his own damn proverbial sword in the shape of self-sacrifice to Sir Gator McBiteyFace.

My eyes latch onto a small pile of sticks, and I force my face into a mask of concern as I meet his playful gaze. "Do you think if I bang some sticks together, it will ward off the gators?"

Jason lets out a deep chuckle and pats my thigh, "It didn't work for Meredith Blake. It's not going to work for you. But if you want to give it a go—" He sweeps his arm out toward the pile. I turn to him slightly and swat him against the chest. The sudden movement causes his body to jerk and his hand to slide from my thigh to just over my vajay.

Time freezes. Goosebumps creep over every inch of my skin. I'm far from unsullied, but his touch brings me back to the blushing virgin I was during our first time together. With the stars above us, the warm breeze blowing along my heated skin, the fact that he just referenced The Parent Trap, and his hand dangerously close to my private region, I can almost forget all that's happened between us. Almost.

Our past takes a hammer to those butterflies in my stomach, and I clear my throat while shifting slightly. The movement causes his hand to fall to the side of our bodies. I don't chance a look at him to see if he knows it was purposeful. We aren't there. I don't know if we ever will be.

Friends. That's what I can give him.

"You see those two stars to the left of Orion?" I ask and point to the two semi-bright stars.

Jason follows my finger and nods.

"Canis Minor."

"Little dog, nice." Jason responds.

"Wow, learned a bit of Latin, did we?" I playfully jest.

"It was one of the languages I took at ASU before I withdrew."

"One? You took others?"

"Mhm. German and Spanish."

I turn my head to look over at him in shock. "Damn, Jace! Say something to me in German."

"Wenn man dem Teufel den kleinen Finger gibt, so nimmt er die ganze Hand."

"Well, that sounded angry. What did you say?"

"It means: If you give the devil your little finger, he'll take the whole hand. Basically, if you give them an inch, they'll take a mile. It was my professor's favorite proverb and his reasoning for never giving an extension on an assignment."

I giggle. That sounds like something a crotchety professor would say. "Did your Spanish professor have any special proverbs?"

Jason's face screws up in thought. "Ojo."

"That's it? What does Ojo mean?"

"Eye. She would slowly glare across the class when we were in the middle of exams and hiss the word. It essentially meant she was watching us."

"Interesting. It's kinda like back in high school. Miss Davis always said the empty jar on her desk was to collect the eyeballs of kids who couldn't keep them on their own papers. I about shit myself when I came in one day to a pair of eyeballs floating in a brown, chunky liquid, and Shane Mandorf had a bloody bandage over his eye sockets. For like two seconds, I forgot it was April Fools. Seriously. We almost had to rename it to Brown Thursday."

His rough timbre warms my insides. I miss this. Just chatting and laughing. We've always had an easy connection. We can do this, right? The just friends thing?

Jason

My feelings are conflicting. This is fucking amazing, and I'm so damn happy to be here with her. It's fleeting, and that crushes me. She's got a huge wall between us, and that pisses me off. I have no right to be mad, but I am. I've broken through those walls once before, and I can do it again.

"So why did you leave school?" Charlotte asks absentmindedly while her eyes trace the cosmos. What a loaded question. I really don't want to bog down our only night together with tales from the past, especially when they are as shitty as mine. So, I'll deflect. I'm good at that. What's something she probably won't want to talk about? "Why did you leave Alaska?" I ask.

Silence stretches on between us. The topics we don't want to indulge in drift away on the midnight breeze.

"Can we not take a walk down memory lane tonight? I just want to be here with you in this moment. Is that okay?"

She nods, and a look that resembles relief slides over her face. There's only one thing I really want to know. "Are you happy?"

Her answer is immediate. "No. Are you?"

"No." I answer honestly. I haven't been happy since... well since 2005.

She threads our hands together and squeezes mine without taking her eyes off the sky. A sign of solidarity, maybe? A coming together of two miserable souls, seeing each other's reflections in the dark.

We stayed in the park until the sun began to crest over the horizon. I didn't want to leave our grassy knoll for anything. But I waited until the last possible moment before I had to drop Charlotte off. Like the gentleman I am, I walked her right up to Savvy's door. Okay, I really just wanted to prolong our goodbye for as long as I could.

"What happens now?" Charlotte asks.

I blow out a small breath and brush some strands of her hair across her forehead. "Now, I ride off into the sunset with a burly, hung-over douche and think about you for my fifteen-hour flight."

She smirks that sassy smirk that I'd love to kiss right off her mouth. "Just for the fifteen hours? That's all I'm worth?"

I snake my hand behind her head, firmly grip her neck, and pull her into my chest; she comes willingly. "Sweets, I doubt if you'll ever be off my mind ever again. But I'm trying not to sound like a desperate twat here."

A small smile crests her mouth, a genuine look of appreciation for my candor. And because I'm a glutton for punishment, I take it a step further. I press my body forward and crowd her up against Savannah's door. I raise my left arm to rest against the door frame. I tower over her, and being this close, she has to strain her neck to look up at me. I don't miss the flash of lust in her eyes as she takes in my position. I crook my forefinger under her chin, "You are worth every goddamn thing. You are worth more than all the colors in the spectrum. You are my color. The only color I see."

Tears gather in her eyes, and we simply stare at each other. Unmoving. Not speaking. Just looking. *Seeing.*

After what feels like an eternity of getting lost in the chocolatey forest of her irises, my gaze juts down to her mouth. I don't miss the clench of her jaw as she notices.

"You are worth more than all the snowscapes I've ever tried to capture, more than the stars I've wished upon in the quiet of the night. You are the heartbeat in every stroke of charcoal, the melody in every line I draw." Charlotte swallows hard, and when I meet her eyes again, hers have traced a path down to my mouth. She watches my lips intently as I speak. I lower my voice to a hoarse whisper, "And that? Is priceless."

Her hand reaches between us, and she fists my t-shirt. Her pull has so much force that our lips crash together. Neither of us push for more than a passionate, close-mouthed kiss. So many words sit unspoken on our lips. So much hurt, confusion, and remembrance.

I break the kiss first. *She's not ready.* Our chests heave and touch with each gasp of air. I press my forehead to hers, and both of our eyes shut. We stand for several minutes, soaking in each other's presence. I don't know what's going through her mind, but I really wish I didn't have to fucking leave right now. My phone has buzzed no less than twenty times in the last ten minutes. No doubt, Jacobs is having a shitfit that I haven't shown up yet.

"I gotta go, Sweets."

She nods but still hasn't let go of my shirt. I gently place my hand over hers, and with my other hand, I reach into her back pocket and pull out her phone. My fingers find the familiar numbers, and I shoot her a look of disbelief. "Really? Still using 3825?"

She shrugs a shoulder, "What? It is my favorite word."

I shake my head at her and huff out a laugh. I slip the phone back into her pocket after adding myself to her contacts. "Oh, I remember. And if I'm not mistaken, it was your favorite activity, too." She laughs, and I wish I could bottle the sound and take it with me wherever the fuck I end up. My phone buzzes again. "Okay, I really have to go now. I don't know if

39

my phone will work after I leave my first destination. Do me a favor and text me your address."

She reaches for her phone, and I place my hand over hers to stop her. I softly shake my head and pull her into my arms, hugging her like it's the last time. For all I know, it could be. "Do it after I leave. And tell me one good thing that's happened to you over the last couple of years. I love you, Charlotte. Take care of yourself."

She begins to open her mouth, and I place a finger against her lips to stop her. "Please don't say anything. I won't be able to walk away if you say anything else. Please, Sweets. Just text me."

She nods, and I place another kiss on her head before turning around and walking away. I wasn't kidding. I would fucking break if she said anything else. I also didn't want to hear her say anything other than I love you, too.

Chapter 6

Charlotte

As soon as I enter Savvy's room, I softly close the door and sink down against it. Burying my head in my hands, I let the tears loose. Every word he said was like another dagger to the ice around my heart. But the thing about ice is that it's similar to glass. The shards do as much damage inward as they do outward.

Nothing makes sense anymore. Everything he said to me tonight has me questioning everything I've said and done since that day at his house. I hate feeling this out of control of my own thoughts. I can't trust my memories. I can't trust my past. How can he say those things to me? He doesn't know what he's saying. If he knew... if he knew my history, he'd run for the fucking hills.

I want to believe him so badly. I'm so damn desperate for something to believe in that I can't trust myself.

Warm hands caress my shoulders, and a quick kiss is placed on the top of my head. Savvy sinks down to the ground beside me. She pulls me against her body and lets me cry.

"You deserve so much, Charlie. I want you to be happy. I want you to find someone who deserves you. Someone who

41

will love you through the darkness. Someone who sees your scars and doesn't shy away from them. I've always followed my gut. It rarely ever steers me wrong. And Charls? My gut says Jason could be that guy for you. He fucking loves you, dude. I grilled him so hard before I agreed to bring you here. He didn't break once. You've had a rough go of things, and no offense, but your judgment fucking sucks."

Damn. Shots fired.

"I stayed out of the Zach shit because you begged me to, and look at how that turned out. Don't get me wrong, you don't *need* a man. You are a strong, capable woman, and you will do amazing things regardless of the dick you ride. But you deserve a partner, and you know if I liked pussy, you'd be top of my list, but alas, I'm strickly dickly. I bet with that pierced tongue of his, Jason could make you see those stars you love so much." She bumps her shoulder against me slightly.

Before I can give her my response in words, my head offers my thoughts by shaking back and forth. "I can't, Savs. After everything with Zach, and even knowing the truth now about Jason, my fucking heart hurts. I can only pretend to be an unfeeling robot for so long before I crumble."

"So don't." She rebuts resolutely.

"Don't?"

"Look, if any man is worth the salt in his spunk, he will wait. So, make him wait. Do you, boo. This is the age of Charlie. All I'm saying is, don't close the door. Leave it cracked just a little bit. For when and *if* you're ready. Just..." she gently pulls my head out of my hands to face her. Her face is blurry from the wall of tears, but I blink them away as best I can.

"Please don't leave me again, Charls. I can't go through that a second time. Jesus, I—" Her voice breaks as she tries to hang on to her composure. We sit in silence for a few minutes before she sighs and leans our heads together. "I just want you to be happy. The shit you've been through is fucked. If anyone deserves to ride off into the sunset on a wave of never-ending orgasms and hot chocolate, it's you."

Savvy stands, pads back over to her bed, lays down, and places her unicorn sleep mask over her eyes. Just like the last ten minutes never happened. I'm left shocked and confused. Did I just imagine that whole interaction?

"You have thirty minutes." She declares from her sleepy state.

"What?" I ask, voice still hoarse from the tears.

"You get to be a sad bitch for thirty more minutes while I snooze. Then we are going to head to the cantina and let some boys buy us brunch before going to see that stupid mouse and his friends."

* * *

This is the greatest day of my life! Alaska has zero amusement parks, and I've been too preoccupied with school to see what else Alabama has to offer. Contrary to her pissiness about it earlier, Savs is living her best life right alongside me.

We walk arm-in-arm down Main Street with matching ears and polka-dot skirts. Sav got me a cotton candy that is bigger than my head. She even got me an autograph book, and every time we pass a character, they sign it and take our picture. Goofy grabbed a handful of Savvy's ass, and I think it turned her on a little bit.

We wait excitedly in line for the teacups. I had a video cassette of the mouse and his world when I was a kid. In it, the characters all rode in the tea cups with giant smiles on their faces. Spinning around and around. I was so envious. I can't believe it's finally my turn to ride them.

"Okay, maybe we should've waited until after the teacups to get the cotton candy." Savvy admits as she rubs my back with one hand and holds my hair out of my face with the other.

"Worth it." I say before spewing chunks into the trash can again. My eyes squeeze shut with every heave, and it makes my head spin as if we are still on the ride. My stomach lurches again. Surprisingly, pure sugar making a comeback is nowhere near as vile as alcohol doing it.

After puking up the contents of my stomach for ten minutes, I'm ready to rally. We grab a pretzel and head to the giant mansion, which is apparently haunted.

"Um, the fucking graveyard is amazing!" I shout over the murmurs of the rest of the line-standers for the mansion. "Here lies good old Fred. A great big rock fell on his head." I laugh and point to the gravestone as we pass it.

"What a shit way to go. Makes you not want to take life for granite..." Savvy says.

I roll my eyes, but actually, that was a pretty good one. "You know what they say. When life hits you in the head with a rock, live like it's your last day, or you'll be QUARRY." I joke, but it falls flat.

Savvy pats my back as we step into the elevator, "Good try, Charls, maybe next time. It's a hard rock life."

"Ugh, I hate you. Now, let's go get fondled by some ghosts."

* * *

After a much-needed shower and the best sugar-induced sleep

44

of my life, I pull my phone out and hover over Jason's contact info.

Me: I dropped you a pin with my dorm's addy on it.

  Me: Safe travels.

Way to go, Charlie. You sound like a dumbass. *Loserville ahead, population: me.*

Three dots pop up on the screen immediately.

Jason: Got it. Thx will do. Aren't you forgetting something?

Me: What did I forget?

Jason: Tell me your 1 good thing.

One good thing. What an ask. How fucking pathetic am I that I can't think of even one.

Jason: Don't overthink it. It can be a small thing.

How did he know I was about to spiral? I think back over the last two years, and there's a whole lot of shit. Some I can't bring up without diving into the nightmare surrounding it. If I tell him about Ari, then I'll have to explain how we came back together and the facility. If I tell him about the facility, then I have to tell him about the drugs. If I tell him about the drugs, then I'll have to tell him about Priest. No, that's all too much. Let's keep it simple. For now.

Me: I made 3 new friends.

Jason: What are their names?

Me: Genny, Reggie, and Sariah.

Jason: Reggie a dude?

Me: Mhm.. why?

Jason: Is he gay?

I could tell him that Reg is married to Sariah, but this is too funny. Jason has always been super possessive, and I kind of like it when that side of him comes out. He always stays just

45

this side of controlling.

Me: No... again, why?

Jason: No reason.

Sure, no reason. I totally believe you.

Me: He's very much into women.

I shouldn't poke the bear. It's not a lie. Sariah is, in fact, a woman.

Jason: *thumbs up emoji*

Cue internal eye roll. Jason is such a guy sometimes. But I think it'll be good to let him sweat a bit.

Jason: Kk, I'm boarding my next flight. I have no idea what commo will be like, but I'll reach out when I can.

Me: Be safe.

Jason: I love you. Don't say anything back.

My heart stutters as I look at his last text. I trace my fingers across the words over and over, wanting them to be true.

Chapter 7

June 2008

Sweets,

Phone commo is basically non-existent, so I decided to go old school. There's something nostalgic about putting pen to paper, don't you think? There's an air of mystery. We can say what we want. We can be who we want. Our tales are confined to these four corners of parchment.

So. Let's recap the last two months (well, as much as I can anyway). This is nothing like I expected. So far, it's been a lot of traveling to different locations and waiting... and waiting... and waiting. I've been using that time to hit the makeshift gyms at the places I've been assigned. I'll be swole in no time. I've always wanted a super-defined V cut. Maybe a certain bratty blonde might like it, too?

Anyway, if you ever wondered what it would be like to shower in an improvised locker room in the way of not at all private stalls in a connex, it fucking sucks. I've seen more dicks flopping around in the last two months than in my whole life. Shower shoes are an absolute must-have. Hate to break it to you, Sweets, but dudes are gross.

Wanna know something pretty cool? As soon as you get on an international flight, the legal alcohol age goes right out the window. As long as you're over eighteen, or at least look it, they'll give you all the booze you want. I knew our first location was going to be in a dry country, so I got hammered somewhere over the Atlantic. Wanna know something not so cool? I had to hurl in an airplane bathroom after someone shitted.

I know it'll make you smile to know that we hit a pocket of turbulence as I whipped my junk out to take a piss and ended up getting it on my boots. So there I was 36k feet in the air, scrubbing my shoe in that tiny metal sink with one eye closed. Why one eye closed? Because that's the only way I could see just one image instead of two. I might've imbibed a little too much. Just a little.

And this time, I didn't have a sweet little blonde to nurse me back to health.

Can I tell you a secret? I think I drank so much because I was a little afraid of what was to come. Diving head-first into the unknown is terrifying. I wish I could share more with you, but you know, NDA and all that.

Since there's been so much downtime, I've been able to do more drawing. I hadn't been doing much these days. Wasn't feeling very inspired. But seems like lately, all I've had is inspiration. Weird, huh? Wonder what the change could be...

I've included one of my latest pieces.

I love you. Don't say anything back.

-J

PS– Tell me one good thing.

I CHOOSE YOU, CHARLOTTE

Chapter 8

July 2008

Charlotte

"Are you sure about this, Charlie?" Reg asks for the millionth time. His voice is laced with concern. I'm surprised he's managed to stave off the lecture that I know is hanging heavy on the tip of his tongue. But I've thought long and hard about this, and I believe I'm making the right decision for me.

I set down the lamp I was in the middle of bubble-wrapping and walk over to him. I wrap my arm around his waist, and he rests his arm across my shoulders. "I am. I know it seems like I'm being impulsive, but this just feels right, you know?"

I've talked at length about this with Dr. T. I haven't been happy here. In school and just Alabama in general. Though Dad and I have been working to repair our relationship, I know he's still with Alexis and call me petty but fuck that bitch with a rusty crowbar. It's not enough to keep me here. Aside from Genny, Reg, and Sariah, I have no one here. I'm a pariah at school. Word about Rebecca got around, and even though I am the fucking victim, people give me a wide berth.

Not to mention that being in the same state as Zach makes

51

me feel like I'm slowly suffocating. I never leave my dorm unless it's for classes or meetings. I'm terrified I'm going to run into him around town. I may have kept my composure the last time we saw each other, but now that a few months have passed, I'm left with hurt and anger. A lot of fucking anger.

"But, who's going to run lines with me and eat the pickles from my sandwiches? You're being real selfish not thinking about how your decision affects *me*, Charlie." Reg huffs with a sassy playfulness. He loosens his grip, and I head back to finish packing.

"Will you at least let me drive with you? It scares me to think about you driving across the country by yourself. Do you know how many weirdos are out there?"

I laugh, "Reg, I am the weirdo. Don't worry about me. I'm actually looking forward to the solo road trip. I think it'll be good to clear my head. I've got a whole itinerary planned! I know you love a good plan. Look—" I riffle through the stack of papers on my desk with my route and stop. "See." I point at the starred destinations.

"Charlie. What in the hell are you going to do in Vicksburg, Mississippi?"

I shrug, heat blooming my cheeks as I answer. "It was the first thing that popped up when I searched my route. What? A girl can't like old war relics? That's mighty sexist of you, Reg. I may have to tell Sariah about this. You know how she feels about chauvinists."

Reggie swats me with the stack of papers, "Oh hush. I just want to make sure you're safe."

"I know, and I love you for it. But I'll be fine. I've got my handy-dandy mace, a stun gun, and a set of handcuffs."

"They're furry! Anyone would be able to break out of those."

"Eh, potato, pahtato."

"And what in the world is in Norsville, Texas?" Reg asks with a pinched face.

I smile, "Someone very important."

He shimmies his shoulders and waggles his brows. "Oh la la, a previous liaison perhaps?"

"Something like that." Keeping my promise to Ari is easy when people jump to their own conclusions. I just won't correct him. She wants her whereabouts under wraps, and I am a woman of my word.

Reg quirks a brow at my vague response, "Okay, okay. Keep your secrets. So, how long have you allotted for this journey of self-discovery?"

"I don't really have a timeline. I figure I'll stop when I want to. I'll explore when I feel like exploring. As long as I'm across the border before the first snowfall, I'm golden."

* * *

Looking around my empty dorm room, I know I've made the right choice. I feel nothing. No pang of regret. No uncertainty about staying. Just a big ol' nothing.

After turning in my key and leaving AU for the final time, I climb into Sariah's minivan. Willow's soft snores float along the quiet of the space. I forgo sitting shotgun and sit in the seat beside the sleeping newborn. She's so beautiful. Chubby, rosy cheeks that beg to be squeezed. The cutest button nose I've ever seen. And very patchy, slightly auburn hair. She's a total doll.

Keeping my voice low, I take a moment to thank Sariah for the ride and for letting me spend my last night in Alabama at their house.

Reggie, the saint he is, took my new car— courtesy of Grayson Johnson, in to have the oil changed and all the bits inspected for safety. He's such a dad. Willow is one lucky girl. She'll never have to find out one day that her hero was anything but. Reg worships the ground Sariah walks on and would rather set his pubes on fire than hurt her in any way.

My last night was perfect. Pizza and movies, chatting, and coloring. Perfect. Genny stopped by to say her goodbyes and give me her sponsor spiel. Reach out. Find a meeting. HALT. Serenity prayer. Et cetera ad infinitum.

I've got new oil, full tires, and a cooler full of snacks. My new Club Masters slide onto the bridge of my nose with practiced ease. I grip the steering wheel, and damn, I think I missed a movie montage moment by not getting a set of fingerless black leather gloves.

I mailed my response letter to Jason— well, Jason's company's shady ass PO Box. Apparently, the mail is gathered and then secretly flown to whatever covert location they're at.

I kinda like trading snail mail. The anticipation builds, and he keeps me on my toes. I never know what's going to come out of his mouth—err, pen. My heart felt so full when I unfolded his sketch. Jason was always extremely protective of his art. So the fact that he willingly shared it with me unprovoked gave me "tinglies," as Ari would say. The Celtic cross was beautiful. I just wish he would've told me what the words meant.

* * *

Jason,

Where do I even begin? Let's get the burning questions out of the way first. So these dicks that were flopping everywhere, what are we talking size-wise? Any super distinguished traits? Curves? Veins? Scars? Turtlenecks? Piercings?!

Don't lie. How many times a day do you have to see some dude's O-face? With shared living quarters, I'm sure it's nonstop.

If y'all don't have internet, what are they using as inspiration? Nudie mags? Polaroids? Highlight reels?

*Okay, enough about dicks. Where do **you** box the one-eyed champ, with what frequency, and what is **your** inspiration?*

Okay, now I'm done.

By the time you read this, I will be somewhere in the Midwest or the western US. Savs told me that she revealed exactly zero about my life, and we didn't have time to discuss it in the one night we had before you left.

So, I'll give you a brief recap.

I was enrolled at the University of Auburn, where I wanted to pursue nursing. However, I wasn't happy with the school, the program, Alabama, or life in general. An opportunity came up back home, so I'm making a solo trip back to Alaska.

I'm a little afraid to ask, but I have no idea what you did when you left AK. What have you known about my life since then?

Getting smashed on an airplane is never a great plan, Jace. So you got what you deserved, HAHA. Some shitty smell and piss on your shoes were on the no-biggie list of things that could've happened on that tin can of death. Could've plummeted to your death. You could've had a medical emergency. A bird could've been sucked into the engine! I hate to fly if you couldn't tell. That's one of the reasons I'm making this drive.

If you get this before September, you'll need to send your response letter to the address I've listed below. If it gets there and I've already left, she'll mail it to Mary's — I'll leave her addy below, too. That's where I'll stay when I get back— in Savannah's old room until I can get on my feet and get my own place.

It'll be so weird to live completely on my own. Even in the dorms, I never felt truly alone with so many classmates around and tons of amenities. But I want to plant my roots in River View and buy a house.

Tell me something about you.

Be safe.

-Charlie

Charlotte Johnson
   C/O Aurelia Fletcher
   111 Horsetail Lane
   Norsville, TX 73211

Mary Mitchell's Addy
   6789 Always Sunny Ln
   River View, AK 99876

PS- For the first time in my life, I don't wake up wanting to die... that often. I find hope even if I have to create it. North to the future, I guess— How's that for a good thing? Got real deep, real fast, huh? You regretting this friend thing yet?

Chapter 9

July 2008

Charlotte

I am going to fucking piss myself. Why are there no non-creepy-looking places to pee in this town? Why did I think it was okay to drive for six hours straight with a 32oz slushy— blue mother fucking raspberry, obviously— and not have a bathroom stop planned? Oh, I know why. Because I'm a fucking idiot.

The sign for Vicksburg is like seeing a desert oasis when you've been walking the barren hills for days in the scorching heat.

I decided on a self-guided driving tour of the military park. The weirdo who runs the guided tours had a real "stuffed bodies in my basement" vibe, and I wasn't about it.

I pull the car over when I reach a small round monument. The four columns in the front remind me of ancient Roman architecture. Stepping out of the car, I look around, but there's not much traffic. There's a heaviness to the air, similar to that of a wet blanket left in a hot room. The smell, though... it's death. A lot of it.

Gazing across the expanse of the grounds, my mind flits to soldiers on opposing sides. Gunshots. Stabbings. Hand-to-hand combat. Fear. Blood. Anger. Death. So many lives lost. So many mothers lost their sons. So many wives became widows. So many children grew up without a father, brother, uncle, or grandfather.

I'll never understand.

Death.

I get the irony. Self-inflicted perma-naps, I get. Taking someone else's life... that's unfathomable to me. Though I've sometimes wished death upon those who hurt me, I was never strong enough to pull that trigger.

A brief montage enters my mind. *Courtroom full of people. Black hair. Black Dress. White Chucks. Blood. There's not enough bleach for this.*

No matter how much of it infects my life, its necessity remains a mystery. Its hold on me, though faint, is never fully out of reach.

Always one bad decision away. Death waits, lurking in the shadows. Sharpening his scythe, humming a tune that sounds like, in the end, it doesn't even matter. Always at the ready to float his ethereal ass over and harvest my stained soul.

I don't want to be here anymore. I'm all too familiar with death and darkness.

Ten minutes later, I'm back on the road. I've slammed an energy drink, and I think I'm good for another few hours.

* * *

Maybe I need to get glasses. As soon as the sun went down, every light became a glowing orb of blurriness. The good news is that it's summer, and daylight hours are longer. The bad news is that I will not be driving at night if I can possibly help it.

My headlights illuminate the sign for Shreveport. Making the post glow with blurry white letters against a backdrop of a field of green. The billboard was definitely easier to see. Fuck me. I think I might have to get my eyes checked.

Pulling up to my accommodations for the evening, I quickly find an open spot. Not wanting to hoof it so far with a bunch of crap, I chuck my backpack over my shoulder and make my way inside.

My senses are immediately assaulted, and my brain stutters, trying to find something to cling to.

Smoke hangs heavy in the air as I make my way across the entrance to the check-in desk. Chatter seems to ebb and flow with the sounds of dings, whoops, and coins dropping.

About 30 feet away, a very sassy-looking lady stands behind the desk. Her fuzzy brown hair is half up and half down. She is donning a white button-down uniform with a black vest atop it and a slightly crooked name badge that I can't fucking read from here. She doesn't even acknowledge my existence.

An amazing smell flits around the space and wraps itself right around my pleasure center. It's so weird how smells can trigger intense feelings. Good or bad.

Frozen in the center of the walkway, I look around to try to find the source of the alluring smell that can only be described as the nectar of the Gods.

"That, Cher, is the world's most delectable cuisine." A deep voice with a smooth-as-silk Cajun French accent says from behind me. His breath tickles the light sheen of sweat that's broken out on my neck from Louisiana's warm and humid night air.

A wave of shivers works its way across my shoulders, and I don't dare move a muscle. The hustle and bustle around me seems to have faded away with the spoken words of this mysterious voice.

Another smell mixes with the mouth-watering scent of perfectly cooked steak. Leather. Tobacco. Whiskey. And just a hint of orange. That smell hits a different kind of pleasure center. The kind with a direct line to my clit.

My stranger rumbles out a small laugh. It echoes around my body like a warm melody, rich and resonant, with a spark of mischief dancing along the deep notes.

"Well, maybe not the *most* delectable. I can think of another mighty tasty treat that I love to lose myself in." His words have caused me to experience synesthesia. Much like the smoking caterpillar, I swear the words he doesn't say float around me in physical form.

Divine. *White.*

Sensual. *Orange.*

Warm. *Pink.*

Wet. *Blue.*

Hard. *Green.*

Explosion. *Yellow.*

Pleasure. *Purple.*

Sex. *Blood Red.*

His words and voice drip sex. A dirty promise of the highest forms of ecstasy, preceded by the world's *second* most delectable cuisine.

Heat envelopes my back when he moves closer. His breath tickles my ear as he says, "I don't mean to be so forward, Cher, but I'd love to give you a tour and have you for dinner."

My gulp is audible as his words sink into my body right before they hit my mind. Before I can turn to address this enigmatic seductor, a high-pitched, scratchy voice calls out. "Oh, bonswa, sir. What can I do for you?" The fake, forced French dialect makes my lip curl up in distaste. Try hard much?

Um, what the fuck. My irritation is a polar plunge for my libido. Did this bitch just ignore me in favor of the tasty stranger?

A large, veiny, tan hand shoots out beside me. The glinting gold of his wristwatch captivates my attention. The way the lights bounce off of the clearly expensive piece of jewelry pulls me in. Lulling me into a sense of calm.

He doesn't address her, but his palm stops her dead in her tracks. She has the good sense to look embarrassed before busying herself with menial tasks.

I can't help it; I snort.

Fuzzy McFakeFuck shoots me a quick glare as the stranger makes his way around me. My breath catches when I take him in from head to toe.

He's a bit older, I think. Jet black hair with just an ever-so-slight dusting of gray around his temples. Combed back and gelled lightly, but not so much that the waves of his hair are no longer prominent. Strong jawline that's just barely visible through a tidy, tightly cut beard. His large, robust frame seems sewn into his deep navy suit jacket. The suit pants are crafted perfectly for his muscular legs. Just tight enough to show what must be sinewy flesh. Down to shiny leather dress shoes that are fucking huge. You know what they say... big feet... big pocketbook.

After my —probably too long— perusal of the Creole Adonis

in front of me, my gaze finally made its way up to piercing ocean eyes. Eyes twinkling with amusement and heat.

He tilts his head to the side as he regards me. "Tu as bien vu, Cher?" *Did you get a good look, darling?*

With what I'm sure is a very un-cultured puzzled expression, I say, "Tu... what?" Jesus Charlie. Way to look like a damn dim-wit.

He shakes his head softly and chuckles. "Charmante." *Charming.* His hand reaches out and takes mine. I watch in rapture as he brings it to his lips. The surprisingly soft bristles of his mustache caress my skin as his warm lips press a kiss to the top of my hand. My cheeks immediately heat under the uninterrupted eye contact. He might as well be kissing other parts of my body.

His heated words come out in an erotic purr, "What do you say, Cher?"

My pussy says hell the fuck, yes. But that bitch often gets me in trouble. Would it be easy to have hot, anonymous sex with this sultry rando? I'm damn certain. I'm in a state I will never step foot in again, for one night only. One night to live out some wild and crazy, passionate fantasy.

"I can't." My voice sounds foreign, even to my ears. I'm almost a little surprised at the words that erupted from me. Excuses flutter around my mind, but each sounds more ridiculous than the last. How can I explain that I'm just not there? Mentally or physically. I'm not in the place where I can take the mustache ride his hand kiss silently offered. I'm a mess. And also on a self-imposed celibacy journey.

So, even though it pains me, I pull my hand back and offer him an apologetic smile. He returns it with sincerity as he nods and pulls a black card out of his pocket.

"I understand. Please accept this," he says, placing the card in my hand and gently closing my fingers around it. "This will give you anything you desire in the casino or hotel: any beverage, meal, or item in the gift shop, any service at the spa. It's also the only key to the Penthouse in the left tower. My suite."

My jaw drops as I look at the card with a gold foil Fleur-de-lis embossed in the center. I look back up at him quizzically. "What? I mean, why... what... who are you?"

My stuttering appears to amuse him. He squeezes my arm gently and bends down to place a feather-light kiss on my cheek. "Leave the card on the entry table of the suite. Though you won't be experiencing it with me this evening, I'd still love to give you an unforgettable night," he lightly chucks up my still-open jaw, "Bonne nuit, bele." *Goodnight, beautiful.*

When I settle into the softest bed I've ever laid in, with a belly full of the most mouth-watering steak of my life, I say a quiet thank you and goodnight to my mysterious Frenchman. The last image to dash about my conscience is of a dark boy with stormy eyes and a secret notebook. *Is he the reason I wouldn't indulge in a spicy dip in that sexy bowl of gumbo?*

Chapter 10

Charlotte

My dreams were hella X-rated last night. The strong man with the tantalizing tongue was without a face. But he fucked me until I almost blacked out on a canvas covered in the brightest of colors. A harmonizing of rainbows and flesh played out below our writhing bodies. When I came, sketches poured from the ceiling. I reached out to one that fluttered slowly to the floor, and a gold-foil Fleur-de-lis was splashed across the paper. But instead of the elegant symbol I saw last night, this one dripped blood red from each point onto a split tongue in the center.

I damn near humped my pillow when I woke with an intense ache between my slick thighs. Damn this fucking self-imposed celibacy tour. I decided my pussy makes too many decisions for me, so she gets no attention from me or anyone else until further notice.

After an easy, breezy four-hour drive from Shreveport, the sign for Norsville shines like a beacon against the scorching Texan sun. The fucking traffic coming through DFW almost made me turn right the hell around and go a different route. But I want to see her. Scratch that. I *need* to see her.

Anticipation grips the entirety of my body as I pull up to a very large metal archway with **STARLIGHT CANYON** written across it. And I swear to God, a tumbleweed rolled across the roadway. A motherfucking real-life tumbleweed!

So obviously, I thrust the gear shift into park and jump out to take a video of it. Savs will get a kick out of this country hick shit. As soon as I pull my phone out, the tumbleweed... well, tumbles the hell away from me, and I give chase while starting to film. "See this shit, Savs? You told me these things only existed in old, cheesy ass western movies. Liar, liar, may your vajune hairs set on fire!" I try to get a close-up when it comes to a stop, but every time I get within a few feet of the prickly bush, it rolls away again. When I've got enough shaky footage to compete with that "documentary" about the witch in the woods, I head back to my car.

The long driveway is well... long. Waves of dirt float through the air behind me like smoke signals to announce my arrival.

Cows!

I try to put my phone into video mode but hit a pothole, and it flies out of my hand onto the passenger-side floorboard. *Damnit*!

A chuckling form with fiery hair waving around her face with the breeze waves me in. The car is barely in park before I'm flying out of it and running like a damn linebacker at Ari.

"Oof." Ari splutters as we tumble to the ground, and I end up on top of her. Grinning at each other from ear to ear, I lean down and boop her nose with mine. "Hey, Red."

"Hey, Charlie. How many beignets did you eat on your drive? I think you broke a rib."

I jerk my face away in mock horror, "Moi? How dare you! Like three..."

65

Ari snorts out a laugh and murmurs under her breath, "More like three hundred."

A loud whistle interrupts our banter, and we both turn towards the noise. The sun blazes brightly as a large body comes closer. The features are completely encased in shadow with the sun directly behind them.

Very dirty and very large cowboy boots stop in front of our faces, and a deep rumble that's damn near a growl comes from the large man wearing them. "Cherry. All good here?"

"Just peachy, Cal. This is my bestie, Charlie. Charlie, this is my... uh... this is Calvin. His family owns the ranch."

"Howdy, ma'am," he greets with the tip of his cowboy hat, but oddly enough, he has no real Southern accent. I still can't see his face with the sun at his back. I look up at him with one eye closed from the brightness and nod my head but pull a disgusted face. "Ma'am? Yuck, please don't ever call me that again. Just Charlie will suffice."

"Well, *Charlie*. You mind getting off Cherry?" He all but sneers at me.

Ari rolls her eyes, but her cheeks pinken at his grumbles as I make a big show of getting off of her. I reach out a hand to help her when Calvin thrusts his out and pulls her up. The act is done with the utmost care and gentleness. It's such a juxtaposition to his huge size.

Calvin takes time to brush the dust off of her and cups her cheek while whispering to her. I can't quite make out what he's saying, but she places her hand over his and nods. Her lips curl up in a classic Ari shy smile as he rubs his thumb across her cheek. I'm interrupting an intimate moment and now feel like a weirdo for staring. Seems like they are awfully cozy for your typical employee/employer relationship. I make a mental note to interrogate the hell out of her later about this man.

After what seems like forever, Calvin pulls back from "Cherry" reluctantly and shoots a glare my way. Hot damn, this man is gorgeous. "You could've hurt her jumping on her like that." He chastises.

Ari taps him lightly on the chest with the back of her left hand. "Don't be mean to my friend, Cal. If she didn't jump on me, I would've jumped on her. I'm not such a delicate flower, you know?" her voice lowers, and I can barely make out her next words, "Not everyone is out to hurt me." Ari tries— and fails— to be stern to this brick shithouse of a man who towers over the both of us. And his. Fucking. Face. Crumbles. His shoulders sag, and he lets out a shuttering breath while nodding at her.

Holy shit. What is happening here?

I bite my top lip hard to prevent myself from smiling and laughing out loud. I'm getting the sense that Channing Tatum's twin brother here is a wee bit protective of my girl.

They stare at each other, seeming to have a conversation with just their eyes. Finally, Calvin breaks away and smiles at me. It's a bit forced, but I'll take it. He nods to my car, "You mind if I carry your bag for you?"

I want to be a smart ass so bad right now, but I imagine that this man isn't often so welcoming to strangers, or maybe just people in general, so I force it down and go with politeness. "That would be great, thank you."

With an ease that I certainly didn't possess when I struggled to get the suitcase in, he has it out and trudges ahead of us to a lovely-looking farmhouse.

I lock arms with Ari, who's trying desperately not to make

eye contact with me. Oh, hell no, we are talking about what just happened. "Um, Ari, what the fuck was that?"

"What?"

"Don't what me. You know what."

She shrugs.

"That man might as well have pissed all over you back there. For a moment, I thought he was going to throw you over his shoulder and take you back to the cave he crawled out of."

"He's just protective, that's all." She offers quietly, but I don't miss her eyes trailing him as he walks.

"Protective or possessive?" I ask, also watching the fine specimen in front of us. What an ass. Literally. The man's ass is so ripe and peachy you could take a bite out of it.

"What's the difference?"

I bump my ass against hers, "The difference is whether he sees you like a little sister who needs protecting. Or as a step-sister he secretly bangs in the pantry in the middle of the night."

Her gasp causes the cowboy to spin around and lock eyes on her. I giggle to myself. "Option number two, then." Ari doesn't respond, but her lips curve up in the tiniest of smiles, and I know I'm right.

* * *

I would have never in my life thought that I would attend a real-life hoe-down. This isn't just any hoe-down. It's an exclusive one. Ari was very hush-hush about the whole thing. Just said I needed to dress for the occasion. To her, that meant *lots* of denim, shiny teal cowboy boots, topped with a very heavy and stiff white cowboy hat.

She plaited my hair on two sides, but since it is so short now, the whole thing is held together with bobby pins and two hair ties.

When we pulled up, I noticed a few things.

1. The humongous, decaying barn which seems to be the only building as far as the eye can see.
2. There seem to be only two modes of transportation besides Calvin's jacked-up Ford: horses with four legs and iron horses with two legs.
3. There is *a lot* more leather than denim.

"If anyone gives you any grief tonight, let me know. They know to give Cherry a wide berth, but you—" Cal takes a moment to size me up and down. Not in a "hey, you look hot tonight" way, but more in a "how fast can she run in that dumbass denim miniskirt and cowboy boots" kind of way. "You ain't from around here, and the Villains always get the girl in this town." Before I can question him on, well, anything he just fucking said, he slides an arm around Ari and pulls her to the entrance, leaving me trailing behind them.

A very portly gentleman sits at the entrance on a metal stool that appears to be on the brink of collapse. He nods to Calvin, his eyes never landing on Ari... *interesting.* They do, however, shoot straight to my tits. He eyes my denim bustier with keen interest. I'm about to tell Old Man River where he can stick that interest when my eyes land on the leather vest he wears over a ratty, stained gray t-shirt. On his left breast, a white patch is stitched with black Old English letters: **"LUNCHBOX"** and below that another white patch: **"TREASURER"**. On his right is a **"1%"** patch. I immediately avert my eyes and speed up to catch Ari's hand.

The inside is nothing like the outside. This is clearly a "members-only" type of place. Though it's not modern in design by any stretch, it's very tastefully rustic. Made to look vintage while being in flawless condition. Longhorn skulls decorate every main wall. Instead of barstools and table tops, there are half-moon red velvet couches with a table in the center and one lone flickering candle in a crazed red vase atop it.

Seductive jazz whispers softly in the background. Every eye seems to fall on me as we make our way deeper into the... I don't know what to call it, but it's definitely not a fucking hoe-down. I feel so stupid in this getup. Ari is going to get a kick in the ass from me when we get back to her place. I'm afraid if I do it now, Calvin will rip my leg off and beat me with it.

We settle into our seats, and I take advantage of Calvin leaving to get us some drinks. I asked for anything in a closed bottle. I don't know if I'll ever trust someone to bring me a drink again.

Fucking Rebecca.

Chapter 11

"You dirty little liar!" I shout under my breath at Ari and throw a crumpled-up cocktail napkin at her chest. Those big doe eyes peer back at me in bewilderment.

"What did I lie about?" she asks, true concern laying heavy against her words. Ari's too good for us. By us, I mean the world at large. She's a goddamn angel.

"Damnit, Ari, stop giving me the puppy dog eyes. I'm trying to be fake-mad at you right now." I hold my hand up to block my view of her face so I can continue. "Oh, I dunno, let's count the ways, shall we? First, you let me come out in this *ridiculous* outfit—" Ari pulls my hand down and shakes her head vehemently, "No, no. Charlie, you look beautiful, I swear. You are the most gorgeous woman in this pla..."

My pointed glare stops her rebuttal. "As I was saying. Clothes. Second, why wouldn't you tell me you had a... feral beast who wants to suck the pure virginal soul right out of your lady bits? And lastly! Why the fuck didn't you mention the whole 'biker' thing?"

Ari wrings her hands together in her lap while hanging her head in what appears to be shame. Why am I such an asshole?

I scoot over, keeping my legs as closed as I can so the leather-clad hooligans don't get a free show, and wrap my arm around her shoulder.

"It's complicated, Charlie." She whispers against my cheek.

"I've gathered that. You didn't do anything wrong. If anything, I'm just happy to see someone so obsessed with you. And a little jelly, if I'm honest." I joke and rub her arm in a comforting manner.

Ari is strong as fuck in spirit, but she is so delicate emotionally. She doesn't like to upset anyone, even to the detriment of herself. I hope Calvin is the person who can change that for her. To show her how fucking strong she truly is. And he had better worship her the way she deserves, or I swear to God, I'll chop off his balls and shove them right up his ass.

"You're growling. Who's the feral beast now?" Ari laughs and lightly elbows me in the stomach.

"I've never claimed to be anything but an unhinged crazy person." I shrug and peer around at the crowd. More people have filled in, and I notice a stage in the back center that I didn't see when we first came in.

A skinny kid, probably around our age, in a plain black vest, hauls a drum kit to the back of the platform. As he positions it in just the right spot, the lights glow on the name stitched across his back, **"PROSPECT"**. He disappears behind a red velvet curtain for a moment before popping back out with another piece of equipment for the stage.

I watch the prospect go back and forth until a full band setup is put together and going through sound check. Calvin makes his way back over to us, dropping a red drink with a cherry in front of Ari and a bottle of some light beer with an opener in front of me. We cheers and continue watching the band set up.

The lights dim, and the band takes their places, but notably, the singer is missing. The raucous noise throughout the club settles, and the stage lights cut off, leaving everyone on it covered in a shroud of darkness.

When the spotlight beams on, it lands on a bowed head full of onyx hair hovering over the microphone.

A melodic strum of a guitar flows into the crowd, and the room seems to fade away as the singer lifts his head and begins to sing. His eyes land right on me, and my body freezes in place. Vibrant emerald eyes. *It can't be... no, no, no. He can't be here.*

My chest rises and falls rapidly with the breath I can't seem to catch. My palms instantly dampen, and my vision blurs.

Zach?

* * *

The breeze caressing my face as I stare out over the town has just the right amount of bite to it. Cool enough to anchor me to this spot, not so cold that it steals the breath from my lungs.

A loud boom draws my attention, and I walk to the cliff's perimeter to inspect the sound. As I near the edge and peer down, I'm met with a familiar scene. A beige sedan is alight with flames. Dry leaves tumble in the breeze, and a raven sings his melancholy.

When I meet the raven's gaze, instead of his midnight orbs I've become accustomed to, I'm met with illuminating green ones. The verdant stare that has looked upon my body in laughter... in lust... in love... in goodbye.

When the raven opens its maw, instead of the bird song he normally sings, the sound comes out, "Charlie". It flows out of his mouth in urgency. He's trying to get my immediate attention. But for what?

"Charlie." He urges again.

What is it, Raven?

"Charlotte!" He shouts at me. I continue watching him. Neither of us moving.

My eyes shut against a burst of wind, and when they reopen, the raven is closer, and his emerald gaze has shifted to sky blue.

"Charlotte, please..." he pleads, his voice morphing into a familiar feminine pitch. Another gust of wind forces my eyes closed again.

When I finally compel them to open, I find Ari leaning over me with my face cradled in her hands. Her eyes laden with unshed tears and panic.

We blink at each other for several seconds before she speaks. "My gosh, Charlie. Are you alright?"

I wheeze out a huff of air, "I'd be better if there weren't this weight on my chest."

Ari looks concerned at Calvin and then back at me. "Oh no, should we call an ambulance?" she asks no one in particular.

Calvin and I meet each other's gaze, and he reaches out with a huge hand to rub delicately at her shoulder. "No, Cherry. I think she'll be right as rain as soon as you get off of her."

Immediately flushed in embarrassment, Ari launches off of me, and Calvin reaches out a hand to help me to my feet. As I stand on wobbly legs, my vision swims similarly to getting off of the anti-gravity ride at the fair.

Somebody places a sweating glass of ice water in my hand, and I bring it to my lips and sip slowly. My eyes close, and I fight against the dizzying sensation. A warm hand rubs soothing circles on my back. The denim creates friction against the exposed areas my top doesn't cover.

"That'a girl. Slow sips. Nice and easy." A deep, lyrical voice coos in my ear. Warm breath flutters along my skin and tickles the baby hairs that fly loose from my braids.

Slowly, with the glass still poised at my lips, I spin to the man behind me. Not Zach. Up close, their differences couldn't be more obvious. Where Zach has sandy hair, this man has deep black. Likely dyed, but the shade of his eyebrows leads me to the conclusion that his natural is quite dark as well.

The emerald stare I saw glimmering in the spotlight is but colored contacts. I now see clearly a slim lining of brown on the inside ring of the iris. And the body, while similar in height, weight, and tone, is beautifully decorated. Ink peeks out from under his shirt. There's not a stitch of this man that doesn't have a story playing out on his skin.

A kind smile pulls up on his lips, and I find myself mirroring the gesture. The hand that was rubbing my back has moved to my arm. It's almost like he can't help but touch me. We stare at each other for a long moment before Ari clears her throat softly, breaking the spell. It's then I realize just how silent it is in the room. My eyes widen as I slowly move my gaze from the singer and see that all eyes in the room are on me. Fuck my life.

Some stares are filled with boredom like I'm a ditzy girl throwing a fit for attention. Some are laced with annoyance, mostly those who seemed to be really into the band. Shit. The band. My eyes snap to the stage where the rest of the band still remains in their positions with their instruments. The microphone stand is the only thing out of place. Instead of its upright position, it lays haphazardly across the floor in front of the stage. Like the singer leaped off the surface, and it fell behind, forgotten.

"So, do you have a name?"

I spin back to the singer and cock my head to the side. I'm still trying to get my brain to catch up with the events that are going on. "Huh?"

A smirk kicks up on his strikingly handsome face, "Or can I just call you mine?"

We stare at each other again, eyes locked like we're the only ones in the room. I bring the cup to my lips again, doing my damnedest to keep a straight face. Humor twinkles in his eyes, and I immediately lose our unofficial game of chicken when I sputter a laugh into my cup.

He cheeses hard and reaches a hand out for me to grab. "Come on, Clumsy Clara, let's get you in a seat. Unless you want to sit on *my* seat?" He waggles his brows while maybe hitting on me? I can't really tell if he's serious or not.

For some reason, I can't form normal human words, so all I offer is a correction, "Charlotte."

"Even better." He responds while ushering me the few steps to the other side of the booth. A seat that has a splendid view of the stage. Guess that's not an accident.

Ari, Calvin, and I take our seats once more as singer heads back to his rightful place. He winks at me as the band kicks up again, and he belts out a heavy metal rendition of a popular love ballad. *Swoon*.

Two hours later, I stand, whooping and hollering in applause as the band completes their set. Earning me a wink from the leading member.

He jumps off the stage and stalks our way. With practiced ease, a tall brunette wearing a leather skirt so short it's basically a pussy curtain pulls out the chair opposite me. As he sinks into it, she places a beer in his hand and drapes a leather vest onto his shoulders. He watches me intently as he slips his arms through the holes. When it settles in place, my eyes immediately jump to the white name tape on his left pec, **"CHARMING, VP"**.

The brunette hovers by his side, waiting for some kind of instruction, it seems. He pats his thigh, and she slides on it. The material of her skirt skids across his jeans, pleating it just enough to give our table a flash of her completely smooth flesh pocket. Gross.

I tilt my now warm beer up to him in cheers. A lascivious grin overtakes his face as he drapes one heavily tattooed hand onto the girl's fishnet-covered thigh. Ari sucks in a sharp breath beside me, but I don't break our stare. I simply watch his hand inching its way up until he flicks his forefinger through her downstairs lips. It's like he wants a reaction out of me. He expects me to shy away from the overtly sexual display. Little does he know, I've been the girl on the lap. Nothing fucking shocks me anymore.

When he doesn't get the reaction he's hoping for, he clicks his tongue and tips his head to the side, effectively dismissing her without a sound or breaking eye contact with me.

Deep chuckles from my right oscillate between us, and Calvin speaks up, "Charlotte, this is Charming. Charming, this is Cherry's girl, Charlotte."

"Charlotte." Charming chews on my name like he's sucking the sweetness right out of my vajay. He hums, and I feel compelled to bring him into the circle who can call me by my nickname. "Charlie. You can call me Charlie."

He leans forward, placing his thick, corded forearms on the tabletop and licks across his lips. Making a big show of looking me up and down, "How long you in town for, *Charlie*?"

I internally giggle. Charming is right. This man has probably never had a girl turn him down in his life. In another life, I'd be sitting on his face by now. But I don't want to alienate the people in Ari's life and what appears to be the Vice President of this biker gang. A little flirty banter never hurt anyone, right?

I lean forward, matching his stance, and drop my voice to a deeper rasp. "Undecided. Maybe a few days. Maybe a few weeks." I mimic his earlier perusal of my body and shrug my shoulder lightly, "You offering to be my tour guide?"

Charming lets out a full belly laugh and slaps his palm on the table. His gaze cuts to the large man beside Ari before returning to me as he tells Calvin, "I like this one. Don't scare her off, Cal."

We spend the rest of the night sipping beers and trading funny stories of our pasts. It's so good to see Ari smile. She doesn't notice the way Calvin watches her. His eyes are glued to her as he hangs on every word. His very presence is protective. He constantly angles his body towards her. I love this for her. And I don't give a fuck how big and bad he is or who his friends are; if he breaks her heart, I will Lorena Bobbitt every motherfucker in this place.

But beware boys; unlike Mrs. Bobbitt, I will dip your amputated weens in a vat of acid. There won't be any dicks coming back from that.

Chapter 12

August 2008

Charlotte

For an Alaskan girl who loathes doing "outdoorsy" things, these last couple of weeks at Starlight Canyon have been transformative. I started to feel like I'd become one with nature. That was until Harrison, the sorrel American Quarter that is "the epitome of a gentle giant"— Ari's words, not mine— bucked my ass off his, and I landed like a sack of bricks in the dirt.

Thank God Ari convinced me to wear a sturdy set of jeans when I was hell-bent on rocking some Daisy Dukes. You know, because it's a bazillion degrees outside. If I had gone with my original attire, I would've been much worse off than the sore tailbone, cut on my left shoulder, and bruised ego I walked away with.

But, no matter how much she's tried, Ari has yet to persuade me to get back on a horse. I'll admire them from afar, like a far, afar.

She's a captivating sight when she's working with the horses in the arena. With a few clicks of her tongue and a gentle pull on their lead, they are putty in her hands. I've never seen such a natural animal whisperer. It makes sense that these beings trust Ari, heart and soul. They can sense her goodness and sincerity. Shit, I would let this woman lead me around by a lunge line if she wanted to.

I sit on the metal bleachers outside the arena and watch Ari working with Samson. The Thoroughbred is a new addition to the ranch. From the little information we were given, he was neglected and abused at his previous home. Starlight Canyon offers rehabilitation, and they have a good relationship with law enforcement in the area. So when animals are found to need fostering, rehabbing, training, or simply a forever home, they come here.

Calvin's mom is the sweetest hardass I've ever met, Helen Latham. She looks exactly as you'd imagine a hardworking, badass rancher would. Tall, thick, and strong, with long brown hair plaited down her spine and a penchant for flannel. Has never seen a manicure a day in her life but has the manners of a Southern debutante. She's just good people.

Calvin also has a brother, Devin, whom I have yet to meet. He's apparently a bit of a troublemaker, and I'm pretty sure the fact that we haven't crossed paths is no accident.

I finally broke down and told Ari about the whole Jason thing and gave her more details on my epic shitstorm with Zach. We talked for hours about my emotional instability and why I'm on a self-imposed boy break. It's too easy to forgive and forget. It's too easy to let someone make my body feel good. It's too easy to stuff everything that hurts me back into that box in my mind. I've done easy long enough. It's time for me to do *right*.

We've been back to the Hoe-Down — which is a name and

not an event— a few times in the last month that I've been here. In my normal fucking clothes and not that cowboy hooker Barbie shit. Just like, normal hooker Barbie shit. I'm getting used to being surrounded by leather-clad villains. Norsvillains. The motorcycle club that Calvin isn't quite a member of but has deep ties to. Devin is a member, and surprise, surprise; Charming is his bestie.

Charming and I have exchanged flirty barbs and heavy eye contact, but I always brush off his advances. Even the ones where he doesn't have his fingers inside someone's pussy while he's talking about mine. The debauchery that goes on in the clubhouse should repulse me. Instead, it fascinates me. The human condition is a pox on the universe, but also, very entertaining.

I've watched so many people fucking; you would think I just walked onto the set of *"Norsvillain Skin Shed 6"*. I've seen more cheeks clapped than a nun at a catholic school.

Fight nights are my favorite, though. There's nothing like watching a bunch of sweaty, fit men knocking each other around, except for when they let the Sweet Butts go at it. That's the cutesy little nickname they give to the groupies that hang around the MC. And trust me when I say that is the nicest thing I've heard them called. They seem to love it, though.

Watching a bunch of catty women go at it in a boxing ring is fucking hilarious. Not a one of these girls can fight with proper form. They are so stereotypical. Scratching, pulling hair, biting, slapping, and shit-talking. There is no TKO happening with them. They simply go at it until members get bored of seeing a mediocre catfight. I swear I've been so tempted to climb between the ropes and pop a girl one good time with a closed fist just so they can see what the hell they should be doing up there.

We've grown into a comfortable routine. Ari and I stay in the gorgeous farmhouse. It's cozy. It has two bedrooms, one bathroom, an open kitchen, and a living room area. The two of us occupy the space perfectly, if I do say so myself. And though Calvin stays in the main house, he is at our place nightly. I think I'm starting to grow on him. A little. He's not very talkative, at least not to anyone but Ari.

* * *

I have good days and bad days. Today is a bad day. I'm having more of those than I have in a while. I don't want to talk to or be around anyone. Ari knew by my face this morning. She simply smiled and squeezed my arm as she headed out to start work. We are so alike sometimes. Even Savs, as much as I love her, always wants to "make it better". Ari understands that sometimes you don't need to make it better. You need to feel it. You need to process it. And then move past it.

About two weeks ago, Calvin showed up at the farmhouse with two ATVs. Each with a **STARLIGHT CANYON** logo on the back fender and an attached GPS unit. He stomped into the living room, where I was vegging out on the couch watching a true crime documentary, and threw the keys at me. Told me to "get off my ass and go explore".

With 500 acres to explore, I've found a few places I like to be alone. I mount the ATV and find the one I want on the GPS. I know I should probably wear the helmet, but I feel a little reckless today. Flying across the ranch's grounds at an irresponsible speed is the highest I get nowadays.

Twenty minutes and several bugs to the face later, I climb off the heated metal steed, leaving it behind for a lone Black Hickory. The area around the solo tree has faint scorch marks. I felt drawn to it immediately. There's something about being the last one standing when the world around you is burning.

I take up my usual position against the tree: Butt planted on the ground, and my back firmly pressed against the bark. The sun is at my back, and the branches offer a slight reprieve from the blazing rays. I pull the small journal out of my back pocket and remove the pen I shoved in my bun. Before I open up to the page I'm dreading, I tip my head skyward and breathe in the deep, smokey odor of the tree. Like I'm asking for permission to write the words that hang heavy on my heart today.

"If this is a shitty idea, give me a sign." I huff out a breath of exasperation, and when a nut doesn't fall off the tree and gouge out my eye, I take it as a sign to stop being a little bitch and write the damn letter. He'll never see it anyway.

* * *

Dear Zach,

This is the first and last letter I will write to you. I want to say I hate you. For a while, I tried to convince myself I did. You know the phrase "there's a thin line between love and hate"? It's a common saying for a reason. The strong emotions that have to be invoked to feel either of those things are very similar and can be so all-consuming that it's often mistaken for hate.

But I don't hate you. I can't. And that makes me want to hate you even more. But I fucking love you. I think a part of me will always love you.

I just want to know why. I know you fucking loved me. There's no way you faked it for that long and that deeply. So, why?

What was it that pushed you away? What made our love so easy to give up? I'm so tired of feeling unlovable, Zach. I need to understand why you did this to us.

I'm not a little girl pining for her "one true love". I believe people can have many loves in their lifetime of equal importance. If you'd found that with someone else, you could've told me. I would've understood. I would've been hurt for sure, but I would've let you go. Because all I want is your happiness. If that's not with me, then so be it.

So I guess that's what I can say now. I hope you're happy, Zach. I truly do. I've cursed you and called you every name in the book, but ultimately, I want you to do what's best for you.

And doing this is what's best for me. I'm letting you go, Zach. I'm choosing me. I'm not unlovable. I just need to find someone who loves me in the forever way.

I'll never regret you.

The only thing I will continue to grieve is the loss of my boy best friend.

When I think of you, I will try to do it through a lens of love and not devastation. I'll try not to recall the sights and sounds from the video. I'll try to scrub the image of you broken in my doorway from my mind.

I'll try. For you. And for me.

I want you to have an amazing life. Travel the world, be a football star, start a Southern Rock band, whatever strikes your fancy—just be you.

As for me, I'll be okay. I know my happily ever after is just around the corner. He'll see me... he'll hear me... and he'll choose me. Forever.

With love and just a pinch of hate (I'm still a human, sue me.)– Little Bit.

Fuck you, though.

Chapter 13

Charlotte

"I can't believe it's your last night in Norsville. Are you sure you can't stay?" Ari pouts while she watches me stuff my semi-clean clothes back into my suitcase. She thinks I haven't noticed that every time I put a few things in, she takes one back out and sets it back on the pile.

"Ah, Red, I'd love to live out your *'Little House on the Prairie'* fantasies, but alas, I do have to make it back to Alaska in time to get things prepped for my new job."

"Is it going to be weird seeing Dr. Turner again?" Ari asks while the little sneak pulls a set of socks back out of my suitcase.

I snatch it from her hands before she lets them go. She doesn't even have the sense to look ashamed. If anything, she's smug about it. "We won't be working in the same facility. He's moved over to the adult care clinic across the street. Even when we do cross paths, I think it'll be okay. We are both adults. We agreed that what happened between us was inapprops and in the past."

"I was really worried to get him in touch with your therapist. I didn't want to cross a line. But I just knew you were made for this position, Charlie. You can be a part of something important. Those kids need you. *We* needed you..." she chokes out the last few words. And I know what she means. I need to be what we needed when we were in Starry North.

Dr. Turner reached out to Ari and a few other residents for statements on the illegal operations and abuse that took place during their treatment. After one undercover sting operation, several arrests, and Small Dick Rick getting tased for resisting, the facility was shut down. I would've loved to see Nurse Hatchet Face's face when it all went down.

Dr. Turner left California and got a group of private donors to take over and revamp the place. It reopens in October, and Jensen reached out to Dr. Thitters as a friend and suggested talking to me about an opportunity to come on board. As a Chemical Dependency Counselor. Courtesy of Ari's nomination.

At first, it seemed like a crazy-pants notion. But then, the more I thought about it, the more it warmed my soul to be able to be there for those kids in the most vulnerable position of their lives.

I wasn't happy at school. Obviously, my love life went to shit. And while I do miss Reg, Sariah, and Genny, I went to college because that's what you're supposed to do. Or so I thought. I've always wanted to help kids. Now, I can.

I put down the stack of underwear to the side of my suitcase and sit beside Ari. "You didn't cross a line. I'm glad you talked to him about me. You knew what I needed when I didn't. I want to move forward in my life, and I felt like I couldn't do that while I was paddling in a circle in Alabama. I hardly saw my dad because I refused to set eyes on his whore. Reg and Sariah were settling into their roles as new parents. Genny is constantly taking on new sponsees. It was the perfect time for a new adventure." I wrap my arm around her shoulder, and we rest our heads together. "And the fact that I don't have to go to school anymore? What a fucking bonus. School is so lame. I've never been a fan."

Ari chuckles lightly, but the sniff at the end is a tell-tale sign that she's shedding some tears.

I was already mostly on board with making the move back to Alaska and taking this new position. But when I found out that you don't even have to have a degree. Shit, that contract basically signed itself.

I don't care about making a ton of money. I want to make a difference. That's enough for me.

"Hey, enough of this sad-sack bullshit. I want to have an unforgettable night with one of my best friends. So—" I pull her to her feet and usher her out the door with a slap on the ass while hollering after her, "Put something on that would make your momma blush, Red. We are going out!"

* * *

We had to drive forty-five fucking minutes away to find a tavern not in the middle of BFE. Saturday night was clearly a shitty time to come. We are smashed in like sardines, and it reeks of Brute and sweat.

We finally find a small, sticky table to sit at with our beers and wait for our food. Occasionally batting off the drunken randos who keep hitting on us. Can't two youngin's with fake IDs enjoy a night out without the penis wielders spitting horrible game at them?

I demolish a basket of onion rings in a very savage way, chasing it with a vodka soda. That was zero percent sexy. I'd love to see those fuck boys come back over here after that animalistic display.

Ari goes up to order another basket and drinks for us. It seems like a lot of the people who were here are part of a bar crawl and have since moved on to the next. Thank God.

After three vodka sodas, my child-sized bladder is screaming at me, so I excuse myself and go to the restroom. Feeling pretty proud that I had minimal stumbling on the way.

The artwork decorating the hallway to the bathroom is nothing like I would've guessed for a dive bar. On the right, there are several groups of family photos. Many with one old man and two small boys, a few with the boys and horses, and a very large painted canvas of a younger version of the old man in overalls and a little girl on his shoulders.

I smile at the love shining through each image. Clearly, these people love each other fiercely.

On the left is a trail of hand-carved stars. I place my fingertips across the grooves as I walk. The path of stars abruptly ends at the co-ed bathroom door; I look a little further to see it pick up again at the other side. All the way down to the wall at the end of the hallway. The wall at the back depicts a massive valley with wild horses running in the starlight and a full moon in the upper right corner. *Fucking beautiful.* I think as I enter the bathroom.

I throw a safety cover on the toilet and crash down on it in the nick of time before my bladder fails me. A loud bang startles me as the door to the bathroom slams closed behind whoever entered.

89

I do my business and exit the stall to wash my hands. I turn to look for paper towels, and I see a lean, tall guy hovering over the towel dispenser. His back is to me, so I can't see what he's doing. He doesn't seem to mind that I'm just standing behind him, waiting like an asshole.

His head dips a little, and I hear a sound that I'm all too familiar with. I fight against the onslaught of memories and wants that crash into my body. It sounds again... and again... and again before his head lifts, and he turns towards me with his finger running across his front gums.

His face immediately turns lustful. He eyes each of my hands, and without turning from me, he reaches back for a handful of paper towels. He walks the towels over to me, getting way too close for comfort. Even in the dim lighting of the bathroom, where his pupils should be dilated from lack of light, they remain small as a pinprick.

We stare at each other as I dry my hands. A barrage of thoughts slam into me. *Could I have just a little? Would it really be that bad? Just a taste. One taste would be okay.*

My tongue slides across my bottom lip without permission. The man watches in fascination before trailing the same finger he just rubbed against his gums across the wet pout.

I could fold my lip into my mouth.

Just a taste.

"Charlie?" Ari's voice filters through the snowy thoughts, and I jerk away from the man and quickly wipe my sleeve across my lips.

He peers behind me at Ari, and his lips kick up into a shit-eating grin. He situates himself against one of the sinks with his arms folded. "Ah, so this is why I've been banished from my house."

My head whips back and forth between the man and Ari. "What's happening?" I ask the room in general.

Without answering, Ari grabs my hand and starts to pull me towards the door. "Come on, Charlie. I'm calling Cal to come get us."

A boisterous laugh fills the small bathroom and reverberates off the tiles. "No need to worry, Prudence. I can take *Charlie* home."

My head swims with liquor and the need to get high, "That's not her name. It's Ari. And I'm going nowhere with you."

The man crowds us against the closed door, and Ari grips my arm tightly. She needn't worry, though; I'll never let someone hurt her.

Before I can tell the fucker to get lost or lose a testicle, Ari's phone rings, and she brings it to her ear. It's Calvin. I can hear his deep timbre from here. She tells him where we are and that we are in the bathroom with D. She reaches between us and holds her phone out to him, "It's for you."

D takes the phone with a smirk, "Yo, big bro. Long time no talk. But I now see why. This hot little number is the reason you haven't let me come home, isn't she?"

Oh fuck. This is Calvin's brother. The troublemaker.

Whatever Calvin says, Devin rolls his eyes and mimes a mouth yapping with his hand. "You got it, bro; I'll keep them nice and safe until you arrive." He hangs the phone up while Calvin shouts and tosses it back to Ari. "Prudence, why don't you go get yourself a Shirley Temple and a lollipop? Charlie and I were in the middle of a conversation, and I'd like to get back to it."

Three loud knocks rap against the wood at our backs. "D, get the fuck out here now. Charming is on the phone."

Devin rolls his eyes and runs a finger down my cheek, "Raincheck, Charlie. Duty calls."

Ari and I move as a unit out of his way and take a collective breath when he leaves the room. I spin on Ari, "What the fuck was that? Why did he call you Prudence?"

Ari blows out a breath and tucks her hair behind her ears before pulling her sleeves to cover most of her hands. "That is the reason we wanted to keep him away from you. He is bad news, Charlie. He's a member of the Norsvillains, but he's also an addict. He calls me that because he thinks I'm a prude. It's a long story. I don't want to ruin our night with his antics. Cal said Charming is closer and will be taking us home."

"But you didn't drink much. Do you not feel okay to drive?" I ask.

She shakes her head. "I'm fine. But that's just the way he is. They'll have a prospect take my car back, and the two of us will ride with Charming."

When Charming enters the bar ten minutes later, Devin is nowhere to be found. That's for the best. I can't believe I even let myself have second thoughts on my sobriety. Maybe I need to lay off the booze as well. I clearly don't make the best of decisions.

Ari lays down across the large leather bench seat of the back of Charming's truck and immediately falls asleep. I chuckle, looking back at her from the front seat. Soft country plays on his radio, and I let my eyes wander over him. He doesn't really look the part of the Vice President of a motorcycle club. Definitely looks the part of a lead singer in a band, though.

His tattooed hand rests on the gear shift loosely with all the confidence of a skilled manual driver—a skill I do not possess, regardless of the countless people who've attempted to teach me.

"You can slide on over here if you want a closer look." He teases.

I roll my eyes, cross my arms, and watch the nothingness go by us while we make the drive back to Norsville.

As we pull up to the farmhouse, I look back, and Ari remains asleep. I take the opportunity to have a chat with Charming. "I'm leaving in the morning." I tip my head towards Ari, "Take care of her, okay? This is—" I gesture to his cut and back to the bikes outside the barn next to the farmhouse. "— intense, and she's important. Just... take care of her, please."

The normal smirk he wears is nowhere to be seen. He nods sharply. "She will always be safe here. We take care of our own. I promise."

I nod back and take off my seat belt. "Okay. Because if you don't, I'll fucking kill you." I look him square in the eyes so he can see the truth in my words. The smirk makes a comeback. "Sounds sexy. Y'all get going now. Take those cute asses to bed and have a pillow fight or something. Call me if you decide to explore each other."

Ari stirs and opens her door, "Why do you have to be such a boy, Charming?" He shrugs and gives us a wave before pulling away.

* * *

"I'm going to miss you so much. I'll come visit soon. But after winter. All the Alaska has left my system after living in California and Texas." Ari says as we hug tightly. Calvin stands like a sentinel a few feet away from us. He was kind enough to haul my luggage back to my car.

"I'll miss you too, Red. You better. Maybe you and Savs could be there for my birthday? We'll figure it out. I love you. Don't let these biker fucks push you around, you hear me?" Calvin growls from his perch at my barb. I pay him no mind. Though I'm sure he could crush me with little to no effort, I'm important to Ari, and therefore, he just has to put up with my shit.

"See ya, Big Man. Take care of my girl." I wave and enter my car. Tears prick my eyes, and I know it's time to get the fuck out of here before I start blubbering.

Just as I'm about to shut the door, Ari stops it and leans in, holding out an envelope. "Oh, by the way. This was delivered this morning." I nod and accept the letter. Jason's letter.

I make it to the town limits before I pull over. My curiosity will not let me go another minute without reading his letter.

* * *

Sweets,

I have so many questions. But first, I'll answer yours. To your inquisition about the descriptions of dicks... none of your fucking business! I'm not gonna sit here and describe other dude's junk to you. It's dicks. They look like dicks. With bigger dicks attached to them.

As far as inspiration. Some use pics from home; a lot use porn they've stored on hard drives and brought with them.

To answer your questions about me: Anywhere I have privacy. Anytime something reminds me of my inspiration. Highlight reel, every time.

I agree that I made a poor decision when flying. But I also won't promise it will never happen again.

Lots of people have a fear of flying. The trick is to find the right distraction. Some use movies or music. Others read a book or strike up a conversation with their seatmate. I'd love to see what could distract you 36k feet in the air. Maybe one day, we'll get the chance to find out.

Okay, now that we got that out of the way.

WHAT. And I can't stress this enough, THE FUCK?

Since when are you and Aurelia Fletcher friends?? The last I heard, you humiliated her in high school, like full-on Jawbreaker mean girl'd her.

Nursing? That's amazing, Sweets. I know healthcare has always been important to you. What is this opportunity that's taking you all the way back to the Great North? And why would you stay with Mary and not your mom? Did she move, too?

As far as what I know about your life after we... drifted, basically nothing. I pulled out of school not long after that last time we spoke in the hallway. I finished out school online and left for ASU. I cut off everything from back home. I just needed a fresh start. And to be honest, it killed me to see you with that football player and to hear some of the rumors that were going around about Poole.

I can't begin to explain to you how that ripped my fucking heart to shreds. I was angry, but I never wanted to see you with anyone else.

I got the impression from Savannah that you might have been through some shit. Tell me? I want to know everything about you. The good, bad, and ugly. I want it all.

You'll probably get lonely living on your own. Maybe you need a roommate. Like a 6'2, handsome, very muscular guy with gray eyes and black hair. All jokes aside, you'll do amazing, Charlie.

Something about me... Even with all the darkness revolving around our breakup and all the anger I held, I always knew. I knew that if I ever got another chance with you, there would be zero hesitation.

I was always meant to be yours, Sweets. Even if you'll never be mine.

I love you. Don't say anything back.

–J

PS—I'm glad you don't want to die most days. I can say the same. But every day I wake up and look forward to seeing your exquisite freckled face again is a day I have hope. Tell me another.

PPS— I've included another drawing.

TIME TAKES US ALL

Chapter 14

August 2008

Jason,

I can't believe you're being so stingy with the juicy deets of all the phallic happenings. *Insert eye roll here* I was just curious. All those men alone together, that's a lot of sausages. Wait... is it only men? I just assumed. Are there girls out there, too??

Oh Jace, I don't think I can tell you about my past in a letter. Though, thinking of saying it to your face scares me even more. I'm afraid if I cut myself open on this letter, the bleeding will never stop. And with the last few years I've had... I'm one drop away from exsanguination.

I can hardly answer one question without delving into a dark, dirty hole that I barely clawed my way out of. I'm not there yet. Give me time?

What I can answer is why Mary. Right after graduation... my mom died. Cancer. It hit hard and fast, and before I knew it, she was gone.

As far as Ari and I are concerned, we've... buried the hatchet in a big, big way. She has forgiven me for my past sins against her, and now we are extremely close, like best friends—don't tell Savs.

I didn't like who I became. I never thought I was capable of hurting someone like that. So, I'm working hard to make sure that Charlie never sees the light of day again.

The short answer on leaving college? I decided school wasn't for me. I still want to help people, and I've been offered an opportunity to help kids at a behavioral clinic in River View that specializes in addiction therapy.

In regards to the football player and Poole... those are stories for another day. Are you sure you want to peek behind the curtain? Once you know how the magic happens and the mystery is gone, all you're left with is a broken, sad girl with unresolved trauma and abandonment issues.

I'm surprised your parents didn't clue you in. They hate me, so I figured they'd jump at the chance to regale you with tales of my downfall.

If you really want to know—and I mean really want to know— the next time you have the internet handy, do a search for my name and River View. It won't tell you everything, but it'll give you an idea until I'm ready for you to know more.

I didn't want to start my drive with tears, but here I am, ten miles down a dirt road leaving Ari, sobbing like a baby bitch. Everything's just hitting all at once, you know? I wanted to get this letter out immediately since I just received yours. Send your reply to Mary's address.

Be safe.

-Charlie

PS— I'm worried that when you do the search, you'll see me differently. My heart aches at that. Please, just remember who I am is more than the things I've done and been through.

Chapter 15

September 2008

Jason

I can't fucking wait for the day we leave this Forward Operating Base (FOB). Being downwind from a shit pond is the worst way to wake up. The Ravenwood Collective (TRC) has been tasked with guarding a member of an undisclosed nation's royalty. Their country is currently at war with its surrounding neighbors, and our military has been sent in for support. We've been traveling from FOB to FOB, laying low in between. Trying our best to avoid active combat.

The five members of TRC here with me take turns on guard duty and ushering His Majesty— what we call him since his name isn't "need to know"— to the DFAC, latrine, and MWR (Morale, Welfare, and Recreation). While he isn't allowed internet usage, we've taken to heated matches of table tennis to pass the time when taking a break from working out.

Jacobs and Singer are taking up one position on the left side of the table, while Brown and Olsen are on the right. With the redness of Jacobs' cheeks and slew of cuss words coming out of his mouth, I assume he's on the losing end.

Like the good little bodyguard she is, Lokowski guards His Majesty on the sidelines. Hand on the top of the pistol that rests against her hip. Eyes cutting through the place like she can see threats through the walls.

It's not that the rest of us don't take our job seriously; we very much do, but she takes it to a crazy extent. I guess being the only woman on a team of all men, she feels she has something to prove. She shouldn't. She's earned the right to be here, the same as the rest of us.

I've learned not to try and coddle her or give her anything she can perceive as special treatment. She's one of those women who will rip off your ballsack and hand it to you in a doggy bag for suggesting she couldn't do something a man can.

I was surprised to see her on the plane when we were heading into theater. I'm not one of those douches who think women can't be in combat situations. I worry about myself more than I worry about her. It's instinct for me to protect the smallest and most vulnerable first. I had to learn to look at her as if she were a man just to stop the urge to always check on her when we get into sketchy scenarios. If I'm not focused, it puts us all in danger.

I fall down onto the couch beside His Majesty; as usual, the little scamp side-eyes me and spits out hushed Arabic under his breath. He's not my biggest fan. I don't know if it's all the piercings and tattoos or the long hair, but he sure is a judgy fuck.

I like to mess with him to pass the time. As I collapse down beside him, I ask, "What's good, friend?" He jerks away from me like my mere touch is going to give him a disease. No, what's likely to give him a disease is that noxious pond where they put all the waste. That shit has seeped into my fucking pores, no pun intended.

"I'll grow on you. You getting in on this, Lokowski?" I gesture to the match in front of us. She shakes her head without looking at me. Eyes always peeled for danger. I chuckle and throw a pencil at Jacobs right when he's about to hit the ball. It hits him in the nose, causing him to thrust his own paddle at his face. "What the fuck!" He shouts and shoots daggers at me with his eyes. They are only visible over the paddle that he still holds against his face. I give him my best innocent eyes and point at His Majesty, "He did it!" Causing His Majesty, Lokowski, and Jacobs to glare at me while the other three laugh their tits off.

* * *

"You think we'll get to go home by Christmas?" Olsen asks as we pause our game of who can get the pebble closest to the burn pit. We do a lot of random shit to stay sane out here.

Ryan Olsen is the only one of us with a wife and kids. Of course Christmas would be a priority for him. The rest of the team wouldn't know Christmas from any other random Thursday. I blow out a breath and lean back on my elbows to take in the night sky. It's completely clouded over, but that actually makes for a little warmer air temp. You wouldn't think the desert gets so damn cold at night. "Dunno, bud. Our timeline depends on the movement of the units and the amount of fire we take on."

"The prick won't even acknowledge us, and yet we are to be risking our lives for him. Why is he so important?" Olsen huffs as he kicks a small pile of dirt away.

I get his frustration, but it's not up to us. We have a job to do. Job says to keep His Assness safe and deliver him into the waiting arms of his rich daddy. I change the subject, "What made you take a job with TRC?"

A brilliant smile kicks up on his stubbled face, showing a deep set of dimples. He takes off his hat and reaches under the front inside lip, retrieving a sonogram photo. "Jenna is pregnant. We're going to be a family of five if you can believe it. With the other two kiddos in school now, we are starting all over with a baby. Babies need lots of things, Donovan. They go through diapers like you would not believe. Then there's bottles, formula, creams, lotions, humidifiers, cribs, toys, swaddle blankets, car seats... the list goes on and on."

I stare at him wide-eyed. Damn. I didn't realize there was so much involved in a tiny human. I've heard formula is crazy expensive. But then why... "Why doesn't she want to breastfeed?"

Olsen shoots an unimpressed look at me, "I'm not talking about my wife's tits with you."

"I'm not asking about her tits. Jesus man. I'm just asking, why pay for formula if her tits make milk for free?"

He shakes his head and chuckles under his breath. I'm clearly left out of the joke. "Not that it's any of your fucking business, but Jenna is an under producer. With our first two boys, she tried everything. Cookies, pills, specialists, massagers. But she would get so frustrated and depressed when she couldn't supply enough. So she will try with this new baby, but we need to have an alternative on hand."

"Okay, that makes sense. I've never been around babies, so I don't know the ins and outs of it all. Just what I've seen in movies or heard from random people." I admit.

"Well, for future reference, don't ever question what a parent has to do to feed their kid. Fed is best. Period."

"Got it."

We sit in silence, listening to the wind howl against the small buildings on the FOB. I pull out my notebook and turn on the small headlamp on my forehead.

My most recent piece stares back at me, half-finished. I shade in portions of the feathers, giving it an in-flight type of movement. My pencil moves back and forth across the page, and I lose myself in the angelic sails until footsteps capture our attention.

"Olsen, time to hit the hay. I'll take it from here." Jacobs says as he smacks Olsen on the back and plops down in between us.

"Don't have to tell me twice, Cap. Night boys." Olsen gives us a small salute and wanders off to the connex he's claimed as his own.

I'm about to get back to my drawing when Jacobs drops an envelope on my page. I almost start to bitch him out when I see the handwriting on the front. I try—and fail—to keep a grin off my face. I don't need any bullshit from Jacobs. He already thinks I'm pussy whipped by someone who isn't even mine, and he doesn't let me forget it.

"I thought that would kick your grumpy ass in the dick. It slid off the mail bucket and was on the floor of the command tent. I figured I'd scoop it for you so I don't have to look at your mopey, love-sick face for one more night."

I ignore his barbs and rip the letter open. My eyes scan as fast as they can. Soaking up Charlotte's words like they are the last drops of hope in a sea of despair.

I finish the letter and read it back again. One section sticks out to me the most. *I'm afraid if I cut myself open on this letter, the bleeding will never stop. And with the last few years I've had... I'm one drop away from exsanguination.*

Oh, Sweets... What has happened to you? What could cause this incredibly strong woman to curl in on herself?

"What'd she say?" Jacobs asks as he leans over, trying to get a peek at the letter. I pull my notebook to the side to hide it from his prying eyes and punch him in the arm with my free hand. "None of your damn business."

Jacobs rubs the sore spot on his arm and pouts, but I pay him no attention. I'm eager to get working on my response to her.

But first, I'll finish the next piece I'll be sending with it.

Chapter 16

October 2008

Sweets,

There are mostly men around. Both on my team and in the places we stop in. I can't disclose much of either. Sorry. You'll have to tell that curious kitty to keep her nose out of where it doesn't belong.

I can give you time. I will give you whatever you need from me. I will never push you, Charlie. But I do want you to feel comfortable coming to me when you're ready.

And when you are... bleed for me. Bleed your pain onto these pages. Let it consume you. Give me your pain, pretty girl. Let it consume me. Purge it from your soul, and trust me with it.

And then let it go.

I'm so fucking sorry to hear about your mom. The more we talk, the more I fucking hate myself for letting us go so long without speaking. I'm sorry I wasn't there for you. And fuck. I'm so sorry I'll never get to meet her. Mary seems like a great woman, and I'm happy she was there for you and continues to be. She must be something to have put up with Savvy for twenty years. (I'm joking... kind of)

I'm glad you and Aurelia— or, I guess, Ari— patched things up. For as much as she was always around in high school, I really didn't know her at all. But I know she was a pretty lonely girl, so having you as a friend probably means the world to her.

You are an amazing person. You are so smart and loyal. You like to hide your mushy parts, but I know they are there. When you love, you love fiercely. When you protect, you do so with your whole being. I've never met such a strong-willed pain in the ass. And if we have a daughter someday, I hope she's just like you.

You will do great with helping those kids. I can't even imagine the mindset and vulnerable state they are in to be in a place like that. But if I were in that position, I know having you on my side would make it all worthwhile. You'll go to bat for them, and I'm sure not many know what that's like.

I want to know everything. There's nothing, **nothing** you could tell me that would make me think any less of you. I know who you are, Sweets. I know your heart.

Trust me.

Fuck my parents. That's really all I have to say about that.

I think I'll wait for you to tell me what you want me to know when you are ready. Though now my curiosity is definitely piqued. What could you have done that warranted news coverage?

I love you. You could say it back if you wanted.

-J

PS—She's got a sadness behind her brown eyes, but her halo shines brighter than a million fireflies.

She feels stuck to the ground, but she doesn't realize the wings she's been given will take her far above and beyond the moon that's round.

A queen in my heart she'll forever be. The perfect trinity. My pretty girl. My Sweets. My Charlie.

Chapter 17

October 2008

Charlotte

It took me six days to get from Norsville to River View, and I slept for two days straight after that. Mary has been a saint, letting me stay at her place so I can get on my feet. I used my emergency credit card at the department store because I'm pretty sure my band tees and holey jeans will be frowned upon at my new adult job.

I didn't think I'd be so nervous going back to Starry North. But the nightmares every night for the last two weeks that I've been back in Alaska tell me otherwise. Most of them revolve around being restrained and sedated against my will. Some have SDR taking his groping to the next level and violating me in the worst way. But the ones that have me gasping for air and waking in a panic are the ones I have of Ari.

I'm asleep back in my bed at Starry North. A creak of the door causes my eyes to shoot open; terror fills my body, so I don't move. Wet footsteps squelch along the linoleum as the figure makes its way into the room.

A drip, drip, drip accompanies the strides and only stops when the figure comes to a halt right beside my bed. A thin, pale arm reaches out for my face, and I squeeze my eyes shut tight. The drip continues, the sound deepening as it hits my skin. The liquid runs down my face and settles in the crease of my lips. A metallic tang settles in the air around us.

Hair tickles my cheeks as the figure leans down. Heavy breaths ebb and flow from my skin. Drops continue to fall, and I can't avoid wiping them off now. As I reach up, cold hands wrap around my wrists and jerk me upwards on the bed.

My eyes are forced open with the mighty roar unleashed in the silent room. The sound pings off the walls, and when I look at the figure, I can't make out a face. The long hair soaked in blood drapes over the face.

Shakily, I reach out a hand and move the crimson-soaked locks to find missing eyes. Bloody sockets rest where there should be clear sky-blue orbs.

My hand caresses her cheek, this monster before me, and her arms come up to grasp onto my wrists once more. This time, I see where the dripping is coming from. Monster Ari has two long, vertical gashes along each forearm, starting at the wrist and ending just before her elbow. Blood runs in steady streams out of each side, soaking her uniform and everything she touches.

When I try to speak, she slams me against the wall, squeezing her hand around my throat, and my vision swims, but just before everything goes black, I wake up.

* * *

A knock raps at the large wooden door to my new office. A moment later, a familiar face pops in. "Hey Charlotte, I just wanted to see how you were settling in. You have everything you need?" Dr. Thitters— or Margie, as she demands I call her now that we are colleagues—asks.

She's not my therapist anymore. I'm still looking for one, but I can tell you it damn sure won't be anyone I work with. Margie is now over at the adult clinic with Jensen, but I still feel a bit awkward that she knows all my demons. That's dangerous information in the wrong hands. Though, I do trust her implicitly. She is the picture of professional.

I leave the pamphlets I was folding on my desk and round it to meet her at the doorway. "Yep, everything is great. Janice showed me around, so I'm familiar with the changes to the facility. I'm just doing a little organizing in my office. I'll be sitting in on the group meeting later today just to get a feel for the patients and how things have been going. I don't want to disrupt the balance as much as possible, and though they've only been here a week, that can seem like a lifetime when you are the one admitted."

She nods her agreement and offers me a genuine smile, "That sounds like a marvelous plan. You'll do great here, Charlotte. This will be an enriching experience for them *and* you. I'm going to putter about for the day, so if you have any questions, don't hesitate to reach out."

She turns to walk out, and I waver at the question I want to ask. I don't want her to think I'm just looking for validation, but I kinda am. "Hey Margie?" She pauses and looks back at me. "Yes?" My hands wring together behind my back as nerves start to get the best of me. I spit it out before I lose all courage, "Do you think my age will be a problem? I'm not much older than some of the patients here. I want to be taken seriously by them and the staff. Any advice?"

Margie walks back over and rubs my arm in a consoling

manner. "I believe that is the very thing that will bring you together. You can meet these kids on their level. Not only in age but also in experience. You'd be surprised by how much respect they will give you immediately just knowing that you are one of them."

Wow. I never thought of it like that. I suppose I would feel the same. A lot of people who struggle with addiction, behavioral issues, or mental health often shy away from authority figures. But if they don't see me like that, I may be able to support them on a whole new, more personal level.

"Do they... do they know I was a patient here?" I ask, my voice trembling against my will.

Margie shakes her head emphatically. "No, Charlotte. We do not disclose medical history here. You know that. It's up to you what you choose to share with them. I would just suggest picking and choosing what would be helpful for them to know. Remember, though, we are here to help. Help and rehabilitate, and there are always ones who do not want it and will use whatever they can to their advantage."

"Okay. Good to know. Keep it real enough to connect but vague enough not to give too many personal details."

"Exactly. Don't worry. You're going to do great things here, Charlotte. I'm so pleased you agreed to join us."

My phone buzzes on the desk behind me. Margie takes that as her cue to exit, and I come back to my new comfy chair.
"SAVS"

I put the phone to my ear. "You've reached the office of Charlotte Johnson, a very professional and high-class worker. How may I direct your call?"

Savvy laughs on the other end, "You know that makes it sound like you are a sex worker, right? God, I hope you don't actually say some shit like that."

My eyes roll, as they typically do at some point during a conversation with my best friend. "Of course not, you dingbat. I'm a seasoned career woman now. I know how to carry myself. What are you up to?"

"Just got done with class. I'm heading to the practice room so I can work on my piece for the winter recital."

"Oh, sweet! Are you looking forward to it?" I ask. Hiding my curse from the small papercut I just gave myself folding another pamphlet.

"I was." She states with irritation.

I wait for a few beats, knowing that she'll come out with it eventually.

"Until that stupid, irritating, kiss-ass complained to the instructor, and now it's a fucking duo."

Trying to hide the smile from my voice, I taunt her a bit further by innocently asking, "Who would do that?"

"Don't play coy with me, Charls. You know damn good and well that it's that infuriating, pompous dillhole, Asher."

"Ah, the infamous Asher. Sounds like maybe you guys just need to bang it out. Have you ever thought about that? Maybe all this tension between you is the sexual kind—"

Dead air greets me, and I confirm my suspicions when I pull the phone away. This bitch really just hung up on me. Well, that's not going to shut me up.

Me: You know I'm right! When someone gets under your skin this much, you might as well get under his. Biblically.

Savs: *Middle finger emoji*

Me: Love you. Now, leave me be. I'm at work. At my NOT SEX WORKER adult job.

Savs: *Two middle finger emojis*

Chapter 18

Charlotte

Deja vu hits me hard as I sit in on the meeting. Six patients are in attendance. Four boys and two girls.

The boys all look between fifteen and seventeen. They have that mid-teen air about them. The one that says, "I don't give a fuck about anything and anyone," when really all they want is someone to pay attention and give them praise.

The girls seem to be polar opposites, but they are both around sixteen. The first girl seems bubbly and extroverted. Her speech is excited, and her words come out at a rapid pace. Her body bounces as she sits in the hard plastic chair. I wonder if she's still got a stimulant in her system or if this is just how she is.

The second girl is withdrawn. She hasn't said a word or looked anywhere but at her lap. Shoulder-length black hair drapes around her face, hiding it from the room. I'm assuming that's purposeful. She doesn't want to be seen. Or maybe she doesn't want to see anyone else. Perhaps both.

Unlike her seatmate, this girl is eerily still. Her baggy facility-issued hoodie hides the movements of her chest as she breathes. She doesn't fidget. She doesn't move a muscle.

My eyes trace down to what should be fully white canvas slip-ons to find that this little rebel has doodled all over them. No words, just symbols. I wonder what they mean?

"Okay, gang, that was a really great meeting. I'd like to thank everyone for their shares. Let's all gather in a circle to close the night out with the serenity prayer." The hippy-dippy temporary addiction counselor instructs with way too much pep.

When I don't move to stand, she excitedly waves me over. I walk over and stand next to the quiet girl. I hold my hand out to her even though she refused to hold speedy girl's hand. Her hair shifts just slightly as she peeks over to see my outstretched hand. The prayer has already started, and I nearly drop my hand when she finally takes it.

As we stand together in the serenity circle, hand-in-hand, I feel a kinship to this girl. She seems familiar to me, though I can't quite put my finger on the reason why. But I know she's going to be one I need to get through to. I *have* to help her.

We finish the chant, and everyone grabs their chairs to put them back in the stack against the back wall. Quiet girl grabs hers, and I get a peek of the skin on her hand and what looks like some kind of drawing. I smile to myself. Reminds me of another withdrawn person with black hair.

I walk up beside her and place my chair on the stack, then turn and reach my hand out. "Hey, my name is Charlie. What's yours?"

The quiet girl peeks at me through her thick curtain of hair. Her deep blue eyes pierce into me with the force of a fastball pitcher. She finally looks away from my eyes, down to my outstretched hand, and sneers, "Nope." She shakes her head before walking away from me.

Still standing with my hand out like a fool, the hippy-dippy lady puts an arm around my shoulder as we watch her walk away. "That one is a tough nut to crack. But something tells me that when she does, the world will get a view of the brilliant life seed that lives within. I think *you'll* be the one to show us. She's never participated in a meeting before. Never touched or spoken to anyone. Well, anyone but you."

I will get through to her. I will.

* * *

The smell of lasagna wafts straight to my stomach as I walk into Mary's house. Soft rock plays from the direction of the kitchen, and I hear her singing along.

I tip-toe over and duck along the wall of the archway to the kitchen. Peeking in to see Mary with a frilly apron on— I recognize it as one Savvy made her in HomeEc— singing into a wooden spoon. Something about Josie being on a vacation far away.

My heart twinges with pain, knowing I'll never see my mom like this. We'll never have silly dance battles again. I'll never taste her deviled eggs again. Never see her smile. Hear her laughter. Get advice. Fight. Push each other into snowbanks.

Mary spins, adding a dance move to her impromptu concert, and stops short when she sees me. There's no embarrassment on her face; Savvy got her confidence from somewhere.

"Oh honey, what's this about?" She asks as she strides over and wipes a stray tear from my cheek.

Never one for the "feelings" talk, I opt for smartassery. "Your singing was just so godawful. It literally brought me to tears." I wink at her, and she rolls her eyes and heads back to the stove.

"Dinner's in twenty. Go wash the day off and find better taste in music before you come back out." She chides and adds her own wink.

My feet ache as I slip off the kitten heels that I one-thousand percent will never wear again, and I kick them to the side of Savvy's bed. Well, I guess my bed now.

I peel off my slacks and blue button-down blouse, shimmy out of my bra and panties, and walk into the bathroom to turn on the shower.

It takes longer than I'd like to recover all the bobby pins holding my hair back. I cut it eight months ago, and the stubborn shits have yet to come back in any real inchery. I've also been debating dyeing it. Everything is all new in my life. New home, new job, new adventure. So why not new hair?

After taking a shower and putting on my fuzzy jammies, I make my way back to the kitchen and help Mary plate everything.

We make small talk during dinner, but I think she can tell I am drained. She takes pity on me and dismisses me for the evening with my promise to make dinner and do the dishes tomorrow.

I curl up on the bed and pull out my notebook. I haven't been writing my letters as often as I probably should. I haven't found a new therapist yet, so I really need to get these feelings out so they don't manifest in more destructive ways... like they almost did in Norsville.

I can't get the vision of a bloodied and suicidal monster Ari out of my head. I don't want to talk to the real Ari and possibly trigger her by telling her about my recurring dream. But I can write to the Ari who will never read it.

Imaginary Ari,

I've had the dream again.

But you know what I find myself wondering? Who found you when you took the razor to your wrists? Was it your absent parental units? A neighbor? A friend?

What was your thought process as you pressed the sharpened edge to your skin and watched the flesh separate? Did you hesitate or just make quick, clean swipes?

I don't think I could kill myself in that way. I've always envisioned something fast and with a bang.

Do you cut yourself elsewhere? Did you regret it before you lost consciousness? Did you write a note? I don't think I'd leave a note. It would likely be misinterpreted anyway.

I never told anyone this, but though I've thought about killing myself a lot in my life, it wasn't until after my mom died that I stopped caring about what would happen in the aftermath.

She's the only one who would have never recovered from it. Savvy would eventually move on and lead a full, happy life. My dad has a replacement in his soon-to-be stepkid, so he'd get over it as well—but not my mom.

I think that's what stopped me from taking it any further. But when she died, I stopped caring.

I blame myself for what happened with the drugs and Priest. Yes, he was a complete piece of shit, and I'm glad he's dead, but I came to him first. I started it all. Part of me thinks I wanted him to kill me. Like I knew he was capable and likely to, so I dove in with both eyes closed.

If he killed me, he'd be the bad guy. And I'd be absolved of blame and guilt. I know I'd be dead; however, it's the principal. But I digress...

One day, I'll tell you this in real life, but until you come to me to tell your story, I'll tell imaginary Ari:

I'm so fucking glad you failed. I can't imagine my life without you in it. I want to murder anyone who has ever hurt you or made you feel like you weren't worthy of life. And yes, that includes me. I fucking hate myself for contributing to that in high school.

You are enough, Ari. You've always been enough.

You aren't the problem. You never were.

You are the most genuine and kind person I've ever known. You deserve nothing but the absolute best. And you can bet your sweet, pasty ass that I will be up Calvin's to make sure he treats you right.

Even though it was shit circumstances that landed us both in Starry North, I wouldn't take it back for anything because we were brought together. You are stuck with me for life, Red.

I love you so much. And if you ever try to kill yourself again, I will follow you. I don't want to exist in a world where you don't.

Okay, that's pretty dramatic, but maybe it'll guilt you enough to stay.

Please stay.

If you promise to stay, I will, too.

Damn. That got morbid quickly. I hope no one ever reads these letters. I will be thrown into the psych ward lickity split.

Chapter 19

November 2008

Charlotte

I was reading Jason's letter for the gazillionth time when a knock at the door had me shoving it into my desk drawer. "Come in," I say to the girl I know is on the other side, right on time as usual.

Quiet girl's name is actually Emily. We've been meeting one-on-one for the last three weeks, and she still hasn't opened up to me at all.

She reminds me... well, of me. But no matter how I approach her, she ignores me. When she does talk, it's some sarcastic remark or some riddle that I don't understand. We aren't that far apart in age, but it may as well be a millennium. We have no common ground.

Emily enters and flops down on the armchair across the desk from me. As usual, her gaze goes straight to her lap, and she says nothing to me.

I didn't want to do this. But I'm at a complete loss with this girl. Maybe if I'm vulnerable with her, it will give her a little trust in me.

I take a large breath in and blow it out slowly. *Please don't let this be a mistake.* "Did you know I was once a patient here?"

Emily's head snaps up and her distrustful eyes meet mine. She clearly doesn't believe me.

I nod in assurance, "Yep. I was a resident of room 23. This was a couple of years ago, but I'll never forget it."

She cocks her head to the side like she wants to ask for more information but still doesn't want to speak.

"For as long as I can remember, I've had dark thoughts. They came and went, but I knew from a very young age that I wasn't 'normal'. I was medicated briefly and didn't like how I felt, so I became adept at showing the world what they wanted to see from me. Eventually, it worked. As far as everyone else knew, I was totally okay. But I wasn't."

She sits up straighter in her chair and keeps her eyes on mine, so I continue.

"My mom died a few months after I graduated, and I stopped caring about everything. I fell in with a bad crowd and took to getting high to avoid feeling... anything. I spiraled for a while until I nearly died. Then I was brought here."

"What was your drug of choice?" She asks, and though it's a very personal question and probably super inappropriate for us to discuss, I'm giddy that she's interested.

"Mostly, it was AstraMalum. I was hooked up with the guy who was supplying the town. What about you?"

Emily shrugs very nonchalantly as if we are discussing the weather, "I'm not overly picky. I prefer downers and psychedelics, but I'll do some coke in a pinch."

I have no room to judge. There was a time when I let Erick put anything in my mouth. I didn't question it. As long as I got high.

123

When I don't look horrified or give her a lecture, she eyes me curiously. "You're not going to tell me all the reasons why that's terrible and I should be making better life choices? Or writing down my every word to gossip with the rest of the staff later?"

Jesus. It's like she's me. I said something almost identical to Jensen.

I snort softly and give her the same curious look back. "Do you want me to tell you those things? I think you're a smart girl. I think you know why it's terrible and that you should make better choices. And I would never share your pain with anyone. That is *your* story. You are the only one who gets to decide who knows about it."

"You're not like the others, are you?"

I laugh, "God, I fucking hope not." I slam my hand over my mouth. For fuck's sake, Charlie. Remember, this is your job.

But then, the most amazing thing happens. She laughs. She. Fucking. Laughs.

We dissolve into a fit of laughter for several moments before going back to silence. But this silence is different; it's companionable. We've found some common ground.

I reach into the bottom drawer of my desk and pull something out for her. This is one thing I've really grown attached to since I was given it when I was a patient.

Emily stares at the notebook I'm holding out for her, and I stare at her until she loses our game of mental chicken, and she takes it.

"I was given one just like this. You can use it for whatever you want. It's only for you. You can journal, draw, make paper airplanes, or write no-send letters."

"No-send letters?" she asks.

I sit and cross my arms over my chest, like I'm protecting my own letters with the motion. "Yeah. Letters to people who will never read them. It's a pretty cathartic way to get things out. Anger. Sadness. Love. Whatever you feel. I do it all the time."

"You do?" she quirks her brow at me like she's not sure if she should believe me or not. I reach down into my bag and pull out my own notebook. I hold it up for her to see.

"Hm. Whatever. I guess if it'll shut you up, I'll take it."

I shrug, "Nothing will shut me up. Many have tried and failed."

"You're kinda funny for an old lady."

I gasp and slam my hand to my chest over my heart. "What the hell! I am like four years older than you. Damn, you sure know how to cut deep."

"Those crows feet say different." She deadpans, and I narrow my eyes at her and, like the adult I am, flip her off.

"Take your gift and get out of my office." I instruct with a stern voice.

She sees right through it and salutes me as she walks to the door. Before she closes it behind her, she turns around, "See you at the meeting?"

"Of course." I smile, she doesn't. But that's okay. We've made a ton of progress today. I'm starting to figure out her dry humor, and she responds more to sassery than niceties. Sass, I can do.

* * *

I fall on my bed and grab my phone. I dial Savs. She picks up immediately, but before she can say much more than "hey", I interrupt and tell her to hold on. Savvy hates three-way calls, so I have to hit her with a sneak attack.

The line trills, and Ari's voice comes on, "Hey, Charlie!"

I abruptly tell her to hang on as I merge the calls. She knows exactly what's happening, so she says, "Hi, Savannah! Looks like another three-way for us."

Savvy lets out a loud groan, "How many times do I have to tell you I'm not into pussy. Stop trying to make me have sex with you."

Ari gasps, scandalized. And I laugh.

"Savs, stop scarring Ari. I have something important to ask the two of you."

"It better not be for a fucking three-way Charls. You'll get the same answer as Aurelia."

I roll my eyes. "Shut it. I know what I want for my birthday. The two of you, here. Make it happen."

A loud squeal from Ari signifies she's in. Silence from Savvy makes me a little uneasy.

"Charls. I have nationals that week..." She says softly, regretfully.

"Oh." I try to keep the disappointment out of my voice. She has worked so fucking hard for this. She deserves to see it all the way through and have support and excitement from her best friend. So I add, "That's great, Savs! I still can't believe you ousted that cuntface from Captain. I want a video so I can watch her stupid face doing *your* routine from behind you."

"I'm sorry, Charls. Maybe—" She begins, and I feel like a dick for making her feel guilty.

I shake my head as if she could see me, "No. It's really no biggie. We can celebrate some other time, and then we'll have two things to toast. My 21st birthday and your big win!"

"Are you sure?" she asks, more defeated than I ever want to hear her.

"Positive. What about you, Red?"

Ari chimes in, "I can be there! Hopefully, the snow will be gone. I've grown to like this warm weather."

I laugh, "Hate to break it to you, but it almost always snows one last time right around my birthday."

"Yay." Ari replies with barely restrained sarcasm.

"Okay bitches, I love both of your faces, but it's super late, and I have class in the morning. Bye!" Savs hangs up before we respond.

Ari and I catch up for a few minutes. She tells me all about Samson's progress and that Devin has come back to the house, and Calvin made him give up the drugs cold turkey. I don't know why people think that will work. If you don't want to quit for yourself, it'll never stick. We make plans for her to spend a week in Alaska for my birthday and say our goodbyes.

Before I go to sleep, I find myself thinking about the time Zach found me high on the floor of a classroom. I don't know why that particular memory comes to me. I try to keep him from my thoughts as much as possible.

It hurts. I thought he could be my forever. But he's someone else's forever now.

Chapter 20

December 2008

Jason

"Donovan, how many times are you going to read her letters? You're acting like an obsessive stalker." Jacobs slaps his hand upside my head as he peeks over my shoulder to try to read Charlie's latest letter.

I whack him in the face with the stack of letters. He laughs and holds his hands up, "Okay, okay. So, are you ready for the final transport tomorrow?"

What am I supposed to say? That I'm terrified of convoying over one of the country's most combat-riddled areas. And what if I was? There's no other choice. So I don't share my fears; instead, I say, "Sure thing, Cap. Bright and early. I'll be the handsome fucker waiting in the Humvee for you."

He nods and leaves me to my letters. I read her newest over again before penning my response.

Jason,

Thank you for being understanding, for giving me time, and for not pushing me. You have no idea what a rarity that is. Everyone wants my healing and words on their own timelines, but not you. So, thank you.

Are you sure you want me to bleed for you? Once it starts, it'll seep into your very being and fuse us together for eternity.

I miss her. My mom, I mean. I feel like everyone thinks about their parent's eventual death, but it's always when they are really old and maybe in a nursing home or something. Not in their prime when they had so much life to live. Not when they didn't get to experience a good, true love. Or holding their first grandchild.

It's just not fair. Why do the good ones always die?

After she died, I got really self-destructive, and I went down a scary path for a while, getting involved with some bad people. I found Ari at a time when we both needed someone.

I'm not good with compliments, so I'll just say thank you for the kind words. I'm glad you see something worthy in me, even if it's hard for me to see it myself.

Do you want kids? I guess I kinda assume you do since you talked about if you have a daughter.

I honestly don't know if I want kids or not. What if my damage is hereditary?

I'm actually enjoying my new job. There's this girl; she reminds me a lot of me, and I actually think I'm making a difference for her. That's enough for me. All I want is to be there and help where I can.

You think that nothing you could learn would alter your perception of me. I wish I believed that. When I say I'm broken, I fucking mean it.

Do you have any idea when you'll be coming back to wherever you're living when you're not working?

I do love you. I told you before, a part of me always will.

Be safe.

-Charlie

PS— Have you ever thought about coming back to Alaska?

* * *

I settle into my seat in the main body of the convoy. Jacobs and I are traveling in the center truck with His Majesty. Olsen and Singer are in the lead, while Brown and Lowkowski trail.

Each truck is driven by a member of the military's PSD (Personal Security Detail) that is assigned to His Majesty. They know the terrain and route a hell of a lot better than we ever will.

His Majesty leans down to look through the window. His gaze is firmly on the cloudless sky, which he eyes like the cerulean canopy is holding secrets that it will only share with him.

Jacobs climbs in beside me, and we radio-check with the other vehicles before we start our journey.

His Majesty seems really squirrelly. His eyes bounce back and forth between the sky and the vast emptiness of the desert to each side of us.

I narrow my eyes on him, "What's your problem?" I ask gruffly. He needs to knock this shit off, it's already an intense day. I don't need him adding to the paranoia coursing through my body. Something just feels off.

He begins whispering hushed words in Arabic. His fingers

roam across a string of beads over and over as he repeats the same phrase. I watch his fingers. They run over thirty-three beads before he hits the clasp and begins again.

I hit Jacobs' leg with mine, and when I catch his eyes, I tilt my head at the man across from us. Jacobs watches him for a moment before leaning close to me, "Praying."

It didn't take a genius to figure that out, but my question is: why? Why is he suddenly praying after staring intently out the window at our surroundings?

I don't fucking like this.

A gust of wind rocks the side of the truck. I don't think too much of it until it happens again. I lean down to look out the window, and my jaw drops. I reach my hand back and hit Jacobs in the arm to get his attention, "What the fuck is that?" I ask as I point at the dark red wall that expands as far as my eyes can see.

Jacobs curses and immediately gets on his radio. All of our vehicles stop, and the wind continues to batter us. "Put this on." He thrusts a face mask at me. It looks like one a painter would wear.

One thing you learn in our position is you don't question things. It can be life or death. If you are given a directive, you fucking take it.

The four of us put our masks on, and like someone switched off the sun, we are enveloped in a wall of dusky darkness.

Chaos and fury shake the Humvee like a rag doll.

"Close your eyes!" Jacobs shouts, and I follow his orders immediately. It's a bit too late; when my lids close, it seems as though they glide against a thousand tiny razor blades. It fucking burns.

Two hours.

The dust storm lasted for two fucking hours. As it subsided, the soldiers jumped out to assess the damage. Nothing too detrimental, although the trail vehicle looks as if it was pelted with baseball-sized hail.

Everyone is accounted for, and as we get ready to take off, our driver, Claymore, clears his throat. "Uhm, we seem to have a problem."

The problem was that this dunce never turned off the ignition. All that dust was invited into the intake, rendering the vehicle a very large, very expensive paperweight.

"We don't have a choice right now. We need to split up into the two remaining trucks. Claymore and Donovan head up to join Olsen. I'll take His Majesty back to Lowkowski's truck."

Olsen winks at me when I climb in beside him, "Welcome to the fun truck, Donovan. We're playing ISpy, and it's my turn. I spy with my little eye.... something brown."

The door flings open, and Brown pops his head in, "Donovan, you're in the other truck. I'm here to save you from Olsen's lame road games."

"Hey!" Olsen shouts at the insult.

"Thank fuck. I owe you one." I tell him as I scurry off the seat before he can change his mind.

"It was that mound of dirt over there, by the way!" Olsen shouts at my back. I roll my eyes and head to the other truck.

I climb into the cozy interior to see His Majesty is still on the prayer kick. Great.

"Let's roll." Jacobs says into his radio.

* * *

It's dark by the time we hit the first of two towns we have to drive through. It's disturbingly empty. There are no lights. The only reason I know we are passing buildings is the edge of our headlights bouncing off the exteriors.

I just want to get this day over with.

"Well, this is creepy as fuck. Where are all the people?" Jacobs asks the question on everyone's mind as we all watch out of our windows.

The road becomes bumpier than it has been. Large potholes riddle the path forward, and they are so frequent that it seems impossible to miss them all. Both trucks slow way down to navigate the dips.

It takes less than ten minutes to make it out of the town. The large flat stretch begins to turn more hilly.

"Just through that valley is the last town. We will hit our rendevous point about twelve mikes after that." Our driver informs us, pointing at a narrow opening along two steep hills.

The lead truck comes to a stop as it reaches the end of the valley opening, which brings us to a halt as well. We keep a good distance from each other. "Why are we stopping?" Lowkowski asks nobody in particular.

Our driver radios the other truck. After going back and forth, he says to us, "Something is blocking the road."

"Jesus Christ. This is how scary movies start, you know." I whine and lean my head back.

"What the fuck?" Jacobs yells, his voice booming throughout the vehicle. I look forward, following his gaze, to see Olsen jump out of the truck and disappear towards the front of it.

"Get on that goddamn radio and figure out what the hell he's doing!" Jacobs demands.

The driver obliges, but before we can get an answer, an earth-shattering boom explodes around us.

Glass splinters across my body, and a high-pitched shriek echoes in my ears before my vision goes black.

Chapter 21

December 2008

Sweets,

You never need to thank me for respecting your boundaries. That should be a given. It pisses me off that it hasn't been your experience.

I'm positive that I'm ready for your truth. But let me give you one of mine in the meantime: You don't need saving. There's nothing wrong with you. You are strong enough to save yourself. I will be beside you every step of the way if you want me to be.

You've always held such strength. It kills me that you don't see it. Whatever you've been through, it didn't break you, Sweets. It tested your resolve, and here you stand. You are not broken.

Read that again.

We've both been forced to grow up quicker than we should've. We've taken on parental roles when it wasn't ours to take on. We've suffered the consequences of not being able to just be a fucking kid. So yes, yes, I want kids. I want to give them the life we should've had.

But here's the thing... I know you are set on the "friends" thing for now, but at the risk of scaring you away, you're it for me,

Charlie. I want the life, the kids, the house, the pets, and the happy ending. But only if it's with you.

No pressure.

The fact that you care so much about this girl who reminds you of you tells me everything I need to know about what kind of mom you will be.

I have zero hesitation in saying that you will be an incredible mother to our children. You will give them everything you needed, and I'll be by your side the whole time. Partners.

Is your panic setting in yet?

Mine isn't. That's how sure I am that this is what I want.

My home is wherever you are. I will be back ASAP. This has been quite the... experience, but honestly, all I've wanted since I left was to be back. Don't laugh, but I kind of think I want to get a job at the auto shop in River View. Maybe one day I could open my own. Nothing could make me leave you again, not when I just got you back.

It's your journey, baby; I'm just hoping to hitch a ride and watch the magic happen.

I love you with the whole of me. I hope one day you will, too. But until then, I'll love enough for the both of us.

–J

*PS— My latest piece encompasses my feelings about your strength, resilience, and heart. **This** is how I see you. Don't forget who the fuck you are.*

Chapter 22

February 2009

Jason,

There are many things I want to say. But you don't deserve any more of my time, so I'll keep this short and (not so) sweet.

I ran into your baby momma today. You got a cute kid. He's the spitting image of you. You must be proud.

If you didn't know... surprise!

Jade was right; the Donovan genes really are strong.

As for you and me. Not gonna happen. I had one rule, Jason. One. No secrets. A love child with the girl you swore you didn't sleep with is a pretty fucking big secret.

You almost had me. Almost. Maybe you meant the things you said, maybe not. I'll probably never know. But I am glad I found out now before I let you back into my life and heart.

I'm a glutton for punishment so I'd just like to know, what was the point? Tell me why you hid sleeping with her from me. I'm so tired of dishonest people. Congratulations, you've reinforced that I have no business being with anyone. You're all liars. Letting your dicks do all your thinking. I'm over it.

Just tell me why. After that, lose my contact info.

So, I wish you luck in your future endeavors or whatever.

–Charlotte

PS— I hope you get incurable athlete's foot from the showers over there.

II

Part Two

Chapter 23

February 2009

Charlotte

It's perfect.

I can envision the couch against the wall. The TV mounted above the fireplace. Decorative curtains, black out obviously, over white blinds. An oversized black shag rug under a wooden coffee table. Maybe a dog bed on the left side of the fireplace for my future pup.

"What do you think, Miss Johnson?" the realtor asks as she moseys back into the living room after giving me some time to explore the place on my own.

I finally gave my dad the okay to sell Mom's house. I couldn't go back there—not without her. He gave me all of the equity, which gave me enough for a nice downpayment on my own place and some extra for a nest egg.

"I'll take it!" I say excitedly. I'm so ready for this. I love Mary and am so grateful for her generosity, but if I have to hear the springs in her bed squeak one more time, I'm going to jab a pen in my ear. Don't get me wrong, I'm glad she's getting some, at least one of us is. But that's like hearing my own mom doing it, and yuck. No. Just no.

* * *

The floor creaks as the most recent boy toy creeps towards the front door. Little things like this give me pleasure in life. I wait until his hand is on the knob before calling out, "Have a great day, Dan!"

He freezes like a deer in headlights; his shoulders creep up, and he turns slowly to look at me. "It's Dennis."

I smack my forehead, "Oh, that's right, Dan is the other one. Well, see ya, Dennis!" I hurry off to my room before he can respond.

Mary knocks on my door once before popping her head in, "Really, Charlie? You had to antagonize him? He's already acting like a stage-five clinger; now he's paranoid on top of it. Thanks for that."

I giggle and raise my hand to cover my mouth in fake remorse. "Whoops. That was an honest mistake."

Mary rolls her eyes and looks around the almost empty room. All that remains is the bed, a dresser, and a picture of Savvy and me on the wall. "I'm going to miss you... brat."

I run over and wrap my arms tightly around her middle, and her arms come around my shoulders just as snugly. "I'm not far. We'll still have dinner weekly, I promise. Thank you so much for everything you've done for me."

When we pull apart, we both swipe at the tears flowing down our cheeks and laugh at each other. Mary follows me to the door with my last bag, and we say our goodbyes before I leave for my house. *My house.*

Walking into the 1300 sq ft ranch home, the emptiness

144

doesn't even bother me. I still envision the setup like I did three weeks ago when I put the offer in. I've got the essentials: plastic silverware, cups, and paper plates in the kitchen, a twin-sized air mattress in the bedroom, and a box with my laptop on it so I can watch my shows.

Tomorrow, I'm going to hit the stores for supplies, decor, and furniture. A fresh coat of paint on these walls will make all the difference. I'm thinking a nice slate blue for the living room. Maybe an accent wall in the bedroom. *Who the fuck am I, Bob Ross? Keep it simple, Charlie. At least until I can afford to hire someone to do it right.*

* * *

Good lord, who knew paint cans were so damn heavy? I swipe the sweat off my forehead as I put the fifth gallon in my trunk.

I'm not a dick, so I take the cart to the catcher in the front of the parking lot. A bright rainbow draws my attention to the little boutique beside the paint store. I don't know what compels me to enter this place I have no business being in, but I guess I'm still feeling a bit on cloud nine from Jason's letter.

Soft instrumental music greets me as I enter the shop. A very sweet-looking lady with gray and pink intertwined dreads and a septum piercing smiles and waves, which I return. She turns her attention back to her phone call, and I begin to peruse the aisles.

My fingers dance lightly across the rows of soft, tiny outfits. I feel a small smile turn up on my face. Could I really do this someday? Do I want to?

After things went down between me and Zach, I let that dream go. We had talked about having kids, but it seemed like a pipedream. One of those scenarios that you talk about but can't actually imagine coming true. Maybe that was my body's way of prepping me for the inevitable crumbling of my relationship.

I close my eyes and let my hand stop on a random onesie; I pick it up to inspect it. Tears prick my eyes as I gingerly hold the tiny outfit. It's a deep navy blue with seven stars in the shape of a pot and one star above it to the right. The Big Dipper and Polaris. Alaska's flag. The words "Little Bear" are printed in cursive below the image.

I clutch the onesie to my chest. *Is this a sign?*

"Well, well. If it isn't Charlotte Johnson."

The hairs on the back of my neck stand immediately, and anger floods throughout my body, completely erasing the feelgoods I had moments ago.

I turn to match the face of the familiar voice. We lock eyes for just a moment before sizing each other up. My gaze roams over the girl, taking in her subtle differences since I last saw her.

She's still tall, obviously. But definitely thicker. Her once-long raven hair now cut into a chin-length style.

I eye down her body to the stroller. That explains the thickness, I guess. What unfortunate soul tied themselves with the she-bitch for life? I feel sorry for that sucker.

"Jade." I respond without a care in the world, letting my eyes stray to different areas around the store.

"I didn't know you were back." She says with an ugly twist of her lips.

I shrug, "Didn't know I needed to check in with you."

A shrill cry comes from the stroller, stopping whatever bullshit was about to spew out of her mouth.

"Oh shh, baby, Mama's here." She coos to her spawn as she lifts the miniature human. Its hair is the same striking shade of black as hers. She pats the little tike on the back while rocking in place until it quiets down.

"Well, as much as I'm enjoying... whatever this is. Bye." I smirk and spin on my heels.

"Wait! Don't you want to see my baby?" she asks in a sickeningly sweet voice that makes me want to hurl right here in the baby store.

I sigh and turn back with my arms crossed over my chest. Impatience written all over my body language.

She spins the little boy around, and all the air sucks out of the room. I gasp, and my feet move forward on their own accord. I search the baby's face over and over, but no matter how many times I look, I see the same thing. Onyx hair. Steel gray eyes. Jason. I see Jason. *What the fuck?*

Jade sucks air in her teeth, and when I look back at her, she wears a smug grin that I want to smack off her face. "Looks just like his daddy. Those Donovan genes sure are strong."

What?

I feel like I can't breathe. The room starts to spin around me. I drop the onesie and run for the door with Jade's cackle at my back.

My hands shake as I try to unlock my car. My keys fall to the ground twice before I finally make it to the interior. My lungs struggle for oxygen as my mind swims and tries to make sense of this.

He lied to me. He told me they didn't sleep together. Did he just mean back in school or ever? Why can't I fucking remember what he said? How could he not tell me he has a child?

Fucking think, Charlie.

He said, "Nothing happened. I didn't cheat on you". That's not "I've never slept with her". Did he purposely deceive me?

Anger charges through my body and explodes when my fists make contact with my steering wheel over and over.

I told him. I fucking told him. I had one rule. No secrets. And he broke that. I can't do this. Why do I find myself in this position time and time again?

My chest heaves as I pull my sore fists back to lay in my lap. I stare blankly out of the windshield while my mind races in a thousand directions.

Not again.

Jason is dead to me.

Chapter 24

March 2009

Charlotte

"I can't believe this is our last session. You've come such a long way, Emily. You should be tremendously proud of your progress. I know I am." I gush, probably laying it on a little thick. But this girl has become so important to me over the last five months.

Her smile beams at me from across the desk. It's like night and day. The girl before me is a whole new person. She is healing, sober, hopeful, and, most importantly, she has a future.

"Thanks to you, Cee. You let me be an absolute cunt-face to you until you finally wore me down. You've done more for me in the last few months than anyone else has my whole life. I may be going back into a group home, but I'm going to keep my nose clean this time. Literally and figuratively."

I smile at her and rest my chin in my hand on my desk. "*You* did all the work. *You* let this place help. *You* passed your driver's test. *You* caught up on schoolwork. *You* participated in meetings. That was all you, Em."

She shyly looks at her lap, but through the draped hair, I see the smile on her lips. "I don't know what I'm going to do without you..." she whispers while panic sets into her voice.

I round the desk and kneel beside her, placing my hand gently on hers. "I will be here for whatever you need. Just because you leave this program doesn't mean I drop you like a bad habit."

Fuck. I know I shouldn't do this. It's probably against several rules. "Give me your notebook," without hesitation, she reaches for it on her side and places it in my hand. I pull the pen out of my bun and write my number and address down for her. "If you need anything, you reach out. Anything, Em. Do you hear me?"

She nods her head, a tear leaks down her cheek, and she thrusts her little body at me. I engulf her in the most loving, big sister hug I can. This is why Savvy said I can never work at an animal shelter. My house would be packed wall to wall with the beings no one wanted. The home for wayward beasts.

"Let's go get you packed. Your social worker will be here within the hour. Let me put on my adult hat for a moment and give you some advice. Keep out of trouble, attend weekly meetings, get a sponsor, and never step foot back in this facility. Got it?"

Emily nods her agreement, "Yes, ma'am."

* * *

I tried really hard not to fall apart when I got into my car after work. I have mixed emotions about Emily's release. I can't imagine not seeing or speaking to her every day. I worry about how she will fare in the real world. But on the other side of the coin, I'm so damn happy with how well she's doing, mentally and physically.

I wonder if I could open a transitional type of house for those leaving the facility but not quite ready to be on their own. So many of our patients are state wards. After they leave us, they simply get thrown into the next group or foster home. What if they had another, more supportive place to go? Could I do something like that?

I grab the ticket from the machine and drive into the parking garage. I circle the damn thing several times before I find a parking spot. I pull my phone out to type in her flight info, and sure enough, it's already landed. Damnit.

I haul ass inside, check the monitor to see which baggage claim she'll be at, and head towards it.

The crowd is thick around baggage claim 6. Why wasn't I born with longer legs? I stand on my tiptoes and peer as best I can at the different faces. My eyes finally land on fire engine strands piled up high on her head, and I run. My arms wrap around Ari from behind. She squeals in surprise but immediately turns it into laughter.

I press my forehead against her back, "You're here. You're actually here." I say, muffled, into her sweater. She pats my hand and leans her head back until it rests on mine. "I'm here."

A deep throat clears, and my eyes nearly leave my head. They roll so hard. Why am I not surprised? Of fucking course, he wouldn't let his precious little "Cherry" out of his sight. "Hi, Calvin." I say, my face still pressed into Ari. She squeezes my hand, her silent apology for not telling me her bodyguard was also coming.

"Charlie." He says gruffly, returning my lackluster greeting before walking off to grab their luggage.

He walks behind us the whole way back to my car. Watching his giant ass squeeze into my little sedan is the highlight of my day. Imagine Shaq trying to climb into a SmartCar. It's fucking hilarious, right? His head touches the roof. His knees are damn near to his chest and pressed against the back of Ari's seat. He probably would've been more comfortable in the front, but he insisted Ari take it.

That's how I know; he's a good egg. No matter how PMS-y he is with everyone else, he fucking adores Ari.

We pull up to my house, and I lead them inside. Pointing Calvin towards the guestroom to ditch their luggage. Ari gently pulls my hand, keeping me by the front door. "I'm sorry. He decided at the last minute to come, and I just couldn't say no. I hope this doesn't ruin your birthday."

Am I a little surprised? Eh, not really. I figured something like this might happen. If it was some rando, maybe I would be upset, but Calvin is a good dude, and he makes her happy, so it makes me happy.

I wrap my arm around her shoulder and lead her into the living room. "No worries, Red. The more, the merrier. Just please tell me you're not a screamer..."

She looks at me and furrows her brow in confusion. "Why would I scream? I don't have like night terrors or anything if that's what you mean."

I smirk at her in silence until her mouth takes on an "O" shape. Crimson dots her cheeks. "There will be no screaming." She says quietly.

I tilt my head to the side, "Ari. Tell me you've let that man have a taste of his cherry." She folds her hands in her lap and pulls her sleeves over them. "Charlie!" She hisses quietly, eyeing the hallway in case Calvin makes a reappearance.

I stare at her, eyebrow quirked expectantly. Finally, she nods ever so slightly. I giggle and bump her shoulder with mine. "Atta girl. I knew you wouldn't stay a virgin forever. How was it?"

"None of your fucking business." Calvin huffs as he strolls back into the room. "Stop making her uncomfortable."

I laugh, not put off by his pricklyness at all. "Never! Now, it was a long flight. Why don't you guys go bang one out in the shower and get dressed? Meet me at the door in an hour, and we'll head to the bar for my first legal drink!"

Ari looks mortified, but Calvin smiles at her mischievously before picking her up and throwing her over his shoulder, fireman-style. She screeches but smiles and hits his butt lightly as he carries her to their room.

* * *

The Salty Nut is crazy busy for a Wednesday night. Why the Salty Nut, you ask? One reason. They advertise that every single drink comes with a color-changing straw. If the drink is tampered with, the straw indicates it.

A crotchety old woman owns the bar. She's like *the* original feminist, and I love her. I met her at the sandwich joint in town, and she bitched about the long wait and terrible customer service so dramatically that I laughed so hard I almost peed. She glared at me but continued to talk to me. So we developed a bit of camaraderie, and she told me about this place.

Ari and I stand at the bar waiting for our drinks. She stunned the hell out of me when she ordered a daiquiri. She doesn't drink. Like ever. It's nice to see her permitting herself to have

153

a good time. I'm guessing a lot of that is thanks to the comfort she feels by having Calvin around to make sure she's safe.

"I'm getting on that thing before the night's over." I say with a nod toward the very large mechanical moose. Many country bars have mechanical bulls. But this is Alaska. We have a mechanical moose.

Ari grins at me as we take our drinks from the bartender, "I can't wait." We make our way back to the pool table that we've claimed as ours. Calvin is dominating the billiard balls. He's a damn pool shark.

We play a few games, and Calvin takes the W every time. I thought he'd at least take it easy on his girlfriend, but he seems to be as competitive as Savvy. Ari keeps eyeing the entrance. I've seen her do it a few times now.

I put my straw—that didn't change colors— to my lips and narrow my eyes at her, "What are you looking at, Red?"

Flustered, she shakes her head and then starts talking to Calvin like I didn't just say words to her. Weirdo.

A favorite of mine comes on the jukebox. Notes blare out around the small tavern, something about apple-bottom jeans and furry boots.

I suck down the remnants of my drink and grab Ari's hand. I wink at Calvin when he shoots a glare at me, but he keeps his eyes on us as we make our way to the dance floor.

We lose ourselves in the beat of the music, the alcohol warming our bodies and lightening our inhibitions. We shimmy and shake, laughing and taking turns spinning each other. When the song ends, we are sweaty and in need of another beverage.

We walk back to Calvin, who has refills waiting for us. I eye the straw, making sure it's still blue—trust, but verify.

I challenge him to another game of pool, which I lose. So I stand off to the side and let him play Ari. She peeks behind me at the entrance again and tries to hide her smile as she leans down and lines up her shot.

Warm breath fans out against the back of my neck. "Hey there, birthday girl."

Chapter 25

March 2009

Charlotte

My breath blows hard back into my drink through my straw, sending cool drops of margarita spraying forward. I spin and scream, "Savs!" I hug my best friend with all my might, and she returns it with equal fervor.

I finally pull back and smack her on the arm, "What the fuck are you doing here?" My brain catches up with my eyes, and I take her in from head to toe. Ribbons in her hair. Cheer uniform. Joggers under her skirt. Tennis shoes. Backpack. My eyes widen, and I gasp, "Did you come here from nationals?"

"I wouldn't miss my bestie's 21st for anything. The moment it ended, I ran off that damn stage and right into a taxi to the airport. You should've seen all the men looking at me like I was their wet dream come to life. If I didn't put my sweats on, I was pretty sure I was going to be the cause of a few divorces."

I hug her again. I can't believe she came. But wait... "So, did you win?" I ask.

Savvy scoffs at me and gives me a look that says, come on now. "Of course, we fucking won, Charls. Does this look like the face of a loser?"

I pop a shoulder and sip the rest of my margarita, "I mean..." I tease. She rolls her eyes and looks past me to Ari before catching sight of Calvin. Savvy's jaw literally drops open, and because she has no filter at all, she says, "Jesus, who is this sexy mountain of a man?"

Ari laughs and comes in for a hug before introducing her to Calvin, who essentially runs away to the bar to get another refill for all of us. The three of us catch up on news, gossip, and our drinks before I decide: it's time.

"Ladies and gentlemen, please direct your attention to the Pen. Not only do we have a new face at the Salty Nut, but she's a birthday girl who also happens to be a virgin to the Pen!" The bartender revs up the crowd, and Savvy shouts from somewhere beyond the spotlight that rests brightly against my face, "She's not even a back-door virgin!" Snickers and cheers radiate from the drunken patrons.

I wrap my hands tightly around the antlers. They are firm but fuzzy, and they don't seem very grippy to me. Maybe this was a terrible plan. Alcohol, excitement from being with my friends, and peer pressure had me thinking this was a solid idea.

The moose jolts below me as it starts slowly walking in place. Okay, this isn't too bad. A few seconds later, it picks up pace to a light jog. Besides shaking my tits, it's nothing I can't handle. The crowd cheers, and there's more than one comment about the hope that my top will fall fully down. Which, with the movement and the lack of bra, is a distinct possibility.

Moments later, it cranks up again to a sprint. I grasp the antlers tightly. My ass bounces against the back of the stuffed moose in a side-to-side motion, and I tighten the grip of my thighs against the metal beast's belly.

I'm feeling confident that I can last the full three minutes... until it jolts once more to an all-out dash. My body is rapidly swinging from side to side, and my thighs burn from the exertion of gripping the body of the moose. Savvy shouts, "Only thirty more seconds, babe. You got this. Put them thunder thighs to use!"

Thirty more seconds. Come on, Charlie. The friction burn on my hands is making me hiss in pain, but I tighten my grip further. The metal beast adds a twisting motion to its quick up-and-down movements. Fuck.

The crowd starts a countdown, "10...9...8—" I don't hear the next number as I'm thrown off the galloping moose onto an inflatable pad. I land hard with an "Oof."

A chorus of cheers and aws ripple through the room. Flat on my back, I stare at the ceiling until Savvy appears with a savage grin on her mouth. "Almost had it, tiger. Now, get your ass up, tuck your nipple away, and let's go get shots."

I groan and grab her offered hand with my right while covering my exposed nipple with the left. Great.

* * *

Before my eyes even open, I know that I'm in for a rough day. How much did we drink last night? My everything hurts.

I roll my hungover ass out of bed and stumble over my discarded clothes on the floor. Savvy snores loudly from my bed. I try my best to grab clothes and take a shower quietly.

Thirty minutes and one dry heave later, I make it to the kitchen for some much-needed coffee. Ari and Calvin sit next to each other at the table, chatting and eating breakfast out of to-go containers.

I grunt my hello as I pass them, and once my coffee is ready, I collapse on a chair at the table. Ari slides a container in front of me and places a fork on top. God, if only I liked women. I'd wife this bitch up in a heartbeat.

I eat my veggie omelet and greasy hashbrowns with graphic moans, and Ari giggles while Calvin looks mildly disgusted but amused.

Savvy strolls in ten minutes later. Dressed for the day and looking as fresh as a daisy. Like she wasn't drooling on my pillow, balls deep in sleep forty minutes ago. "Morning bitches. What's for breakfast?"

Ari pushes a container to the last free spot at the table. Savvy wastes no time digging in.

"What's the plan for today, Charlie?" Ari asks.

I rub my throbbing temple, "Well, I don't know how great an idea it is now, but I made us reservations at High In The Sky."

High In The Sky is a resort on top of a mountain. It offers tons of cool stuff to do, including a hot spring and spa. You can ski, snowboard, sled, or tube there.

We make the two-hour drive to the resort, and all decide to start with getting massages at the spa. Calvin verifies all the staff are women. We make fun of him, but he has zero shame about it.

They take Ari and Calvin first. Savvy and I sit on warm, comfy couches in our fluffy robes and sip our cucumber water.

"So, are you going to tell me what's going on?" Savvy asks, though it doesn't sound like a question at all.

I know what she wants to know, but I play dumb anyway. "What do you mean?" I barely get the response out when something wet slaps against my cheek and slides down. "What the fuck?" I look down to see a slice of cucumber on the lapel of my robe.

"Don't play with me. Tell me." She demands.

"I just decided it wasn't going to work out."

"Why?"

"Reasons. Does it matter?"

"Yes." She says flatly.

She's not going to let it go. Savvy is like a dog with a bone sometimes.

"I ran into Jade last month."

"And?"

"And she has a baby. A baby who looks just like him. My suspicions were confirmed when she told me how strong the Donovan genes are."

"That doesn't make sense, Charls. He told you they didn't sleep together. Did you ask him about it?"

"I sent him a letter. Haven't gotten a response yet. It doesn't really matter, though. Does it? You don't get it, Savs. He looks identical to Jason. There's no denying that baby is his blood."

"I just don't get it. Why would he lie? He seemed so genuine. You know I grilled the fuck out of him. I believed him. You believed him. How could we both be so wrong? I'm so sorry, babe. This is all my fault. I shouldn't have brought him back into your life." Savvy apologizes. It's not on her, though. I let him back in. This is on me.

* * *

Four days flew by. It was so amazing to have my two best friends back home with me. And having Calvin party crash wasn't too bad, either.

I dropped them off at the airport a few hours ago and decided to go to Sky Ridge. I haven't been up there since I've been back. It's held so many memories for me, some more painful than others. I wasn't sure if I was ready to face it again, but I wanted to reclaim my space.

The wind whips sharply across my face as I stand on the cliff's edge. I've been to this spot many times, in my mind and in reality. The town still has a dusting of snow across its landscape. Turning the urban quarters into a picturesque postcard.

The sun shines brightly, casting a glare off the glossy covering on the ground. I walk over to my table and dust off the top of it. My fingers trace the words I've written over the years. So much pain on this table.

I kind of want to burn it, but I need the reminder that I've been through worse. I've made it this far, and I'm stronger than I was yesterday.

The pen in my pocket beckons me to let it free. I pull it out and press the tip to the wood.

"Hurt"

I'm tired of giving people the power to hurt me. I'm ready to move forward, and just do me. My work is what's important right now. I'm not swearing off love forever, but I'm not going to chase it anymore.

I won't keep telling people who don't deserve to hear it that I'm worthy. The right man will know. And he won't lie and hide things. He won't cheat and make me feel disposable. The right man will choose me. He will love me, and he will deserve me.

And if Mr. Right doesn't magically come along, then I guess

I'll get that shelter job and fill my home with other discarded souls.

He's out there, somewhere. Looking for me right now. I feel it.

Chapter 26

July 2009

Charlotte

A piercing tone sounds out through my darkened bedroom. Sleep only came just a few short hours ago. Disoriented, my gaze swings from left to right, trying to determine where it's coming from.

As it continues to go off, and I wake up, I gather it's my cell. I swear to God, if Savvy is drunk-dialing me, I will add hot sauce to her aftershave lotion. She'll have great pubes of fire for a while.

Finally, my hand slams down on the phone. When I turn it, the screen temporarily blinds me from the brightness. **"UNKNOWN"**

An unknown call at 3 am? It better not be a telemarketer. "Hello?" Rustling noises fill the receiver, but no words. I ask again, "Hello? Is someone there?"

A sob-filled voice comes on. "Cee?" it says so quietly that I have to strain to hear, even in the still of my room.

Oh my God. There's only one person who calls me that.

"Emily?" I ask, panicked. My hand grips my phone so

tightly that the plastic case groans under the pressure.

"I need help... I don't want to bother you, but I have no one else. I need you."

My body flings itself out of my bed before she finishes her sentence. I grab some sweats and shove my feet in a pair of slip-ons. "Where are you?" I ask, putting my arms in a hoodie and grabbing my keys. The pounding in my chest is so loud I'm sure she can hear it.

She gives me an address, well, an intersection, and begs me to stay on the line with her while I break several laws to get to her.

"Okay, I'm pulling up now." I look around the street, which is blanketed in darkness. I don't see anyone.

"Can you flash your headlights twice?" she asks, muffled like her hand is covering her mouth.

I do. And a bush rustles to my right. Right before my mind spirals on, "Oh fuck, it's a bear, run!" an extremely disheveled Emily comes out of it and runs to my passenger door.

With shaky hands, she opens the unlocked door and climbs in with a small black trash bag, which she tucks at her feet.

The light pink sleep shorts she wears expose her legs. Scratches and bruises riddle a large portion of the visible skin. Did that happen in the bush? The black hoodie covering her upper body has several holes all over the arms, and the hood hides her face from my sight.

I don't linger on the creepy street. As we leave the neighborhood in the rearview, her shoulders relax a smidgen.

"Em, what's going on? Are you alright?" I ask softly. My eyes bounce back and forth between the road and her battered legs.

Emily curls herself over, hugging her legs with her head in

164

her lap, and her body begins to shake violently. We've made it far enough from where I picked her up, so I pull into the parking lot of a 24-hour diner.

Gently, I reach a hand over to her shoulder. The moment I make contact, her body recoils fiercely, and I immediately feel like shit and should have known better. "I'm so sorry, Emily. I won't touch you. Can you please talk to me? I want to help, but I need to know what kind of help to give."

A gut-wrenching sob comes from the small, balled-up form, and it sinks right down into my soul. Her pain is palpable. This girl, this brilliant, smart-mouthed, sassy gem, is breaking right in front of me.

I have to wait until she's ready. I can't push her. Fuck, if anyone knows that, it's me.

We sit in the car for what seems like hours before her sobs slow, and the hiccups recede. Emily sits back up, the hood still covering her face, but I can tell she's staring out of the windshield. She holds a trembling hand out to me, and I immediately latch onto it.

"Em?" I coax. Hoping I've given her enough reason to put her trust in me. I told her she would always have me. This is me living up to that. Whatever she needs, she'll get it.

The time in the car slows to nearly stagnant as her hands slide into the sides of the hood. Where there used to be lusciously thick locks is now a buzzed and patchy mess. I hold back the gasp that wants to escape.

She slowly turns to look at me. As soon as our eyes latch on to one another, I burst into tears.

Her left eye is completely swollen shut, and the skin surrounding it is mottled in varying shades of purple and red. Cracked, dried blood trails lay below each of her nostrils. Her

165

previously light pink pout is split in several areas, and a trail of dried blood comes from the right side.

My free hand flies to my mouth to hold back the sobs as if it is the guard of the floodgates.

"Take me home?" she asks, her voice sounding steeped in broken glass. She doesn't need to elaborate. I nod and immediately head back to my house.

When we get inside, I show Emily to the guest room. She hasn't said a word, but I'm giving her the time and space to feel okay enough to do so. She silently walks into the bathroom and stands in front of the shower, unmoving. I reach around her and turn the knob on to a medium temperature and place a fresh towel and washcloth on the counter before silently making my exit.

I assume she's gotten in the shower, so I hurry to my room, grab a pair of fuzzy pajamas, slippers, and a beanie—just in case— for her to put on afterward, and leave them on the bed.

I lean my head toward the hallway, still hearing the running water, and pull my phone out of my pocket. Trying not to make as much noise as possible, I open the sliding glass door and step onto my balcony to make a call that I never thought I would.

A gruff, sleep-filled voice answers on the third ring. "H-hello?"

My breath quivers, and I take in another lungful of air before speaking. "I need you." The line is silent for a moment before I hear a slight rustling noise like he just sat up in bed.

"Charlie?" he asks, bewildered and very concerned.

"It's me. I need you. Please." I beg.

A groggy-sounding female says, "Who are you talking to at this hour?" and my heart sinks. Of course, he has someone.

I didn't think. "You know what? Never mind. I'm sorry to bother you." I retract quickly.

"No, Charlie. Tell me what's wrong?" he says with a lot of distress and just a little force.

"I just really need your help. Can you come over?"

The phone muffles, and I hear voices speaking back and forth, the female one sounding angry.

"Send me the address. I'll be there right away."

I breathe a sigh of relief and nod to no one. "Thank you... just—" I stutter my words momentarily. "Thank you."

I head back in and tiptoe to Emily's door. I no longer hear the water, but I don't want to rush her. I lean against the wall that's opposite her door and slide down to the floor.

About five minutes later, the door creaks open, and Emily comes out wearing the entire ensemble I left for her. I stand and tilt my head down the hall for her to follow me. We get to the kitchen, and I begin to make two cups of hot chocolate. I know chocolate won't fix the physical or mental wounds, but if it can bring even a tiny bit of comfort, I want to give that to her.

I set the steaming mug in front of her, with topping choices of mini marshmallows, whipped cream, and cinnamon. When she adds all three, a wisp of a smile appears on my face.

My phone beeps with a text, **"I'm outside."** I tuck it back in my pocket before turning to Emily, "Em, I asked someone to come talk with us. You can trust him, okay? And if you feel too uncomfortable, just tell me or give me some kind of signal."

Her eyes widen slightly in panic. They bounce around the room before landing on me, and she gives the smallest nod.

I open the door and smile sadly at the man before me. He is dressed in gray sweats and a navy hoodie, and his hair seems to be tousled with fingers instead of his typical styling products. No primping for him. He simply jumped out of bed and came when I called. He looks good dressed down. I stand to the side to allow him to enter. "Thank you for coming. We're in the kitchen."

"Em, this is a friend of mine. He's here to help."

He walks over to her, keeping his movements slow and steady so as not to startle her. Keeping a respectable distance, he crouches down to her level. No judgment on his face or in his tone when he speaks. "Hi, Emily. My name is Jensen. Is it alright if I talk with the two of you?"

Emily ignores Jensen completely and looks at me with her one good eye. "You trust him?" she asks, placing the entirety of her faith in my answer.

I nod immediately. We've had our *interactions* in the past, and we've kept our distance since I've been with Starry North, but it's no question. I trust him with my life. And in this case, Emily's. "I do."

She takes a small sip of her cup. Jensen and I both take a seat at the table, waiting patiently for her to tell us what happened.

"I was put into a new foster home two weeks ago. I've been doing really good, Cee. Like we talked about. Keeping my nose clean and just trying to make it to eighteen."

I incline my head, offering my belief in her statement.

"When I first got there, it was just the husband and wife and two other fosters. Boys. Fairly young, maybe ten or eleven. They pretty much ignored me but gave me a room and food, so that was fine with me."

She pauses to swirl her cup around and take another sip. Chewing lightly on the marshmallows.

"Then, earlier this week, the boys were sent back to live

168

with their bio mom. The first night they were gone, I heard the husband and wife arguing, so I kept to my room and went to sleep. Later on, I heard a noise, and when I opened my eyes, the husband was standing over me…"

The acid in my stomach churns violently, and my heart picks up pace. It's a feat of strength to keep any reaction off of my face. I think I know where this is going. And if I'm right… I will kill him.

"He was jacking off right over me. Shot his load on my chest and slammed his hand over my mouth when I went to scream. He told me to be thankful that he took care of it himself and didn't wake me for the main event. When he left, I ripped the sleep shirt off and puked in my backpack."

That motherfucker. I barely restrain the growl in my throat. Well, that explains the trash bag. My eyes dart over to Jensen; he has no visible reaction, but the fist on his lap under the table is clenched to the point of white knuckles.

"Sadly, that's not the first time something like that has happened in one of the homes I've been in. It's kinda par for the course. After that, he left me alone for the next few nights. But then—"

That's not fucking okay. It shouldn't be chalked up to "par for the course". These people are trusted to keep these kids safe. What the fuck is wrong with these monsters?

"Tonight, I had just fallen asleep when the creak of the door woke me. I didn't move, but my eyes shot open, and I froze when I heard the footsteps coming closer. It was him."

I hold my breath, waiting for the words I fucking know are coming next.

"He wanted audience participation this time. When I refused, he did this—" she points to her eye. "I was okay

169

with the punch if it was that or suck off this nasty fuck. But he wasn't looking for an 'or' situation. He wanted 'and'."

A small gasp comes out of my mouth on accident. Emily's eye shoots over to me, and Jensen places his hand on my knee. I lick my suddenly dry bottom lip, "Did he.. did he—" Fuck. I can't even get out the words. The room seems like it's getting smaller, and my breathing becomes labored. Projections of what she went through tonight merge with the nightmares of my past. Darkness dots my vision as I struggle to remain tethered to the here and now. Jensen squeezes my knee lightly, bringing me back to the present.

Slowly, Emily nods. "He did."

Chapter 27

July 2009

Charlotte

I abruptly stand up, not caring that the chair tips backward onto the floor, and rush over to her side. I stand over her with my hands hovering in the air, afraid to touch her without permission. No one should fucking touch her without permission. No one should touch *anyone* without permission.

Her arm reaches out and latches onto my leg, and I immediately embrace her. "Shh, I've got you." I can't bring myself to tell her it's okay. It's not.

She continues to hold on to me as her cries soften. With her voice muffled by my legs, she says, "When he was done, he just walked out. I didn't know what to do, so I just laid there. The door opened again a few minutes later, and lighter footsteps entered. The wife. I thought she was coming to take care of me or check on me, something like that. But no."

She abruptly pulls back and rips the beanie off of her head. Showcasing the damage done to her once lush, full head of hair.

"She beat the shit out of me while calling me a junkie whore.

Said I seduced her husband and she was going to teach me a lesson. That I thought I could use my looks to get whatever I wanted, so she was going to take that away. That's when she did this—" She points to her head.

"I'm not sure how long the beating went on for. I just kind of... turned myself off. When she finally left, I dumped out the garbage in the can beside my bed and threw what little belongings I had into it, then jumped out of the second-story window. There was a raspberry bush below it, really fucked up my legs. All I could think was I needed to call you. That you would get me somewhere safe. Please, please don't make me go back there."

I shoot a concerned look at Jensen. He looks contemplative and at a loss himself. I lift my brows and give him a "what do we do" look. He taps his thumb against the table top as he thinks.

"I will always keep you safe, Em. You hear me? Always. You will never go back there again."

"Emily?" Jensen asks in that soothing way he has. Gentle and comforting. She lifts her head to look at him. "It's been a very long and intense night for you. The best thing you can do right now is to try and get some rest. Charlie and I will discuss the next steps. But I can assure you, you will stay here tonight, and you will *never* go back to that place."

I lead Em back to the guest room and tuck her in, giving her an old teddy that was in my closet. She may be seventeen now, but you will never be too old for the comfort a teddy provides you in your darkest hour. We don't speak, but her soft smile is all I need to know; though she isn't okay right now, she will be.

I enter the kitchen again and see Jensen rinsing the hot

chocolate mugs. I lean on the wall and watch him. He is such a good man. He turns, wiping his damp hands on a towel, and folds it neatly back on the counter. "Do you want to go to my car to talk?" he asks. That's probably for the best, I don't want Emily to overhear us talking about her, and it's fucking cold outside.

* * *

"Are you okay?" Jensen turns to me from the driver's seat and reaches a hand out like he's going to touch me. At the last second, he lets it land on the console instead.

"I'm not the concern here." I say briskly. Not meaning to be a bitch, but I really can't focus on me right now. This is about Emily.

Jensen gives me a sad, knowing smile and nods. "Of course."

"I'm sorry. I don't mean to be snappy. I'm at a loss. What can we do?" I ask. Jensen is definitely the more adultier-adult, and I'm in need of direction. I'm feeling way out of my depth here.

"Charlie, you do understand that we are mandatory re-porters, right?" I know he's right. I've heard the phrase, and I've never had an issue with reporting harmful situations. But this... is different. This is Emily.

"What will happen?"

He sighs and rubs his hand through his low-cut beard. "Not a lot, if I'm honest. I've seen this happen too many times. Wards of the state are in abundance. The social workers and proper home placements are not. Many things are overlooked or fall through the cracks. It's an unfortunate truth."

I shake my head. "I'm not okay with that, Jense. I can't let

173

her go back into a placement situation. I just can't. What if she just stays here with me?"

His face softens. "Charlie, you have the biggest heart, and I know you care for this girl, but you can't just harbor a runaway."

"She just turned seventeen! She has less than a year until she's able to leave on her own. It sounds like those wastes of breath won't be missing her anyway."

"They are still subject to home inspections, and if they want to keep collecting their payment, she needs to be in the home. They may have already reported her as a runaway."

"I don't accept that. There's got to be something I can do. Please. Anything?" I beg, on the verge of tears. I've got so much emotion building inside me. I won't let her be put in an unsafe situation again. This is almost like a chance to save a version of myself from five years ago.

Jensen blows out a breath as he stares out of the windshield for several minutes before he turns back to me. "Let me make a call tomorrow. How would you feel about being a foster mom?"

I nod vigorously, "I'll do whatever I need to do. She's not leaving. I won't let her go. I'll fucking Ruby Ridge this bitch if I have to."

He tsks at me and rolls his eyes, "No need for any standoffs, Charlie. I think I have a favor I can call in. Let me handle it, okay?"

I reach over and latch my hand with his, my tears on the verge of spilling over. "I can't thank you enough. I'm so grateful that you showed up, no questions asked, and jumped right into the fray with me."

Jensen's thumb runs light strokes over mine, "I'm glad you

called. This wasn't how I envisioned seeing you again, but it makes me happy that I was the one you put your trust in."

I bite down on my bottom lip, desperately trying to keep my emotions in check. "Did I get you in trouble?" I whisper, unable to meet his gaze.

He lets out a soft chuckle, "She'll get over it."

"I'm sorry."

"I'm not. Can I let you in on a little secret?"

I gulp and nod.

"I could've been in the middle of fucking her, and I would've come running when you called."

I burst out laughing, and when I look back at him, he gives me a wide grin. Touche Dr. Turner. Touche.

* * *

I don't know whose dick Jensen sucked to get things approved so quickly, but he was able to get Emily's emergency placement at my home and my foster license expedited. Within a week, it was all a done deal. Legally. No gunfire necessary.

I used my emergency credit card to get everything Emily needed and filled my house—our house—with every snack known to man. We got her a whole new wardrobe. Though she probably could've just raided my closet, we have very similar tastes.

The highlight of the shopping excursion was my surprise trip to the salon. I called them ahead of time and let them know that I wanted the nicest, calm, and understanding stylist they had, and they delivered. Not even a wince when she saw the state of Emily's face or head. She had enough hair to get extensions. They were hella fucking expensive. And I would pay it, time and time again, just to see the smile back on her face.

It's been two weeks since that first night. Though her physical wounds are well on their way to being healed, and she feels more confident with her new hair, the emotional wounds are soul-deep. I hear the soft cries through our shared wall at night.

Emily's rapist foster dad was arrested. He pleaded guilty in return for a lesser sentence, but at least Emily won't be dragged through a trial and have to see him again. The wife, however, had no repercussions for assaulting Emily. And that brings me to tonight. Sitting back at the intersection that I picked up a battered girl, in all black.

I put the phone to my ear, and Savvy picks up immediately. "You're going to do it, aren't you?"

"You're my best friend, right?" I ask, dead serious. She picks up on the tone right away.

"For the rest of our fucking lives. What's up?"

"If it goes south, I need you to make sure Emily is cared for."

Her voice gets softer, "Whatever you need, Charls. You know that."

"I just needed to hear you say it. Okay, here goes nothing. I'll call you later... I hope."

"You'll call me later." She confirms with no hesitation. Right before I hang up the phone, she chimes in. "Oh, and Charls? Remember, the soft silt at Tim's Creek is not the best place to hide a body. Be smart."

I snicker, "If it comes to that, I'll be sure to confer with you about proper body disposal."

I take a deep breath and leave my phone on the seat. Reaching into the back seat, my hands search until they find what they're looking for.

I roll my neck side to side as I stroll past the very bush that scarred Emily's legs and find the window with the faulty latch. It opens with nary a noise. I crawl in. The stench of vodka is potent throughout the disgusting shack.

I keep my footsteps light as I make my way up the narrow staircase. A TV blares from the room on the left. It's cracked open just enough to flicker light from whatever shit she's watching.

I press the door lightly, peeking around the corner to find the woman I'm looking for passed out. Damn. I really wanted to see her reaction when I first entered the room. I know I should probably feel something for what I'm about to do. Like regret or trepidation. However, the only thing I feel is certain.

Reminiscent of my favorite female lunatic, Harley Quinn, I swing the bat in a circle and let it land on my shoulder as I make my way beside her bed. I look down at the middle-aged, obese ogre and grin as I bring the bat down on her midsection.

A curdled scream leaves her as she rolls to the fetal position, giving me her back. I bring the bat down again against her ribs.

An odor of vomit fills the air, and I slam the wooden weapon into her knee, holding back my own stomach contents.

"Stop! What are you doing? Who are you?"

WHACK!

Another hit to her shoulder. I grin, "Tsk, tsk. So many questions. Just call me Miss Quinn."

She rolls towards me, tears and snot running down her mottled face. I give her a Cheshire grin before pulling my fist back and releasing it in her face. Her head rolls to the side

177

as she groans and grapples with the sheets tangled around her lower body.

I drop the bat at my feet and grip a handful of her greasy locks and lean my mouth down to her ear, "You won't say a fucking thing. Or you'll wish this was the worst thing that happened to you. One fucking word, and I will gut you like the pig you are. Your entrails will dangle from the banister like garland. Nod if you understand." I growl.

She nods fervently, mistakenly thinking this is over. I reach into my pocket and pull out my second weapon of the evening. When the loud buzzing fills the room, she gasps. I give her no time to react before I press the electric razor to her head. Snively sobs convulse through her body, and I simply beam with delight.

Should it concern me that I felt no remorse leaving that house? Maybe. Does it actually? Not in the fucking slightest.

I toss the bat in the backseat and make my way home, whistling along to the pop tune on the radio.

One more demon down.

Chapter 28

September 2009

Charlotte

Life is funny. Four years ago, I was falling head over heels for the dark boy with the secret notebook. The strong, silent outcast. He broke my heart.

Three years ago, I fell hard for a mysterious southern boy—the boy with the savior complex, the sweet golden retriever type. I was certain he was an incredible man who would never do me harm... but he also broke my heart.

A year and a half ago, the dark boy came back into my life. Things weren't what they seemed. We had shit communication. The love was still there, in deep, dark, hidden corners of my being. And I let him break my heart again.

Seven months ago, I decided no more. This is the era of Charlotte doing Charlotte. No more boys. No more heartbreak. Nothing is allowed in my life that doesn't serve me. I'm done letting people take up space in my head, rent-free. Ass, gas, or grass motherfuckers. No one rides for free.

As much as I chant my new mantra—and I chant it a lot—I can't help but feel hurt that Jason didn't even bother to respond to me. It just shows me how much my feelings matter to him. I guess he thought since he was caught out and the jig was up, he might as well ghost me and move on.

It fucking hurts. I don't want to admit it, but it does.

Why do we always want what hurts us? Are we so fucking toxic that we'd settle for less than we deserve?

Why?

Like one of my favorite alt-rock bands says something about not knowing how they got that way, and it's not alright, but they're breaking the habit.

Time for me to clutch my inner Savvy and hold on for dear life.

* * *

"Em! Get in here!" I shout toward the open door of my bedroom. After hearing the world's most dramatic sigh, she plods down the hallway and stops at the door frame.

"What the hell, Cee? You know the finale of *The Deal Breaker Resort* is on. She's finally going to find out that the dude she's been crushing on is her cheating ex-boyfriend's dad."

Jesus. This girl and her reality TV shows. At least this one actually takes place in Alaska. Not a lot of Hollywood magic going on in those remote woods. I roll my eyes very dramatically, matching her sigh, and point to the three swatches of paint on my wall. "What do you think?"

Emily makes her way over to me, scuffing her slipper-covered feet the whole way. Her lip kicks up as she points. "Yellow is fucking gross, Cee. Do you want it to look like a dude who drinks way too much Mountain Dew pissed all over your walls? And this green? Is the inside of a baby diaper after its first round of smashed peas what you're going for?"

Fucking teenagers. There is no way I was this annoying at seventeen. "What about the gray?" I ask, ignoring her whole-ass attitude.

"Boring." She feigns a yawn with a pat to her mouth.

I can't believe I'm listening to a broody adolescent. The green wasn't *that* bad. Okay, maybe none of them were my favorite either. So here I am, making my way to the hardware store...again.

The key to a successful hardware store visit? Act like you don't have a fucking clue. *Those* men— you know the kind— have the keen ability to determine a damsel in distress within three meters. It's like they came equipped with a vulnerability identifier. They appear out of thin air to man-splain the ever-living fuck out of the different uses for a roll of painter's tape. There is a proper way to do it, and as a woman, surely I don't have that knowledge.

If you do actually know what you are talking about, they take it as personal blows to their ego. Like you are chasing after them with pitchforks, ready to revoke their fragile man card.

I think we know by now I could give a flying fuck about hurting someone's feelings. Especially a man who thinks a woman is beneath him. So I strut around the place and refuse to ask for help... even if I need it.

Which brings me to the present, where I stand in front of the wall of paint swatches. Where I've been for the last forty-five minutes because the pervy douche behind the counter is too busy staring at the ass bedazzled with the words "**NAUGHTY**" belonging to one of the many cougars of River View.

It's just an accent wall, Charlie. You're not determining which wire to clip to save the world from exploding. Pick a fucking color.

I slam the metallic purple swatch onto the counter and wave my hand in pervy boy's face. "I'll take a gallon of this."

He blinks slowly at me, like his mind is still computing the words. I give him a pointed look from the swatch to the mixing machine. *Chop, chop, pervy dude.*

I pull out my phone to busy myself while waiting for my paint when my name is called from behind me. I turn to see who it is and lock eyes with someone I really never thought I'd see again.

"I thought that was you. It's lovely to see you, dear." She gives me a wobbly smile like it pains her to be nice to me. I just bet it is. Considering she and her husband have never made me feel welcome in their home. She always looked at me with an air of superiority, like she just knew I'd never be good enough for her son.

You're trying to be a better person. You're trying to be a better person. You're trying to be a better person.

I plaster on my customer service smile, "Mrs. Donovan. How charming to run into you. The clouds have really parted for us today!" Okay, smartass, rein it in.

Her smile falters. "Please call me Nora. I know we haven't had the best interactions in the past, and I'd like to apologize for my part in it."

Sure. Okay, whatevs. "Don't even worry about it, Nora. Water under the bridge. Well," I gesture to the can being placed on the counter for me. "It looks like I'm all set. Great to see you. Let's do it again, or not. Oh, and congrats on becoming a Grandma. You don't look a day over sixty. I bet you are beyond thrilled to have made Jade a permanent fixture in your precious family." So much for trying to be a better person.

I grab my can and hustle out to my car. I climb in and press my forehead to the steering wheel. This is what I get for moving back here. Small towns will always be small towns. Can't go anywhere without running into the people you want to avoid the most. Like an ex's family member or high school acquaintances who've made up this super close relationship with you in their head.

A timid knock draws my focus to the window, where I see a teary-eyed Nora. For fuck's sake. I roll my window down, "Yes?" I ask, trying to keep the snark out of my tone.

"I think we need to talk, dear. Would you join me at The Coffee Hut for a few minutes? My treat."

I want to punch her in the cooter and run away so I don't have to think about that family ever again... but I'm also curious about what she has to say.

* * *

I tuck my foot under my leg and blow on the top of my toasted marshmallow breve before taking a sip. Nora sits across from me, looking uncomfortable as hell. That makes two of us, lady.

"I'm not really sure where to start. When's the last time you spoke to my son?" she asks while twisting her hands in her lap. She seems really rattled.

I knew Jason would come up. How could he not? "He sent me a letter around the beginning of January. I haven't heard from him since. Why?"

"Has he shared much about our... family dynamics?"

My head tilts slightly as I look at her, puzzled. She identifies my confusion immediately and continues.

"I'm going to guess that hasn't come up. You should probably have this conversation with him, but I want to set a few things straight. First, that is *not* my grandson. That baby and his mother are not part of *my* family. Unfortunately, he is blood to Jason. His brother."

I huff a surprised breath at her news, right into the top of my very full coffee cup. I screech when sizzling drops land on my thighs and hand. Nora quickly hands me a stack of napkins, and I dab myself, "His brother?" I ask in bewilderment.

Nora smiles at me sadly, tears welling up in her eyes again. "Yes, dear. Neal fathered that baby. Not Jason."

Taken aback, I gape at her. My mind races with a million questions. "But, that means..."

Nora finishes a few of the questions that were circling my brain. "That he cheated? That he groomed and sexually assaulted a minor? That he's the scum of the Earth? Yes, Charlotte. To all of those. He's also in prison."

How in the fuck did absolutely none of this come up in Florida? Sure, we didn't have a ton of time together, but this seems like a huge piece of information to keep hidden. *That's not fair. I told him next to nothing about my past. I can't expect him to just open all his wounds to me when I've been so closed off.*

"Holy shit." I whisper.

"Holy shit, indeed. I was granted a divorce and all of his assets, so I've washed my hands of the whole situation. Jade is proud of her relationship with Neal and goes to see him in prison, from what I'm told. They can have each other as far as I'm concerned. But enough about people who don't matter."

Nora picks her americano up and takes a sip, watching me over the rim with a thoughtful expression. I feel exposed under her watchful eye. "I'm truly happy you and Jason have reconnected. Our relationship has been... strained, at the very least. But we are working on mending it. He did tell me that the two of you were back in contact and that you had moved back. He also mentioned your mother had passed. I'm truly sorry for your loss." She says softly and reaches a hand over to pat the top of mine.

It no longer sucks all of the air out of the room to hear my mom being talked about. I miss her every fucking day, but I don't want to act like she didn't exist. I want her to be remembered. I nod and slip my hand away under the guise of scratching an itch on my other arm. Emotions are still a complicated thing for me.

So, I was wrong about Jason... again. Fucking hell. And fuck Jade. She knew *exactly* what she was doing when she led me to believe that was Jason's baby. What a cunt.

"I appreciate that. So, speaking of Jason, I may have bumped into Jade earlier this year and thought the baby was his. I sent him a really, really unpleasant letter, and he never wrote back. Is he still deployed? When's the last you spoke with him?"

The tears are back. Fuck. She brings her hand to her mouth, holding back a sob, and closes her eyes. A trail of tears leaks out of each side and slowly slides down. Nora reaches for a napkin, and my heart sinks to my ass. I can't. I fucking cannot hear any more bad news.

"Oh, Charlotte. I hate to be the one to have to tell you this..."

Chapter 29

Jason

I tighten the harness and verify that the latch under her chin is in place, ensuring my girl is snug as a bug in a rug. After my inspection, I trail kisses up the side of her neck. The light touch sends shivers across her skin. "Jace! I'm so nervous. Don't distract me right now!" She stutters out, and I wrap my arms around her from behind.

"Sweets, that's exactly why you need a distraction. Just don't think about anything. I will do all the work. Do you trust me?"

Her immediate nod and submission go straight to my dick, which is now pressing uncomfortably against the strap of my harness.

"Start running." I whisper against her ear.

We both take off toward the cliff's edge, picking up speed. I glance back to make sure the wing is completely open. Our feet leave the ground as the wing fills with air to carry us, and Charlie turns around with panicked eyes. "Is this supposed to happen?" she shouts, and I hold back a laugh.

"Yes, Sweets. This is the 'glide' part of 'paraglide'."

"Don't you dare laugh at me, Jason. I was not meant to leave the surface of the Earth."

I let go of the brake toggle and cup her chin, bringing my lips to hers in a quick but hard kiss. I smirk at her before turning her back to face forward, and she gasps at the sight before us.

"It's the most beautiful thing I've ever seen." She says in amazement, taking in our surroundings from new heights.

And it is. Beautiful, but nothing compares to her. "It is." I agree with her but mean it in a completely different way. She is and always will be the most beautiful thing I've ever seen.

The ride is smooth, and seeing Charlie's pure joy is worth everything we've endured to get to this point.

We pass over a familiar cluster of trees, which she recognizes and spins to face me, showing me the glowing smile plastered against her face. She opens her mouth, but before she can speak, we are hit with a gust of wind. Immediate terror takes over her body. It's no big deal, but to someone who is terrified of heights, flying, and anything of the like, it's doomsday.

I correct us easily, and the ride smoothes out, but I can feel her trembling. "It's alright, baby. See? All good now. Just a little breeze sending us toward our destination, that's all." I coo and rub her back. She doesn't respond but shakes her head back and forth.

"Pretty girl?" I turn her face toward me. Her eyes are squeezed shut, and her mouth is agape. She seems to be struggling for air, but she shouldn't be.

"Baby. Breathe for me." I instruct firmly but with a soft edge.

She continues to fight for air. Fuck. She's having a panic attack. Leaning forward, I place a kiss on her shoulder and press my cheek against the side of her helmet, "Come on, Sweets. Take a deep breath. Can you do that for me?"

187

My right hand rubs circles on her back as I place another kiss on her neck. She trembles a little more but expels a gasp.

I slide my hand around to her ribs, just below her breast, and continue in a circular motion. My tongue traces the shell of her ear, which barely sticks out from beneath the helmet, before working back down her neck. I feel the moan through my lips and smile against her skin.

I work my hand from her ribs down to her thigh and apply more pressure, gliding my glove-covered hand across the apex of her thighs.

Charlie's chest expands with a deep breath, "Mm, that's my good girl. Let's see about that distraction, hm?"

It's this moment that I'm so fucking grateful Charlie made me watch that movie a thousand times. The one where Mark Wahlberg fingerfucks Reese Witherspoon on a roller coaster. I remember her getting so fucking turned on. I had hoped one day, we'd be in a position where I could give her my own death-defying orgasm.

I rub firm circles over her legging-clad clit, thankful she decided on a lightweight material.

Her pulse jumps rapidly against my lips, and I nip it lightly with my teeth. My dick is painfully hard and is experiencing a heavy dose of FOMO. Charlie's breathing comes in clipped pants, and I can tell she's close. I keep a steady pace and rhythm. So many guys fuck up the moment of glory by switching shit up at the last minute. Stay the course, fellas. Don't fucking change anything.

I swallow her release with my mouth covering hers. My tongue lashes around her mouth, absorbing her taste and committing it to the deepest part of me. I never want to be free of her essence.

With my girl satisfied and breathing normally, I guide us in a few gentle turns before descending on top of Sky Ridge.

She nails the landing, and once I detach us, she rounds on me with a brilliant smile and new life in her eyes.

She begins to speak, but when her mouth opens, an ear-piercing beep comes out instead.

I cringe and cover my ears.

Beep.

Beep.

Beep.

Chapter 30

March 2009

Jason

"I think he's waking up." A deep voice murmurs from somewhere around me.

My head is fucking killing me. I fight to open my eyes, but it's like they're cemented shut.

"Donovan, open your eyes, buddy."

Beep.

Beep.

Beep.

"Turn whatever is causing that fucking unrelenting beeping off." I grumble and regret it as soon as I do. My throat feels as if I've swallowed glass.

"Well, that beeping lets us know you're still alive. So no, we won't be turning it off." Who I've figured out is Jacobs, chuckles.

With immense strain, my eyelids finally lift. Blinding light floods my vision, and I slam them closed again. A string of curses and rustling sounds fills the room. "Give it another go, man."

I open my eyes again to a more acceptably dim hospital room. What the fuck happened?

Jacobs blows out a breath, "Shit got fucked up, man. Let's get you checked out by the doc now that you're awake, and we can talk."

I've never seen him this serious. My stomach roils, and the back of my head throbs, but I nod, and he leaves the room to get the doctor.

* * *

TBI? Coma? Feeding tube? Jesus. I wish I could remember what happened. I have bits and pieces of memory from the day of the accident. But nothing makes a solid picture.

The doctor came in and told me my prognosis, checked me out, and ordered some more tests.

If all goes well, I'll be discharged in the next couple of days. But apparently, the real hard work begins after that. Physical and cognitive therapy are on the docket for the foreseeable future.

Once the doc left, Jacobs came back in, and I really took him in from head to toe. His normally put-together appearance is severely disheveled, and a slight limp now accompanies his usual swagger.

"Lay it on me, Jacobs. How bad is it?"

He brings a chair over to my bedside and shakes his head. "Bad."

Jacobs proceeds to fill me in on that day. There was a decoy in the road, and when Olsen went to inspect it, an IED was triggered, killing him immediately. The lead vehicle was close enough to the blast that everyone inside was killed as well.

Either immediately or succumbed to their injuries shortly after.

Our truck managed to avoid complete destruction, our driver and myself being the only ones severely injured. His Majesty, Lowkowski, Jacobs, and I were extracted and taken to an undisclosed medical plaza to be assessed.

I was then brought here to a private hospital in Germany.

More than half of my team is dead. Olsen will never see his wife and kids again. Fuck. Why didn't I switch with him?

"I need to get back. I've got to go see his wife. See if there's anything I can do or any way I can help." With strain, I sit up and start pulling on random wires. Hissing when things begin detaching from my skin.

Jacobs stands and swats my hands away. "What the fuck do you think you're doing, Donovan? Knock that shit off. You are in no position to help anyone. Chill out."

I press against him in a futile attempt to push him away. My strength is zero. Exasperated, my head falls back against the pillow, sending ricochets of pain bouncing around my cranium. My hands immediately cradle each side of my head.

"We've got to go, man. His wife, dude. His fucking kids!" I exclaim as a sob breaks loose. Jacobs sighs and sits beside me again.

"I know. And we will, I promise you that. But you've got to get better first. You'll stay here to start therapy until you're well enough to travel. I'll be going back and forth between headquarters and here to check on your progress. Once the doctors clear you, you'll join me in Texas."

"Then you'll let me go see her?" I ask.

He nods firmly, "Then, I will *take* you to go see her."

* * *

July 2009

I've had perfect vision for twenty years... and one well-placed hit to the head took that away from me. It seems like a small thing to be upset about comparatively, but the fact that I now have to wear glasses or contacts, or I get a headache from hell sucks.

My muscle tone is coming back. I feel stronger. After being discharged from rehab, Jacobs kept his promise of flying with me from Germany back to TRC headquarters in Texas.

When we boarded the first long-ass flight, he gave me a sheepish look that I was immediately suspicious of before handing me a worn-down envelope.

Even though he hadn't opened the envelope, he must've intuited its contents and given it to me at a time when I literally couldn't do a fucking thing about it.

She thinks that kid is mine. She thinks I lied... again. Everything is fucked. I never would've kept something like that from her.

She thinks she's done with me? With us? I don't fucking think so.

I had fifteen hours to write a response of my own. But this one, I will be giving her in person.

After I attend to matters in Texas, I'm coming for my girl.

* * *

August 2009

My heart gallops out of control as we make our way up the driveway of the Olsen family home. Each step rips a piece of my soul out. I have to look his wife in the eye, knowing that if I had just sent him back to the other truck, he would still be with her today.

I took their chance at a happy family away. Subsequently, I caused the worst day of their lives to come to fruition, and I need to own up to it.

Jacobs and I stand shoulder to shoulder in front of the door. As I reach up to knock, he pulls my arm down, "Don't do or say anything fucking stupid, Donovan. I mean it. This isn't on you. I see the guilt written all over your face. Don't put that shit on them, you hear me?"

I don't agree, but I nod and jerk my hand away to knock. After a few moments, a petite brunette answers the door with a bouncing toddler on her hip. The unruly curls atop his head come straight from his daddy.

The fact that this little guy is all that remains of Ryan Olsen breaks my heart. One decision, one stupid, seemingly insignificant event, forever changed the course of countless lives.

A lump forms in my throat, blocking my words from leaving my mouth. Jenna's sad eyes are too much to bear. Like he can feel my hesitation, Jacobs places a hand on my shoulder and greets her. "Jenna. It's been too long since we checked in. How are you and this little guy holding up?" He reaches out to tickle the boy's foot. He giggles and starts kicking.

"Oh, Randy, we're hanging in there, you know? Doing the best we can day after day. Come in, come in," she stands to the side and ushers us into her home. "Have a seat. Did y'all want anything to eat or drink?" We both decline, and everyone sits down in the living room.

I swallow past the lump, "Mrs. Olsen, my name is Jason Donovan. I worked with Ryan, and I wanted to offer my condolences. Is there anything you need, or we can do for you?"

"Please call me Jenna. Thank you, Jason. My Ry spoke highly of you. Said you were always good for a laugh and had a hell of a way with a pencil. You made him feel so welcome on the team. I can't thank you enough for that." She sniffs, holding back tears as she talks about her dead husband. Dead because of me.

The toddler rubs his eyes, and Jacobs offers to put him down for her; she gratefully accepts the help. Clearly, he's a lot closer with this family than I realized.

Jenna and I sit in awkward silence for a moment before we both begin to speak at the same time. "I'm so so—"

"How are you hol—"

An embarrassed laugh from each of us fills the quiet space. I offer my hand out for her to go first.

"How are you holding up? Randy told me a little bit about your recovery. Are you feeling back to normal?"

My hands flap at my thighs, and I try to tighten my fists to quell the need. That's such a loaded question. I give her my best guess at an answer. "I don't know that there will ever be a 'normal' to strive for. But I'm here."

The moment it leaves my mouth, I fucking regret it. Tears stream down Jenna's face as she gazes down at the ring on her left hand. "Yes, you are."

Shaking my head at my own idiocy, I walk over and kneel before her, "Jenna, I'm so sorry. I wasn't thinking. Fuck. That was a dick thing to say."

She shakes her head repeatedly and looks down at me with red-rimmed eyes. Her hand gently cups my cheek. "No. You are here. Thank the Lord for that." My eyes flutter closed as I feel the sting of tears behind them.

"I see it, you know?" she whispers. I open my eyes and search hers before she continues. "The guilt you carry. Randy also carries it. Neither of you are responsible for what happened. Even though Ry lost his life that day, he wouldn't have wanted the three of you to. So the best thing you can do for Ryan? For me? Live. Live your life. Take the chances. Chase the love. Choose happiness. Don't let fear and regret stop you from carrying on."

Jacobs pauses at the entry to the living room, looking like he interrupted an intimate moment. I sniff and pull away from Jenna, who gazes up at him with a sad smile. She stands, and he opens his arms immediately for her, engulfing her with a very tight hug.

They stay embraced for an uncomfortable amount of time. He whispers into her ear, and she nods before reaching up and placing a lingering kiss on his cheek. We say our goodbyes and head back to the car.

"What the fuck was that?" I ask.

He doesn't even bother to look at me. "What do you mean?"

I narrow my eyes at him. "You got something going on with Olsen's old lady?"

Jacobs' jaw clenches, and he tightens his grip on the steering wheel. "You don't know what you're talking about. We're friends. That's all. And Olsen is gone, man. As much as I wish that he wasn't, he is. That woman has been through hell and back. I feel for her is all."

My face softens at his words, and I nod. "You're right. I

didn't mean to insinuate anything bad. It might be a little soon, but you know if you had feelings for one another, that'd be okay. She deserves happiness. You deserve happiness."

He shakes his head, "It's too soon. It's not right. But fuck, man. I've never felt these things for a woman before. I can do one-night stands like nobody's business, but this is so much more."

"There's no rush, Jacobs. You can't help how you feel. If you want my advice? Take things slowly. Just be there for her and let things run the course they're meant to, naturally."

As he usually does when he feels uncomfortable, he deflects with humor. "Oh yeah? And is that what you're doing with 'Sweets'? Taking it slow and letting it naturally run its course?"

I laugh and look out of the window. "Nah, man. She's something entirely different. Your situation is like watching a flower come to life in the summer sun—lovely and effortless. But loving Charlie? It's like diving straight into a hurricane. It's wild and unpredictable, pulling you into a whirling vortex of emotions. You have to fight your way through, but once you do? There's something hauntingly beautiful about it, like finding peace in the midst of chaos. And I never want to come out."

"Jesus, dude. If she doesn't take you back after saying some shit like that, there's no hope for any of us."

Chapter 31

September 2009

Charlotte

The swirling of information in my mind is making me dizzy. A couple of days ago, Nora dropped me right off the edge of a cliff without a parachute.

Thank God Jason is alive. She didn't have a ton of details, but he's alive and back in the States. I've never felt such instant relief in my life. I went from hating him in one second to feeling like my breath was snatched from my body in the span of a heartbeat.

I truly hope that my letter was lost in the midst of the mayhem he was dealing with. I was so hateful and brash.

Emily left for therapy a little bit ago. It's always odd to be home alone. She has become such a fixture in my life, and I wouldn't have it any other way. She is the sister I never knew I wanted. We bicker and annoy each other, it's fucking great. There's love.

There was a time in my not-so-distant past when I convinced myself that I'd never have love in my life. I was just looking at things wrong. Romantic love wasn't what I should've been looking for. Familial love—that's what was missing.

Snuggling further into my blanket, I close my eyes and wait for sleep to take me.

DING DONG

My eyelids open, and I stare at the ceiling for a moment, trying to decide if I want to ignore it and go to sleep or greet whomever it is with my handy-dandy baseball bat. Fuck, maybe my night of vigilante justice has awoken a blood thirst in me... meh, oh well.

DING DONG

I let out a string of muffled curses as I thrust myself out of bed. Whoever it is will have to deal with my threadbare tank and booty-hugging shorts.

DING DONG

For fuck's sake, I am coming. I stomp to my front door and fling the lock open, ready to give the intruder of my slumber a glimpse of sleep-deprived, crazy Charlie. The door swings inward, and the words die on my tongue.

"I believe this belongs to you," Jason says as he holds the familiar envelope in his hand. So he did get my last letter, fucking hell.

All snarky retorts fizzle away with the relief that crawls through my body. I fling myself at him. He chuckles and lets the stupid letter float to the ground while wrapping me up tightly in his arms.

I nuzzle my face in his neck. His scent embeds itself in my skin, and I tighten my legs around his waist.

"Tell me a good thing." He murmurs against my skin.

I pull back and cup both sides of his face and crash my lips down to his. His hands grip my ass tightly as we both try to eliminate any possible space between us.

We kiss for several long moments. As we pull back and place our foreheads together, he gives me that little half-smile I love, "That's a pretty fucking good thing, Sweets."

"I love you." I blurt out, unable to keep the truth inside me for a moment longer. I've been on an out-of-control roller coaster of emotions for far too long. Enough is enough. I could've lost him. I would have never forgiven myself if something had happened to him, and my last communication was that stupid fucking letter.

He looks back at me in confusion, and my heart sinks. "Oh. Um, this is awkward. I thought we were just friends..."

This is where I die. Right here in my skanky sleep clothes. On my porch for all to see. On my tombstone, they'll write, "Here lies Charlie; she died of extreme embarrassment and rejection".

His lips kick up in a sly grin, and he gently grabs my chin, lifting my face to meet his gaze. "I fucking love you, Charlie. And I'm never letting you go, you hear me? This is your only chance. If you aren't in this for life, tell me now. Once I walk through this door, that's it. You're mine, forever."

"Is this like a vampire thing where you have to be invited in or something?" I ask sarcastically with an air of nonchalant-ness.

Jason growls and presses his lips back to mine, and both of us fight for dominance of the kiss. He nips my bottom lip, and I release a small scream into his mouth when his hand comes down firmly on my ass. "Answer."

"You and me, Jace. Forever." No sooner than the last syllable leaves my mouth, he scoops me up in a bridal carry and storms into my house.

Jason

Mine. She's fucking mine. Well, she always has been, but now she knows it. She points me in the direction of her bedroom, and I toss her on the bed. She chuckles as she bounces while I try to contain myself, watching her tits bob up and down. Her barely there tank top does absolutely nothing to hide her erect nipples.

I kick off my shoes and follow her down, climbing over her body and taking her mouth again.

Her breathy moans wake my dick up immediately. I kiss down her neck, sucking at her pulse point. She likes it; she grinds her barely-covered pussy against me while tugging at my hoodie.

I let her remove it. As soon as it hits the floor, her hands explore the hard plains of my chest and stomach. I smirk down at her. I told her I'd be swole and have a defined V the next time I saw her.

"You like what you see, pretty girl?" I slow the pace and gently tug her hair, bringing her face up to mine. She nods and pulls me down once more. I press my lips to hers in a closed-mouth kiss. She trails wet kisses down my neck, sliding her tongue along my Adam's apple and sucking the skin below it.

I let her lead for a moment, gently gyrating my hips against hers. Letting our desire for each other be known.

I gaze down at my girl; her features are coated in love drunk, and she's lost in lust. I watch her writhe beneath me as my hands wander across her body. She's gained some of her curves back since I've last seen her. I fucking love it.

Seeing Charlie open herself up like this has always been my favorite part of her. When she's the most honest and real version of herself.

Her hand slides down the hard ridges of my stomach until she reaches the hidden hardness below my jeans. Her hand strokes firm circles around it, and she presses her tits against my chest. Her need for friction taking over her body.

The conversation I had with my mom yesterday floods my brain at a terribly inconvenient time. She explained her conversation with Charlie and cleared the air, for which I was ultimately grateful. But then she asked if I knew about her past. Without giving me too much detail at my request, she gave me a rundown of the shit that went down with a local drug dealer.

My girl had been so lost in her own mind that she lost her sense of worth. She used her body to disappear. I never want her to feel that way again. She will never need to use sex to get what she wants or needs.

Charlie lifts her hips to meet the back of her own hand as it strokes along my dick. A gasp followed by a moan has me crashing my mouth back to hers. I want to inhale her pleasure. I need all of her sounds.

I press harder into her hand for just a moment. Allowing myself a tiny bit of pleasure before I put a stop to it all.

"Fuck me, Jace. Please." She begs in a breathy moan, her hands reaching for the button of my jeans.

I deserve a fucking medal for doing the right fucking thing.

"Sweets," I reach down to stop her hand. I bring it up and press my lips to her knuckles.

"What's wrong?" she breathes out, her brows wrinkling in confusion.

I sadly shake my head and close my eyes. I open them, place one last chaste kiss on her swollen lips, and look deep into her chocolatey ones. "I'm not ready." *She's not ready.*

Her cheeks pinken with mortification. I move to a sitting position and bring her up with me. "Let's get something to eat, hm? I'm starving."

Looking grateful for the distraction, she nods and grabs my hoodie off of the floor, covering the exposed arousal on her chest. "Sure, of course. Follow me."

Chapter 32

December 2009

Charlotte

Where is it?

I squeeze my ass as far under my bed as I can get, moving random boxes and items that have made their way into this land of superfluous elements.

I know it's here somewhere.

Shimmying out from under the bed, I make my way to the walk-in closet. The satisfying whoosh of hangers gliding along the wooden bars hums around the small space.

I lift, move, and inspect everything I can get my hands on. *Fuck.* There's not that many places to hide things.

My hand slides under a stack of T-shirts, and my fingers meet an out-of-place item. *AHA!* I slowly pull the item out, a grin firmly affixed on my face.

The small, square box sits heavily in my palm. I'm pretty sure I hear angels harmonizing over me as I pull the black velvet ribbon off. The lid comes off with a smooth and satisfying 'POP'.

Ever so slowly, I crack open the matching black velvet

jewelry box. A resounding creak follows, and at long last, the interior is visible.

What is this?

I pull the small, neatly folded red paper out of the otherwise empty box. Taking great care not to rip the contents, I unfold it slowly until the words are laid out in front of me. **"Nice try."**

I scoff and roll my eyes before placing everything back as I found it and tucking the box back under the stack of Jason's shirts. I turn around to exit the closet and freeze. A smirking Jason stands lazily propped against the door frame, looking like the cat who got the cream.

I make a move to storm right past him and murmur, "Dick."

I barely make it through the threshold when he reaches out and takes hold of my wrist. My world swims at how quickly he spins and pins me against the doorway. His large body towers over mine, but I glare up at him all the same.

His lips hover over mine, "What was that, Sweets?"

"I said you're a dick. Did I stutter?" I sass.

He chuckles and runs his tongue over his new snake bite piercings. "No, but you'll be stuttering later when I spank your ass raw for snooping when you were expressly told not to."

A warm fucking breeze gets me wet these days. That's what happens when you go an eternity without a good banging. Jason's made it his new favorite pastime to arouse me with his words and proximity. But then, just to be a prick about it, refuses to actually fuck me. He says he's not ready. I'm not sure how much I believe that. So, in the meantime, there's just a whole lot of innuendo and sexual tension mounting. And eventually, something is bound to erupt.

It just felt natural for him to live with me and Em. He had

a bag full of his clothes the day he showed up at my door and just kinda never left. We've never had an official conversation about anything regarding the two of us and where our "ship" stands. It definitely feels like more than a friendship, but not an official relationship.

All I know is I love being in his arms every night. I love hearing him bicker with Emily over ridiculous things. And most of all, I love how his presence in my life has made everything feel right and calm.

I think I got so good at functioning in chaos that it became what I craved. If my life was going well, I would figure out some way to self-sabotage.

Look at me, growing and shit.

A shudder runs through my body as I envision him doing exactly that. But two can play this game because I'm well aware of Jason's preferences. He loves a brat. Good news! This is a role I was born to play.

Slowly, I press my hand to his calmly beating heart and slide down, caressing the ridges across his stomach and tracing the line down his zipper. I don't press any harder; I simply let my hand rest on top of his jean-covered cock.

"Oh, Jace. You couldn't make me stutter even if you choked me with one hand while spanking me with the other."

His dick twitches, giving away how my words affect him even if his face stays as stoic as ever. I give him a slight squeeze and a bright smile as I twirl out from under his arm. He growls and chases me into the kitchen, where we find Emily frozen with a hand over her mouth, staring at the TV.

"Em? What's wrong?" I ask and come to stand beside her.

She doesn't take her eyes off of the TV but asks, "What school does Sav go to again?"

My brows knit, caught off guard by the question. "University of Central Florida. Why?"

Emily gasps and points at the TV. My eyes slowly make their way across the screen, trying to make sense of the red bar moving steadily across it.

"BREAKING NEWS! Active shooter on UCF campus. All efforts at communicating with the suspect have failed. The campus has been placed on lockdown while authorities make their way through and evacuate in blocks."

Oh my fucking God. Savvy. My hand reaches out to my side in a grabby motion, and Jason immediately places my phone in it.

RING

RING

RING

"Yo... What's up? Oh, that's sweet... Well, hopefully you realized by now that I can't come to the phone. So leave me a message at the beep. Or, you know, just text me like a normal person. 'K, thanks. Bye!"

No.No.No.

I make the call over and over, getting the same result each time until Jason finally pulls my phone out of my hand. "Baby, I'm sure she's okay. Try not to panic until we have more information."

My eyes stay glued to the news report. My best friend is trapped on campus with a madman, and I'm 4,700 miles away. She could die today.

Sobs rack my body as I fall to the floor. Instantly, Jason and Em are right there with me. We don't exchange words. But we all know. These kinds of things never end well.

* * *

I can't help but fidget every second of our drive over to Mary's. My knees bounce at an unreasonable pace as I chew on what's left of my thumbnail. No amount of meditation is going to quell the torrent of anxiety flooding my body.

It's been three weeks since some lunatic shot up Savvy's school. The kid, a freshman, shot and killed four students and a professor. He found Sav and Asher locked in a practice room. He had some kind of infatuation with her, and she didn't even know his name.

After Asher protected my best friend at the cost of being grazed with a bullet himself, he is forever on my anti-shit list.

The terrifying ordeal did have one silver lining. It finally forced those two to admit they had feelings for each other, and now, they are officially a "thing"— because my commitment-phobic bestie refuses a more sturdy label.

We pull up to the familiar duplex, and I'm the first out of the car. Jason chuckles, and Emily grumbles about being "the maid who will grab all the shit, I guess".

I plow through the front door and make a beeline for my chosen sister. I find her in the living room, in a recliner. I throw myself into her open arms.

"Oof, Charls. I'm broken, remember?" She groans into my ear, and I immediately pull back and move gently away from her cast-covered leg. I pat it lightly like that will remove the pain I've caused.

Jason and Emily walk into the room, each with an armful of presents. Mary comes in from the kitchen with a tray of warm beverages and instructs them to put the gifts under the tree.

Asher formally introduces himself to us and dotes on Savvy. She's finally being treated like the queen we always knew she was.

After eating a huge and delicious Christmas meal, made from scratch by Mary, Savvy and I went to her old room. Well, *our* old room.

"Bitch. You didn't tell me he was a short king!" I hoarsely whisper at Savvy while swatting her arm. She has always remained pretty tight-lipped about Asher. I always imagined she'd end up with some 6'8 bodybuilder type. Not a 5'9, average build, and maybe 170 lbs soaking wet. But somehow... it works. And this is the happiest I've ever seen her.

"I don't tell you *everything*, Charls. God. Leave some mystery in our relationship, for fuck's sake." She sighs with exasperation as if we've had this conversation a million times. We haven't.

We catch up for a little bit before being summoned to open presents. We are all grown-ass adults, but you wouldn't know it by Savvy's attempt to trip me with her crutches in order to beat me to the "good recliner".

I giggle at the sight of Jason in a Santa hat, but my heart melts when I watch him put one on Emily, who begrudgingly keeps it on her head. He passes out all the gifts, and one by one, we go around the room to open them.

I got Savs a beautiful, custom book specifically meant for her sheet music. She got me a wearable vibrator. That was fun to open in front of an audience. I got Jace a leather-bound sketchbook. He got me new winter tires for my car and an envelope with my name on it that I'm not to open until later.

None of us knew what to get Asher, so I gave him a gift card to the last remaining record store in town. He beamed at the gift, so... mission accomplished.

Emily is the last to go. When we asked her what she wanted, she wouldn't give an answer, so I got her a handheld video game unit and some new makeup. I thought it would be from both Jason and me, but he apparently had another plan up his sleeve.

"What is this?" Emily asks, looking up at Jason as he places a large, rectangular box in front of her.

"Open it and find out, Gremlin." Jason retorts, smiling at her glare. Gremlin is his nickname for her, for obvious reasons.

Emily rolls her eyes but does as he asks. She quickly pulls the bright pink wrapping paper from the front of the box. Before unwrapping the whole thing, she slams a hand to her mouth, and her eyes dart to Jason. They immediately flood with tears, and she shakes her head before she runs out of the room.

Jason smiles sadly at me and tilts his head in the direction she ran off to. I nod and go in search of her.

I find her curled in a ball on Savvy's bed. I climb on behind her, wrap my arm around her middle, and rest my cheek on her shoulder. We stay in silence for a few minutes before I ask the question that's on everyone's mind. "What's happened, Em?"

She takes a few deep breaths in before answering. "I can't believe he got it."

"Got what?" I ask.

She rolls over to face me. A wave of fresh rain and cedar wood tickles my nose. Jason climbs in behind me, sandwiching me between the two of them, and he answers for her. "An EasyBake Oven."

This fucking man. Every time I think I've seen the extent of his character. He goes on and does something else to surprise me.

A couple of months ago, Jason was watching some action movie while Em and I were putting together a puzzle at the kitchen table. We chatted lightly about a bunch of random things. Somehow, we got on the topic of our most missed-out-on childhood gifts. Mine was a Teddy Ruxpin. Hers was an EasyBake Oven. I had no idea he was listening. This seemingly small gift means the world to Emily. After spending her whole life thinking no one would ever care for her, she's become a permanent part of my family.

We are living proof that you don't have to be blood to be a family. This family is even more precious because we chose each other. There's no obligation to be here. No fake platitudes for the sake of peace. Just a group of misfits bound together with the ties of unconditional love and acceptance.

* * *

Sweets,

By now, I've told you everything in person. I've cleared up any misconceptions you may have had and set you straight on who the one and only woman who will ever carry my children will be.

I also know, because I'm a stubborn bastard, that I have yet to make love to you. You can make fun of me for that term all you want, but that doesn't change the fact that it is indeed making love. Don't get me wrong, there will be plenty of fucking in our future. But the first one? That one will be all love. And it will only happen when I look into your eyes and see the same depth of love reflected back from mine.

You don't need to be anyone but yourself, baby. I don't need anything from you but your time.

Hopefully, this letter finds you before it's been years. If it's been years, I will definitely be a two-pump chump, and you'll have to give me a mulligan.

I was thinking about when we used to go up to Sky Ridge. I would be drawing away in my notebook while you wrote or carved words into the surface of the table. They were always negative. I thought it was your way of working through your emotions or periods of darkness, but that's not it, is it? You wrote those things because that's how you saw yourself.

I can't change how you view yourself; only you can. But I can tell you how I view you instead.

So my latest drawing does just that.

I love you forever.

-J

PS— You are my good thing. Marry me?

BEAUTIFUL INSPIRED SPICY NICE
RESILIENT DEFIANT BRAT
PEACE SWEETS STRONG
KIND AMAZING LOVED
FOREVER

Chapter 33

July 2010

Charlotte

It should be illegal for temperatures to be in the nineties in Alaska. People ask us if we rode polar bears to school, for fuck's sake.

Three good things have come out of this weather:

1. I get to enjoy a refreshing blue-motherfucking-raspberry slushy lakeside while reading my new dark, smutty novel.
2. I get to eyefuck Jason in his swimming trunks, lying lazily beside me in the grass.
3. The rest of the Alaskan vampires, who have an aversion to the sun and heat, have made the swimming hole our personal oasis.

Jason abruptly stands and reaches a hand out for me. "Come on, let's go check out the dock."

I groan, but I set my book down and let him pull me up, keeping a firm grip on my slushy. We walk hand-in-hand to the rickety wooden dock. The only sounds are the flapping of our sandals and a slight rustling of leaves as the breeze dances through them.

The dock creaks and groans from our weight. Thank fuck, there are no deadly water creatures in Alaska. If we were to fall into the swimming hole, the most we'd end up with is a few leech kisses or a mild case of swimmer's itch.

"Where do you think the saying 'An eye for an eye' came from?" Jason ponders as we look out across the water.

I wrinkle my whole ass face at him. He's so fucking weird and random sometimes. All esoteric and deep meanings to every little thing. "Where the hell did that come from? I have no idea."

"So there is a Babylonian law code that dates back to roughly 1754 BCE. In it, there is a principle known as lex talionis, meaning 'the law of retaliation.'"

"Oh my God, Jace. Why the fuck did you ask me if you already knew the answer?" I grumble and then take a large sip of slushy. The cool liquid glides down my throat and carves a welcomed icy path down the rest of my body.

"May I?" he asks, holding his hand out for my drink. I narrow my eyes at him. He knows I don't like to share. But it is fucking hot out, and I do love him. I reluctantly hand my drink over.

He takes a sip from the edge of the cup instead of the straw like a goddamn barbarian. "It was made with the intent that if someone wrongs you, you can have some reciprocal justice."

"Fascinating." I deadpan and hold my hand out for my drink.

Jason swirls the straw around the large plastic cup and smiles at me. "Yeah, I think so too. Hey, do you remember that time back in high school when we stood real close just like this?" he gestures to the lack of space between our bodies. "Yeah, and you had this exact beverage. Whatever happened to it?" he rubs his chin like he's putting a lot of thought into remembering the circumstances.

Fuck. Me.

He blows me a kiss and tips the cup over the top of my head. I scream as the icy treat makes its way across my face, down my breasts, and settles around the waistband of my swim bottoms.

"Oh, you fucking ass—" My words are cut off as we fly through the air. Water engulfs our bodies, and Jason wraps his arm around my middle, pulling me against his body. His mouth slams down on mine, and I wrap my legs around his waist. Our tongues lap each other as we break the surface.

Just as I begin to grind against him, he slowly pulls away and looks into my eyes. The amount of love in the depth of his steel gaze takes my breath away. He reaches up to move some random pieces of hair stuck to my face. "Marry me." He softly demands.

Smiling, I slowly shake my head back and forth. "I'll tell you the same thing I told you at Christmas. I don't want to get married. Ever."

"Fair. Okay, so since you won't marry me, how about you be my girlfriend?" he asks victoriously like he just solved the answer to life. *Isn't that 42?*

My eyes flutter of their own accord at his ridiculousness. But also, it's so fucking sweet. "Ah, this was the plan all along, wasn't it?" I ask while I wrap my arms around his shoulders and tighten my legs against his waist. "Start with an unreasonable ask, so when you ask for something else, it seems like the logical choice. Clever."

"So?" he asks, waiting for my answer.

I press my lips to his and whisper against them. "So, I guess you better give your girlfriend the best swimming hole sex of her life."

He moves us so my back is to the bottom of the floating dock. The wood grains against my skin send heated jolts of pleasure throughout my body. His lips move down my neck as he licks and sucks the damp skin.

It took us over three months to break my celibacy journey, and Jason kept his promise. He made love to me. For hours. And then he fucked me like he hated me. I loved both.

I'll never tell him, but I cried in the shower later that night. I don't even really understand why. But for some reason, my mind chose that moment to think about the fact that before Jason, Zach was my last partner. We had been broken up for over two years at that point, but as I was washing Jason off my body, I thought about Zach.

I think it will always hurt, at least a little, to remember him. But at the most random times, I find myself wondering what life is like for him now. I'm not brave or stupid enough to try to find the answer, but I hope he's happy.

Wanting that for him solidified for me that I was indeed ready to move on. I can't say I regret being with Zach. He loved me at a time when I felt utterly unlovable. I loved him the best way I knew how at the time. But I think a part of me always knew it wasn't forever.

Jason's hand glides down my center, and he pulls my bathing suit bottom to the side. Two of his fingers rub lightly over my clit, causing me to moan aloud and thread my hand into his thick hair.

He slides a finger inside me, "Mm, what's got you so wet, baby? What kind of shit were you reading?"

His finger drifts over my slick walls at a torturous pace, and my hips buck lightly, searching for more friction. "It's called a reverse harem." I breathe and slam my eyes closed as he adds a second finger.

"And what is a reverse harem?" he asks while skimming his tongue down my chest and nips my nipple through the barely there material of my bikini top.

I bite back a moan, "It's one girl with at least three guys. One for each hole, you know?" I grin at his possessive growl. Teasing him to get that caveman to come to the surface is one of my favorite pastimes.

His other hand detaches from its firm grip on my ass as he slips underneath the thin material. His digit teases at my back entrance, and a little gasp escapes me. At my response, his right hand moves in and out of my overly slick pussy with two fingers and circles my clit with his thumb. Jason slams his mouth back on mine, speaking into my very soul. "When we get home, I'm going to fill all three of these holes. Just me. There will never be anyone else. I'll always give you whatever you need. You understand me?"

I nod eagerly and scream my orgasm into his waiting mouth.

* * *

November 2010

Jason

Turkey. *Check.* Stuffing. *Check.* Greenbean Casserole. *Check.*

218

Nasty cranberry sauce. *Check.*

I drop the arm full of groceries on the counter and take a moment to admire the pert ass of my girlfriend who is whirling away making desserts for Thanksgiving dinner tomorrow.

"Hey, Betty Cocker," I tease and kiss her neck, inhaling the sweet vanilla scent. This time, it's hard to tell if it's from her perfume or the cookies.

"Hey, babes, thank you for grabbing that stuff for me. Was the store nuts?"

I wrap my arms around her middle and rest my head on her shoulder. "Eh, it wasn't too bad. But when you look like me, people often keep a good distance."

"They better. I'd hate to have to cut a bitch for getting all up on my man." She scowls like the thought physically pains her.

"Mm, baby you know I love it when your inner psycho comes out. I'm hard already, and I've got to leave to pick up your dad in like ten minutes."

"Gross, can we not fuck in the kitchen. This is a communal area. We talked about this, you uncouth hooligans!" Emily complains, walking into the kitchen with her eyes closed.

Charlie and I both laugh, and I give her a small pat on the ass before putting away the groceries and heading to the airport to pick up Mr. Johnson.

"So, how's my baby girl doing?" Mr. Johnson, who insisted I call him Grayson, asks. The ride from the airport to our place is only about thirty-five minutes, but somehow, today, it feels much longer.

"She's doing great. Work is going really well. She's happy." I don't want to give him too much information. That's not mine to give. But all these things are true.

He nods, "Fantastic. I'm not going to give you the whole 'you hurt my baby, and I'll kill you' speech. I don't know what Charlie has told you about me, but I'm the last guy who needs to give a talk like that. Though don't get me wrong, if you hurt her, I will kill you. But I don't know if anyone could hurt her more than I have."

"I understand. Look, man, I'm not going to blow smoke up your ass and tell you all is forgiven and forgotten, but she's trying. You lose trust in waves and gain it back in drops."

Grayson sighs, and his shoulders droop. "She doesn't know yet, but I've left Alexis. It's been months now, but I just couldn't bring myself to tell her. I stayed with Alexis for so long because I couldn't bear to admit it wasn't what I wanted. I tore my family apart for a woman who was nothing more than excitement and a stroke to my ego."

"Everyone makes mistakes. Your daughter is more forgiving than she'll ever admit to. She's got a heart of gold. And honestly? I think she will be even more understanding in learning your truth. She thinks you chose Alexis over her. I'm willing to bet she'll be a little relieved to know that wasn't the case."

"She gets that heart from her mom. Amelia was such a good woman. I'll never regret anything more in my life. Take it from me, son. New and exciting means nothing against loyal and unconditional. I'll carry my remorse for the rest of my life. Never make my mistake."

I shake my head and meet his eyes. "Never."

* * *

Charlotte

The table is set, the drinks are poured, and the music is playing. What am I forgetting? Something just doesn't feel right, and I can't figure out what it is.

Jason carves the turkey while Emily and I bring the rest of the food to the table. My dad sits at the head of the table with Mary to his right, followed by Savvy and Asher. Jason will sit opposite my dad, with me next to him and Emily on my right.

I take my seat. Jason brings over a plate with turkey. I motion for everyone to fill their plates. We take turns passing sides and laughing at Jason's hack job on the turkey. He scowls at us and throws a pea at my head.

I look around at my family, missing the one member who couldn't be here. Ari is spending the holiday with Calvin's family, which I get, but we miss her presence all the same.

We all look around at each other, and I shrug and smile, "Okay, well, dig in."

Jason snaps his finger, "Oh wait!" He abruptly leaves the table and goes to the fridge. He comes back with a large, rectangular plastic storage container and places the lid off to the side before laying down deviled eggs on my bread plate.

Three of them.

And proceeds to place exactly three eggs in front of everyone else. I stare at the eggy goodness, and tears gather along my lashes.

I blink up at my boyfriend with watery eyes. He bends down and places a kiss on my forehead. "Couldn't forget the eggs."

"Never."

Chapter 34

June 2011

Charlotte

I can't believe it's been five years since I graduated high school. I also can't believe I let Savvy and Ari convince me to go to the stupid reunion this weekend. The only reason I'm going is because they will both be here, and I also want to see the Frankenstein'd mess that is Shelly Devaney's face. Whispers have been floating around about her botched surgeries. That's what she gets for picking on me. Bitch.

I really give no fucks about trying to impress anyone. My gorgeous boyfriend would think I looked sexy in a paper sack. I have a successful career that gives me more fulfillment than I could've asked for. I have an amazing circle of friends, even if we are scattered around the country. I own a home. Okay, maybe I could rub it in these judgy bitches faces... just a little bit.

So that brings me to my current predicament: I'm standing in front of my wardrobe, debating whether I want to go smoke show, bombshell, or mouthwatering. I hold two pieces side by side. On the left is a gray sheer button-down with a matching pencil skirt that grips and accentuates every curve I have. Very professional chic with a hot dose of bow-chicka-bow-wow. On the right is a cream-colored long-sleeve sweater dress with a cinched waist that goes perfectly with my black thigh-high boots. Very girl next door with a side of daddy issues.

Hot breath fans over my shoulder, and I feel the rumble of his voice before it reaches my ears. "Are you teasing me, Sweets? This—" he reaches out a finger to stroke the short hemline of the sweater dress. "— will get you bent over and fucked somewhere inside the school."

I bite my lip to hold back the simultaneous moan and laugh that wants to come out. Instead, I kiss his cheek and press my lips to his ear. "The dress it is, then."

Jason abruptly spins me around, causing me to drop both outfits on the floor as he crowds me against the shelves. "You can wear the dress *if* I can pick the panties."

"Deal." I immediately agree. I don't need his permission. We both know it. But he likes to take charge, and I like to pretend I let him. Besides, I don't have any underwear that will leave lines. It's all thongs or boyshorts, so if that makes his possessive caveman settle, so be it.

* * *

Soft curls fall around my face as I take the rollers out. My fingers gently thread through them, separating the strands. I check myself over in the body-length mirror. The dress fits amazing, like a second skin. I went for a subtle smokey eye look with deep red lips. I rarely wear lipstick, but if there's even a chance that things will get sexy, I want to be prepared.

Nothing makes Jason more feral than seeing me dressed to

the nines and then getting to smear my lipstick while fucking my face. It's the whole good girl gone bad aesthetic. I get it.

Savvy and Ari are meeting us at RHS. Not surprisingly, Asher and Calvin are accompanying their ladies. I can't wait to see Adam react to seeing Savs after all this time. Jason and I have a bet that Adam will make a fool of himself. Jason thinks he'll play it cool. I think he'll act like an idiot and embarrass himself.

I'm hoping Chad skips the event altogether. He may be a year younger than us, but word around town is he's been shacking up with Josh Hilston's ex-girlfriend, Lisa. I'm thinking there's going to be some drama tonight, and I am here for it.

Jason looks fucking edible as he walks into the bathroom. Dark wash jeans cling to his muscular legs. A plain black tee sits below a black bomber jacket. And my favorite all-black Chuck T's on his feet. He's abandoned his ballcap in favor of hair products to keep his new, shorter locks out of his face.

He stands behind me, and we look at each other in the mirror. His eyes carve a fiery path down my body before tracing my side with his hands. He dips down and taps my right foot. I lift my leg slightly, and he slides it through a thin, black material before doing the same with my left. He slowly brings the panties up until they are in place. The rigidity resting against my clit tells me exactly why he was so keen to choose my undergarment.

Jason places a hot kiss on my exposed thigh before pulling my dress back in place. His piercing stare meets mine in the mirror again, and he waves a little black remote in his right hand. Ah, shit.

"You better watch yourself tonight, pretty girl. You never

know when something might happen." He punctuates the end of his sentence by sending a powerful jolt to the vibrator. My hands immediately clutch the countertop as my eyes widen at him.

"Are you serious right now?" I gasp, pressing a hand to my chest to calm the rapid beating.

"Very. Tonight, like every night, your pleasure belongs to me." He growls and sends a sharp slap to my ass cheek.

I yelp in surprise, but a grin kicks up on my face. I school my features into a pouty, submissive look, "Yes, sir."

His eyes heat and narrow before he bares his teeth and sinks them into the exposed flesh of my shoulder. "Get your beautiful ass in the car before I tear this fucking thing off of you."

* * *

"Did you just pour peppermint schnapps into my drink?" I ask Savvy in suspicion. She winks and pats my cup to push it upward toward my mouth. I take a swig and immediately cough. "Jesus Christ, Savs. It's straight booze!"

"I just want you to have a good time." She says, taking her own sip and scanning the room. She smiles and waves to her adoring fans.

"Liar. You want me to trip on my face and make an ass out of myself."

She scoffs, hands her drink over to Ari, and grabs Asher's hand. "Like my girl, Shakira says, this ass don't lie." She slaps her own ass as they walk away.

"Yeah, I don't think that's what she says!" I shout at her. She waves me off and begins to shimmy around Asher on the dance floor. The poor guy has zero rhythm but is happy to be in Savannah's orbit and has the biggest smile on his face.

Jason and Calvin have bro'd up and are chatting about some mechanic nonsense. The auto shop Jason works for has just begun taking on motorcycles, and he's eager to learn everything he can about them.

I convince Ari to make a lap with me. She's hesitant, as usual. These people and this place don't exactly inspire pleasant memories for my friend. But if anyone so much as looks at her wrong, Harley might have to get some batting practice in. Good God, have I become a psychopath? Nah. Maybe... nah.

Thankfully, some of the people I dreaded running into have not been in attendance. I think if Jason were in Erick's presence, he'd come undone. And as much as it makes the kitty purr to think about my man defending my honor, all I want is a good, chill night with my friends. I am a little sad to see that Adam didn't make it, either. Less drama for Savvy, I suppose.

I point out some of our classmates who are a little... worse for wear to Ari. We snicker, well I snicker. Ari shakes her head at me, but I get a few giggles. Shelly's face really will haunt my dreams. But also, fuck her. A banger comes on that I haven't heard in forever. Something about bringing sexy back. I pull Ari onto the dance floor, and we move to Sav and Asher. The four of us make a square and begin to bust out all kinds of retro dance moves.

I can't bend over in this dress for fear of flashing my ass to my classmates, so I stick to moves like the robot and running man. We cut up for a couple of pop songs when a slower, more sensual melody flows.

A sweet, nerdy kid I recognize from a math class we shared

taps me on the shoulder and stutters out a dance request. I make eye contact with Jason, who glares daggers at the poor guy, but I smirk and blow him a kiss before accepting.... Jimmy! Jimmy's hand.

In my boots, we are about the same height. Jimmy puts his hands in a respectable place on my hips, and I lay my forearms across his shoulders. There's plenty of room for the Holy Spirit. We sway back and forth, and a gasp is yanked out of my body as an intense vibration attacks my clit.

My head whips over to see the smug look on Jason's face. He blows me a kiss before kicking the power up a notch. My arms grip tighter over Jimmy's shoulders as my knees wobble. I bite back a moan. My breath hitches, and Jimmy looks at me with concern. "Is everything alright, Charlotte?"

I try to plaster a nonchalant smile on my face and wave off his worry. "Just peachy, Jim."

Another powerful jolt. A moan slips out.

Jimmy's cheeks heat, and his grip tightens on my hips. "Actually, it's Tim. But, if you'd rather it be Jim, that's okay with me. I'll be whoever you want me to be." Not Jimmy says all breathy-like and closes the gap between us. I feel his erection for a heartbeat before his body is removed altogether.

Jason has a firm grip on Not Jimmy's shoulder, "Mind if I cut in?" he growls, not looking at Timmy but glaring me down like this is my fucking fault.

Timmy stutters out a weak protest, but Jason pulls my body to his and cuts Timmy completely out of my sight. I imagine he'll just give up and walk away. I'd feel worse if I wasn't so fucking turned on right now.

"You're going to pay for that later." Jason whispers against my ear as we move together slowly.

"I can't wait." I say against his neck, the resulting shiver across his body adding to my arousal.

"Maybe I'll just take my payment now, since you're so eager and all."

Before I can give any sassy retort, the vibration begins again at a steady, unforgiving pace. Jason presses my body firmly against his as my legs threaten to give out. I rest my face against his chest and bite down on his pec, pulling a deep groan from him.

"Come for me, Sweets. Right here in front of everyone. But don't make a fucking sound."

My mouth opens in a silent scream as white-hot pleasure hits me in waves. The strong vibration wringing every last drop of orgasm out of me and attacking my over-sensitized clit. "Please turn it off." I beg.

Jason peers down at me, his gaze bouncing from my eyes to my mouth before crashing our lips together. With a hot but chaste kiss, the vibration stops. I pant and smile against Jason's mouth. "BRB lover, I now have a situation to attend to." I point my gaze down, signifying my wet as fuck panties. He laughs and sends me off with a pat to the ass.

The line for the ladies' room is ridonkulous. Fuck that, the wetness in my panties has turned cold, and it feels fucking gross. I shuffle my feet, keeping my thighs pressed together, and head for the other bathroom down the hall.

I push open the door and am promptly hit with the smell of sex and groans. Looks like Jason wasn't the only one with dirty thoughts coming into tonight. I debate turning around, but I can't stay this way all night. Eh, fuck it, we're all adults. What's a little exhibitionism among the graduating class of 2006?

I round the corner and come face to face with the lust-blown eyes of my ex-boyfriend. His gaze immediately lands on mine and carves a filthy path down my body. His hand moves in time with the head of curly blonde hair that's pressed against his crotch.

Nauseating slop sounds echo off of the tiled room. My heart pounds in my ears, and I think it may just thump right out of my chest. A loud gasp halts the blonde's movements, and I realize it came from me.

She locks eyes with me and pushes back straight away, but Zach stops her with a firm grip on the hair in his hand. "Shh, don't worry about her, darlin'. It's nothin' she ain't seen before. Ain't that right, Little Bit?"

I'm going to throw up. I have no words. What is happening?

Zach groans and reaches over with his free hand to what I now see is a line of powder on the windowsill. He snorts the line down and lazily looks back at me while thrusting into the blonde's mouth.

"Want some?" he asks, holding the rolled-up bill to me. A tear breaks loose as I stare at the boy who used to have my heart. A boy who I believed loved me more than anything. "I won't even invite my buddies to run a train on that sexy ass. You can have this all for free. Spin around for me, sweetheart; lemme see how the years've treated you."

"Who are you?" I ask with a sob because I truly don't recognize this person. I spin around and slam out of the bathroom, right into Maxi's chest. He gives me a sad smile and wraps his arm around my shoulder, leading me back into the multipurpose room.

I go willingly, turning my head one last time before we leave the hallway. Zach stands at the door, staring after us. His arms

229

braced on the door frame, his pants low on his hips. Gone is the charming Southern boy, replaced by this angry imposter. No expression on his face; he simply watches. I keep his stare until tears blur my vision, and Maxi ushers us back into the reunion.

Chapter 35

Jason

Some big guy with braids walks through the doors with Charlie tucked under his arm, and I see red. With Cal hot on my heels, I storm over and slam my palm against his chest. "What the fuck do you think you're doing with your hands all over my girlfriend?"

Charlie steps in front of him and places her hands firmly against my chest, but I keep my glare steady on him. Charlie's shattered voice breaks the spell immediately, "Jace. Please."

I wrap my arms around her and tilt her chin up to look at her face. Tears stream down, and I shoot the man an accusing look. Before I have the chance to kill the bastard, she calls out for me again. "Jason. He didn't do anything. Please."

"I'm Max Whitaker. You can call me Maxi. Everyone does." He smiles and holds a hand out for me to shake. I don't. I turn my attention back to Charlie, and Maxi walks away. Cal shuffles off after placing a squeeze on my shoulder.

"Baby? What's wrong?" I ask, gently pushing her curls out of her face and wiping away the mascara under her eyes.

She opens her mouth, and a loud bang causes everyone to gasp collectively. A tall, blonde dude stumbles in with his arm draped around a chick who looks freshly fucked. Charlie sobs into my chest. I hold her tightly, confused as fuck.

Shouting from where the drunk dude walked in draws everyone's attention. A thin, dirty blonde woman is yelling at the guy who can barely stand. I can't make out exactly what she's saying, but he says something to her, causing her to glare at the woman beside him. A resounding slap fills the air.

The music screeches to a stop.

"I'm your fucking wife, Zachariah! Why the fuck would you think it's okay to hook up with some gutter slut right in front of me?" she screams. He seems completely unfazed. As a matter of fact, he grins at her, dimples popping from his tan face.

He lazily looks around at the crowd that's gathered until his eyes fall on me. They shoot down to where my girl is pressed to my chest, and he laughs. There's no joy to this laugh. It makes cold shivers run down my spine.

He rolls his eyes at his wife. "Such dramatics, Melanie. Go get yourself a drink or somethin'. Maybe she'll lick your pussy too if you ask real nice."

Melanie glares daggers at him, but his focus is directed right at Charlie. Who has now pulled back and is returning his stare. Her body trembles. What the fuck?

"Well, well, well. Ain't this just the cutest damn thing you've ever seen?" He slurs to no one in particular as he makes his way toward us.

My body tenses and Charlie links our hands together, giving me a squeeze. I don't know what this guy's problem is, but it's about to get a whole lot bloodier if he doesn't back the fuck off.

"So, he cheats on you and breaks your fragile little heart and gets a free pass. But I do it, and you tell me never to contact you again. Tell me, Little Bit. What did it take? Hm?"

"I don't know who you are or what your fucking problem is, but you better back the hell off right now." I hiss at him. My words don't deter him at all as he continues forward.

"Did he fuck that tight pussy like I did? Did he give you pills? I know how much you'll do for those. Ain't that right, *Charlotte*."

"Don't." Charlie whimpers. I've never seen her so timid.

He splays his arms out wide and shouts to the room. "Step right up, one and all! If you've got some pills and maybe some cash, you too can fuck any hole on her body. Bring your friends, she don't mind!"

That's it.

I shove Charlie behind my back and step right up to this preppy douche. *Preppy douche.*

Motherfucker. This is the guy she dated after me. The heat in my blood intensifies. I slam my palms into his chest. He wobbles back a few steps before righting himself and laughing. "Ah, the first love. You're the reason she was so damaged. So I guess it's your fault she became a whore."

The gut-wrenching cry from behind me cracks my heart. I look back at Charlie and find her wrapped in Savvy's arms while her best friend aims her ire at this dude. He's clearly beyond caring because he continues.

"Tell me, Jason, is it? Yeah. Jason. Does Charlotte ever let you hit it from the back? I tried while we was together, and she was *such* a fuckin' prude about it. Like she hasn't taken countless dicks up the ass. Am I right?" he scoffs and waves his hand towards her before holding it up in a high-five to me. I don't return it. My fists ball up, and I'm about to lay this

233

motherfucker out when a flash of red cuts across my sight.

CRUNCH

Zach goes down like a drunk sack of potatoes. Out cold. I blink my surprise at Ari, who is cradling her right hand. Cal immediately rushes over to her and inspects it. Holy shit.

"Jace." Charlie's broken voice calls out to me, and I hustle over to her. "Take me home, please."

* * *

Charlotte

I have no tears left to cry. Literally, no liquid is left in my body. Jason brought me home alone. Only after promising my best friends hourly updates. I just can't bring myself to be around anyone right now.

Jason hasn't pressed me for information. He let me know he's here when I'm ready, and I'm grateful for that. He stayed in the living room while I took a shower for so long that the water turned to ice.

Wrapped in a towel, I collapsed on my bed and cried until I had nothing left. My head throbs. My throat is sore. My nose is red and raw. And that is nothing compared to the state of my insides right now.

Zach knew how to eviscerate me completely. And he did. He took the worst pain of my life and made a public mockery of it for no other reason than to hurt me.

Why would he want to continue hurting me? I didn't make him cheat. It's clear that's just the type of person he is since he cheated on his fucking wife tonight, also.

Wife. Wow. I just can't wrap my mind around that monster

inside Zach's body. That wasn't my sweet, southern boy. That was a demon. And since when does he get that fucked up? A few beers, sure. But being that drunk? Doing coke?

Setting aside the complete obliteration of my heart, I now have to tell Jason the full truth about my past. Something that should've been on my fucking terms. Zach took that from me, too.

I wrap my blanket around my body and walk to the living room. Jason sits in the dark with his head in his hands.

I'm grateful Em is staying at her boyfriend's house tonight. I don't want her overhearing what I'm about to say.

The shuffle of my blanket causes Jason's head to snap up. I move to stand in between his legs. He promptly wraps his arms around the back of my thighs and presses his head into my stomach.

I run my fingers through his hair. Soaking up the last few moments before I blow his world apart and possibly change his perception of me forever.

"I have some things I need to tell you."

III

Part Three

Chapter 36

July 2016– 5 years later

Charlotte

A single line stares back at me. Taunting me for having a broken body. One thing. My fucking body was made to do one thing. Have babies. And I can't even do that right.

I slam the pee stick in the garbage can and wash my hands aggressively. Ripping the towel off the holder to dry them while muttering curses at my reproductive organs. I flick the light switch off and storm out of the bathroom.

"Went that well, huh?" Jason asks as he lays butt-ass naked on our bed. What was I mad about again? Oh yeah.

"Yeah, go ahead and make fun of the damaged girl. Yuck it up, dickface." I complain as I fall onto the bed beside him and curl up on his chest. His arms cradle me instantly, and the stress starts to ebb away.

"It'll happen, baby." He urges with a kiss on my head.

I'm glad he seems so certain because I sure as hell am not. We haven't used any form of birth control for the last three years.

At the time, we both decided that if it happened, then it

happened. But it never happened.

Every time my period is late, I rush to get a pregnancy test. It's always negative. And, like some cruel twist of fate, I start to bleed the very next day. Just another reminder that my body is fucking useless.

You would think, after countless disappointments, that by now, I'd be numb to it. Which to be fair, most of the time, I am. But for those few seconds, as I wait for the lines to appear, I have a spark of hope. And it's crushed immediately when the result window stays at one line.

I know I shouldn't compare myself to other people, but Ari got pregnant on the literal first try. She let Cal hit it bare, and he gave her a baby for her troubles.

Savvy got pregnant by accident and felt very inconvenienced by the whole thing until she went to that first ultrasound.

Hell, even Emily has good eggs. She's donated some to her boyfriend's older sister to help them extend their family.

And here I stand, a twenty-eight-year-old barren hag. Jason may as well cut his losses now. He's still young enough to find some fertile myrtle to pop out his spawn like a pez dispenser.

I'm so tired of the intrusive questions from everyone around me. Strangers or not. It's always, "When are you getting married?" or "How many kids do you want?" or my personal favorite, "You're not getting any younger, when do you plan to start a family?". Just a little tip for the clueless nosy Nelly's out there, stop fucking asking people these questions. The answer to all of the above is NONE OF YOUR FUCKING BUSINESS.

Why does my reproductive timeline or government-dictated union matter one goddamn bit to your life? It doesn't. Fuck off.

I keep trying to convince myself that I will be content if it doesn't happen, that being an auntie to a fiery four-year-old girl and an inquisitive two-year-old boy is enough for me. But is it? Would it be?

I nod against Jason's chest because what else can I do? He doesn't seem concerned, so I might as well spare him from the barrage of anxiety and worse-case scenarios going through my mind. "Oh, I forgot to tell you, Margie called and asked me what color I wanted on the walls of Ellie's House."

Jason crunches forward, smooshing my head against his lap as he stares down at me, excitement lighting up his face. "Does that mean...?"

I nod as a wide smile breaks out across my face. "It does. Your beautiful, brilliant, and philanthropic girlfriend has enough investors to make my dream a reality."

I laugh as he jumps up on the bed and launches himself on top of me. He peppers kisses around my face before cupping my cheeks with both hands. "You are fucking amazing. I am so proud of you. Though I never got the chance to meet her, I know your mom would feel so honored to be a namesake for such an important cause."

Tears slip out from my lashline as I blink. Emotion clogs my throat, keeping my words inside. All I can do is nod.

* * *

I can't believe this is real. Walking around the new transitional facility I've opened feels surreal.

Ellie's House has been my brainchild for the last five years. When I started at Starry North as a CDC, I experienced first-hand just how badly society lets our youth down. Even though the facility is a million times better than when I was a patient, it's still very clinical. Meant to be a temporary fix to a long-term problem.

I wanted an option for more. For the Emily's of the world. The ones who've fallen through the cracks and have been left behind. The ones whose help runs out the second they turn eighteen, and the government no longer gives a shit about them.

I give a shit about them.

Between the people I've fostered relationships with over the years working at Starry North, Margie's knowledge of rules, regulations, and law regarding a nonprofit project of this magnitude, and Jensen's endless connections, Ellie's House became a reality.

EH will not open for its first residents for another couple of months, but it's well on the way.

The first hurdle was acquiring a large, three-story cabin that is nestled among twenty sprawling acres of land. It had been unoccupied for quite some time and was in desperate need of a facelift.

I immediately hired Savvy Spaces to do all of the interior upgrades and overhauls. I couldn't think of a more perfect person for the job. And the fact that I get to be my best friend's first official client in her new interior design business? That's just icing on the cake.

Emily suggested offering work placement training, educational advancement assistance, and even animal care therapy. I loved all of her ideas. She didn't even need to put together a slideshow presentation to pitch them, but she did anyway. It was the most entertaining hour and a half of my life.

Jensen has offered to come in once a week for continued one-on-one therapy for the residents. His new wife, a veterinarian, has also volunteered her time to help with animal care therapy.

Once we get EH off the ground, the next step is to open a similar facility for adults. Margie has already offered to head that project, and I'm grateful for it. The youth program is where my whole heart resides, but having so many people in my life excited and willing to be a part of something risky but incredible is unreal.

Gravel crunches as a car pulls up the long driveway. I make my way to the front entrance to greet my bestie. "Knees to chest bitch, I've got things to do!" I tease as she waddles her way up the stairs, huffing and puffing in exertion.

Her middle finger stands tall before her hand falls to cradle her stomach. "You try sprinting around all willy-nilly with a watermelon strapped to your stomach. And just for funsies, every time you take a step, you pee a little."

I snort but bend down and place a kiss on her very swollen belly. Baby number two is due any day now. Asher wanted to wait until after the baby was born to start this project, but the thing he didn't account for? His wife will do whatever the fuck she wants. Whenever the fuck she wants to. So here we are, doing the walkthrough and making a plan.

After three hours, four bathroom breaks, and two snacks, Savvy and I finished the walkthrough and hammered out a rough outline of what needed to be done. She's going to get some swatches and plans together for us to go over. I can't wait to see what she does with the space.

I was spent by the time I walked into our dark house. Jason's truck was parked in its usual spot, but when I walked up to the door, I could tell no lights were on. He left super early this morning, and we've only texted a few times throughout the day. I just want to grab a shower, maybe play a round of hide the salami, and crash the hell out.

Melodic sounds of soft rock carry down the hallway. Our bedroom door is slightly cracked. I press against it and slowly peer around. Flameless candles decorate the windowsill, nightstands, dresser, and pathway to the bathroom.

Following the lighted path, I enter the warm, darkened room and inhale a burst of lavender and mint. A light flickers as Jason comes into view. He sits atop the counter with a lone flameless candle in his hand that he just turned on. The sight of my boyfriend topless in just a simple pair of black flannel pajama bottoms does tingly things to my nether region.

"Welcome home, baby. I drew you a bath." He purrs and gestures to the full, steaming tub behind me. I eagerly disrobe, eating up the way his eyes trace my every movement.

Like every couple, we have our problems—arguments, stubbornness—but in this arena, we are in sync like a 90s boyband.

Naked as the day I was born, I saunter toward him. His legs widen to accompany my body between them. I wrap my arms around his neck and lean it to give him a kiss when he hisses in pain.

I immediately draw back, searching his eyes with concern. But I didn't expect to find... uncertainty? "Jace? What's the matter?"

Sheepishly, he looks down at his lap, and his hands flap beside him on the countertop. My heart picks up pace at the motion.

"I love you." He says without hesitation.

"Okay... and I love you. Why are you being weird?" I ask.

Jason's hands come up to my shoulders and rub lightly down

my arm and back up. "Marry me." He says. Like he has countless times over the last few years. There's never any big speech or grand gesture. He doesn't even ask a question. It's a demand. A demand that has the same response each time.

I shake my head and roll my eyes. "Not this again. Stop trying to bring the government into our relationship." I joke, and he chuckles.

"Okay. But if you don't want to marry me, then I'll just have to come up with another way to make you a permanent part of my life."

"Well, that doesn't sound creepy and murdery at all... Don't mind me, I'm just going to send a quick text..." I pull out my phone and playfully make a show of dialing 911 before he swats it out of my hand with a laugh.

"Get your sweet ass in the bath before it turns cold." He tilts his chin toward the tub as he makes his demand.

I lace our fingers together and pull him forward. "Join me." I say and place an open-mouth kiss on the middle of his sternum.

"I'd love to, but... you know how I said I had a crazy busy day?" he asks.

My brows crease in confusion. "Uh, yeah?"

"Well, I didn't mean at work. I took the day off."

My eyes widen, and my hackles raise. "And what did you do all day when you led me to believe you were working?"

Jason smirks at me, and the flicker of anger that was beginning to brew kicks up to an inferno. Before I can unleash holy hell on him, he brings the candle to the left side of his neck. I squint my eyes, trying to make the dark patch come into focus. Is that...?

"You got a tattoo? Of someone's lips?" I ask, a splash of uncertainty climbs up my spine.

"Not someone's. Yours."

I blink wildly in shock. "What? How?" I move closer to inspect the deep red pucker that now takes up a large piece of real estate on his neck.

Jason reaches into the top drawer to pull out a familiar sticky note. I left it for him a few weeks ago when I left town to help my dad pack up the rest of his house in Alabama in preparation for moving back to Alaska. I didn't want him to wake up without a morning kiss, so I put on my darkest lipstick, kissed a sticky note, and left it on the bathroom mirror for him.

The inferno still rages, but instead of anger, it's transformed into utter adoration. He got a piece of me permanently etched on his skin. Forever, my mouth will be visible to the whole world. He's marked himself as mine, unbeknownst to me. And I fucking love it.

I press him back against the counter and carefully but firmly pull his face down to mine in a heated kiss.

He smiles against my lips, "Well, I'm glad this is your reaction to me carrying a part of you with me forever. If you had been upset, that would've made this really awkward…" Jason pulls back and slowly lowers his PJ bottoms. I'm momentarily distracted by his bared cock in all its strong, thick glory before my eyes latch onto the very large tattoo on the entirety of his left thigh.

Tears prick my eyes as I look from the tattoo back up to his molten steel gaze. My usually unflappable man is incredibly uneasy waiting for my response.

"Jace. She's beautiful." I whisper and place my hand up to my lips.

And she is—just as beautiful as the first time I saw her, eight years ago, in a letter. The sketch of the formidable warrior-maiden in her battle armor sits regally on his skin. Her resilience and beauty shine through the swirls of black and gray ink. Her graceful braids rest along the breastplate and act as an arrow to a set of initials.

"CBJ"

Chapter 37

October 2016

Charlotte

"I'd like to thank all of you for being here with me today. The opening of Ellie's House has been a much-anticipated event for so many. The first residents will be moving in at the end of the week. This program will change and enhance so many lives. And none of it would be possible without the people standing next to me," I gesture to the group of people on my right. Jason, Savvy, Emily, Jensen, and Margie. "as well as our incredible investors who have asked to remain anonymous at this time."

It should bother me that I've never met these mysterious investors, but I trust Jensen with my life. If he vouches for them and Margie doesn't raise red flags, then they can keep their anonymity.

With the ribbon-cutting ceremony, news interview, and countless photos and questions from members of the community, Ellie's House is officially open.

The media circus disperses, and my friends and I enter the house for celebratory drinks and to eat our weight in pizza.

Jason has been warming up to Jensen. Well, at least he doesn't actively scowl at him anymore. After I was forced to divulge the nightmare of my history to Jason, we spent the next twenty-four hours going through our pasts. We no longer had any secrets or omissions between us.

Nothing has ever changed how he looks at me. I never knew how much I needed that. Someone to know and understand my pain but know that it isn't what defines me. I'm more than the fucked up trauma that I've endured. I never needed saving. I needed a partner. Someone to stand beside me, not in front of me.

Jason is that partner.

I may have turned down his countless "requests" to marry him, but the truth is that he already has me forever, without a paper. I know it makes no sense, but with everything that I've been through, what my mom went through, and hell, even Mary, marriage just isn't in the cards for me.

"Charlotte?" A sweet voice calls out from my left.

I take a deep breath, stand and nod. "That's me."

"Follow me, please. We'll be in exam room six."

I finally let Ari convince me to make an appointment to talk about fertility with my doctor. Jason volunteered to have his sperm checked first since that's a really easy thing to do. Turns out his swimmers are just perfect. I'm the problem. But I already knew that.

* * *

I type "PCOS" into the search engine and wait for the results to pop up. I want to find out everything I can about polycystic ovary syndrome. This sounds like some fairy-tale made-up horseshit for when the doctors have a bunch of symptoms that don't point to anything specific.

You have irregular periods? PCOS.

Your mustache grows in a little thick? PCOS.

You gained a little bit of a tummy pooch? PCOS.

You tired all the time? PCOS.

You get moody? PCOS.

Are you a woman? PCOS.

After having a giant wand shoved up my hoo-ha, the search party for my ovaries turned up nothing out of the ordinary.

My gyno wrote a referral to a fertility specialist and called it a day. I should expect to hear from the specialist's office sometime between now and the end of time. Great.

I slam the car door behind me as I head toward the grocery store. After the day I've had I think I deserve a treat, or six.

The delectable smell of sweetness wafts around me as I peruse the bakery section. This place is renowned for its tiramisu—well, as renowned as a small town in Alaska can be. I pick up my prize, tasting it on my tongue already, and head to check out, grabbing a pint of ice cream and a container of frozen cream puffs along the way.

"Jace! I got a sweet treat for you!" I shout as I pull my goodies out of the bags and display them on our kitchen table.

"How many times do I have to tell you? Your pussy is the sweetest treat there is." Jason chuckles but eyes the tiramisu with heavy want.

"Oh, okay, so I guess you have no need for this—" I lift my shoulder and scoop up the tiramisu container, holding it away from him. He narrows his eyes at me and simply reaches over my head to grab it. Curse this fucking shortness of mine!

We sit at the table, plates be damned, and fork into our

dessert. Both of us moaning and groaning at each delicious bite of fluffy mascarpone and licking our lips after each pass of coffee–soaked ladyfingers.

Talking over the mouthful he's working through, Jason says, "You know what would make this even sweeter?"

I lift a brow and fork another bite into my mouth. "Hm?"

A squeal rips out of me as Jason abruptly stands and lifts me from my chair. He lays me on top of the table and yanks down my leggings and underwear in one fell swoop. He collapses back in his chair, hooks both arms under my knees, and slides my body right in front of him.

I gasp when a cool sensation spreads over my pussy followed by the hot trace of his tongue. He laps the rich delight up in deep, even strokes. "Mm, perfect."

His tongue dips inside me and swirls around, making me grab hold of the table edge. I bellow out a moan. Dizzying pleasure courses over me as he continues circling my clit with his tongue and pressing his fingers inside, and curving up to hit a spot that sends intensifying pulses throughout my body.

On the cusp of an orgasm, Jason pulls away. My eyes thrust open, and I make a very displeased noise when his body comes over mine. "Eyes on me, Sweets." He demands, forcing my chin in place to watch him. Our lips clash together, and he plunges his tongue inside my mouth.

Sweet mascarpone floods my taste buds with a trace of feminine essence. Tasting my favorite indulgence with his favorite indulgence mixed together in an erotic offering keeps me on the edge.

Jason sucks my tongue into his mouth and tastes the combination of tiramisu and creme de Charlie. The resulting moan of pleasure bubbling up from his chest, coupled with his fingers back on my clit sends me over the edge.

My eyes lock onto his lust-coated silvery orbs as waves of pleasure pulse throughout my entire body, and I explode in a scream against his mouth. Jason works me through my orgasm until my body jolts in sensitivity.

"*That* is definitely my new favorite flavor." He proclaims and thumbs a rogue piece of cake off of the side of my mouth and sucking it into his.

He pulls me up to stand, and I link our hands together, leading him into our bathroom. I reach in to turn the water to Satan's sauna—as he likes it— I join him under the spray and stroke his still-hard cock.

"My turn." I grin before lowering to my knees.

* * *

I fling my purse onto the empty passenger seat and turn the ignition on. The November chill is settling across the state. It's snowed a few times, and it has yet to stick, but we know it's just around the corner.

After I latch my seatbelt in, I go to put the car in reverse, but... *what the fuck*? My feet don't reach the pedals. They definitely reached when I drove home last night.

Leaning over, I fumble through my bag until I grab hold of my phone. I find the contact I need. "Hey baby, miss me already?" Jason jokes because I've left him less than three minutes ago.

"Always my love. Hey, um. Weird question. Did you move my seat?"

"Uh, no? What's wrong with your seat?" he asks.

"It's slid back several inches, and I can't reach the pedals."

"Do you want me to come check it out?"

I reach down and grab the bar beneath the seat. It slides forward to where it should have been and locks in place. I shimmy my butt a bit to make sure it's going to stay. "Nah, it's no big deal. If it happens again, I'll bring it to the shop, and you can diagnose the hell out of it. I know how much you like that." I tease.

I say my goodbyes to Jason again and head to Ellie's House. We now have five residents. All females, three are seventeen, and two have recently turned eighteen. But unlike the state, I still care about what happens to them now.

Do I need to show up multiple times a week just to check in? No. The staff is fully capable and communicative. But this is about the kids. I want them to see my face often. I want them to know they can trust me and believe that I want the best for them.

I can't save everyone. I'm not so delusional as to think I could. But I will do everything that I can for every person I can. There will not be a quantifiable amount where I will feel like I've done my part. I've done my part when I'm dead and have passed it along for someone else to pick up where I left off.

I know it will always be an uphill battle, and I will constantly have to prove myself, but I will. Over and over because everyone deserves to feel cared for and secure. Safe.

Chapter 38

December 2016

Unknown

I've been watching her for weeks now. Hiding in the shadows. Identifying her routine and the comings and goings of her boyfriend. Doing small things to let her know I've been there.

She still walks around on a cloud like she's safe. Oh, if she only knew.

She doesn't look over her shoulder when she walks alone in the store. She should.

She doesn't check the backseat when she gets in the car. She should.

She doesn't double-check that all the windows are locked before she goes to bed. She definitely should.

Safe? Not even close.

I'm coming for you, Charlotte.

Soon.

Chapter 39

January 2017

Jason

Maybe she's been working too much. Between her shifts at Starry North, constant visits to Ellie's House, and weekly NA meetings, she's run ragged. And is starting to lose her marbles a bit.

She's been accusing me lately of doing juvenile things to annoy her: moving her car seat, eating the center of all the Oreos and putting the cookie part back in the package, and changing every contact in her phone to "Estrellas" *stars*.

I can't tell if she's fucking with me or she's really losing her goddamn mind. I've convinced her to take a vacation for the first time in the last five years. She needs a lot of chill with a hefty side of dick.

So, I booked us a cabin up north for a few days. It's isolated but gorgeous this time of year. If the website is to be believed, each cabin is separated by at least one mile, has its own hot tub, and offers breathtaking views of a lush mountainscape.

To be completely honest, I could use a break, too. I've been working nearly as much as Charlie. Though I knew owning my own business would come with some intense hours, I didn't anticipate feeling this run-down. I need a break from the shop, and they are all sick of me being up their asses.

I started seeing a counselor a few years ago after having a weird bout of controlling behavior with Charlie. It started with me just being anxious when I wasn't with her. I would consistently feel this sense of foreboding. It grew to wanting to know exactly where she was and what she was doing at all times. But the worst part manifested when I started to tell her where she could and couldn't go.

She was not having any of that. So, she gave me a choice: get help or get out. I immediately sought out a counselor who specializes in PTSD and deployment trauma. Turns out, I had a lot of shit to unpack and work through.

Having no control over the deaths of my team members, my own injuries, and the subsequent issues that followed led me to need to have an abundance of control of the world around me.

It didn't help that in the back of my mind was all the pain and danger she was in for those few years we were apart. I wanted to kill that drunk fucker at the reunion. The only silver lining to that disastrous night is Charlie and I had a huge heart-to-heart. I wonder how he'd feel to know that instead of creating a wedge between us, we are closer than ever.

She told me the details and extent of her drug use, the *parties* she attended, surviving being forcefully committed and drugged just to end up with a psycho disguised as a friend at school who also fucking drugged her.

I told her about all the shit with my family, my attempt to drown myself in meaningless sex because I didn't feel worthy of anything more than that. I had put Charlie out of my mind.

Completely erased her existence from my life.

I will never make that mistake again. I may have leaned too hard in the other direction. My heart was in the right place, and I simply wanted to keep Charlie safe. But, I smothered her aggressively and snuffed out her individuality. Her light dimmed because of me, and it's taken me a long time to forgive myself for that.

* * *

My truck is loaded with our luggage, and Charlie shouts as we prepare to pull out of the driveway. "Wait! I don't think I unplugged my straightener. BRB." She jogs up the porch and disappears inside.

I'm flicking through my phone to set up a vacation playlist. Some rock to get us pumped, some country to make my girl all mushy, and a few love ballads to get the baby gravy train in motion.

Charlie refuses to talk about the baby situation. Or rather, lack thereof. There's nothing specifically preventing her from having a baby physically. She received the PCOS diagnosis, began mitigating medication, changed our diet, and started exercising semi-regularly. All the things she was told would increase the chances of conceiving, we've done. And yet, still no baby.

I've always been take it or leave it with the thought of having children. I'm down if it happens, but if all I ever have is Charlie, that's enough for me. But I know her internal clock is ticking away like a bomb, and it's poised to rip her apart from the inside out. I'll do whatever it takes to make her happy.

My phone buzzes with the notification of a new text message.

Unknown: Be careful with that one. Old habits die hard.

   Me: Who is this?

   Unknown: Consider me a concerned citizen with first-hand experience of Charlotte's games.

   Me: Fuck off. Delete my number.

   Unknown: If you don't believe me, that's on you. You'll find out eventually.

BLOCKED.

That was fucking weird. The chime of the open door brings my attention back to Charlie climbing in the truck. She smiles sheepishly, "Not only did I not leave my straightener on, I realized I haven't even used it in a few days."

I laugh as we pull out of the driveway, the weird text interaction all but forgotten. I wait until we get about fifteen miles away to gasp and look at her wide-eyed. "Did you turn the oven off?"

Charlie's jaw drops, and I watch the ping-pong match in her brain as she retraces her steps. Not wanting to give my girl a heart attack before our trip, I pat her thigh. "I'm just fucking with you, Sweets. I double-checked all heat sources before we locked up."

"Ugh, I hate you." She folds her arms and sulks, looking out of the window.

I squeeze her leg, "No, you don't." My hand slides higher and settles against the warm apex of her thighs.

She sighs, "No. I don't. But that wasn't nice. Pedal to the metal bud. You owe me for that one. And I think I'll take my payment in the form of you on your knees for me while I fuck your face."

Fuck me. My dick jumps at the thought. My controlling habits are still very present, just put to better use now, but when she takes the reins... it's so fucking sexy. I love watching the power roll through her body when she takes what she wants. And Queening is my favorite scene.

"Yes, Mistress."

* * *

Excitement thrums through my veins as I carry an armful of firewood back to the cabin. I've imagined every surface I want to take Charlie on. Pressed up against the kitchenette counter. Her pretty pink lips wrapped around my dick in the multi-person jetted tub. Eating her pussy on the bathroom counter. On her knees, bending over the hearth.

My dick is rock solid when I enter the cabin. The only light comes from the dying fire. I softly place the stack down beside the fireplace and strip off my gloves, jacket, and boots. Soft snores and crackling embers are the only sounds to be heard.

I strip down to my boxers and stand at the end of the large four-poster bed, watching the love of my life rest. The chokehold this girl has on me— has always had on me— blows my mind. I've always felt like an old soul deep inside. But the moment I saw this absolutely strong, fiery, and breathtaking creature, I knew I had to have her.

We nearly fucked it up. A couple of times. But we've learned. We've grown. Together. I've never been more sure about anything in my twenty-seven years than I am about my devotion to Charlotte Belle Johnson.

She says she doesn't believe in soul mates, not in the traditional sense, but more that the soul can recognize its counterpart in more than one person. I suppose I agree with the point of having multiple influences to make up a soul tie, but that doesn't necessarily mean romantically. Can you love more than one person in your life? Sure. But all I care about is I love *one* person for the rest of my life. She was my first, and she will be my last.

I crawl onto the bed, taking care to keep my movements light and gentle. As much as I would love to bury my cock in her all night long, she is exhausted to her core. I wrap my body behind her, and unconsciously, she burrows back against me and lets out a contented sigh.

If this were my last day on Earth, I wouldn't have changed a thing. Everything that's happened in our lives brought us here to this moment. It's taken me a long time to let go of the survivor's guilt— or at least most of it— and embrace the gift I've been given in a second chance. At life itself but with the person who makes that life worth living.

My last thought as my eyes grow heavy and my arms tighten around my girl is: I wouldn't change a single thing about her. Except for her last name.

Chapter 40

January 2017

Unknown

A romantic, remote cabin, how sweet.

Not for the first time, I recorded her when she was behaving like a total slut for the boyfriend. I've watched it over and over. Studying her movements. His sounds. What he likes. What she likes.

I hope he didn't feel special. It's not like she's picky about who she lets fuck her. Whores are like that. If you've got the payment, they've got the holes.

I wonder if she's found the gift I left for her yet?

It was amusing to search for a place to leave it in the cabin. Not too obvious, but it will be puzzling nonetheless. It's been an exhilarating game of cat and mouse. Only the mouse has no idea the cat is on the hunt. Using a large branch to cover my footprints in the snow—what fun!

I can't wait to continue our game.

I wish I didn't have to leave to go back to River View to prep for phase two. I would've loved to get her reaction on video.

Patience.

I've waited eleven years... what's a few more days?

Chapter 41

January 2017

Charlotte

This is the weirdest juxtaposition of temperature I've ever experienced. My back is lit up like a furnace. My front trembles like I took a polar plunge.

Jason's arms tighten around my middle as I try to shimmy out from under the covers. I still until I hear his breath even back out and launch myself out into the arctic air of the cabin as gracefully as possible.

The fire is nearly out. *Fuck me,* it is so cold!

I grab the afghan off of the armchair and drape it around my shoulders before shuffling over to the stack of firewood. I grab a couple of kindling pieces and set them in the fireplace. When they begin to catch, I horribly stack a few logs, but I'm freezing, and I was never a boy scout—girl scout—whatever.

Warmth emanates from the newly revived crimson blaze. The ice in my bones begins to thaw. One more log. That should keep for at least a few hours. Long enough that I can crawl back in bed to snooze before waking Jason the same way he woke me yesterday, with my mouth wetting him to prepare to take me.

As I reach out toward the dancing flames, a crinkle sounds from beneath the log in my hand. Immediately thinking it's some kind of weird crinkling poisonous spider, I flap my hand quickly against the wood to try to get it off of me.

Shocker, it's not some weird new crinkly spider. Just a little piece of plastic. My eyes narrow on the back of it, some kind of writing or something is on the other side of it. Interest piqued, I reach down to pick the baggie back up and flip it over. A scream is ripped from my throat as the log that I was previously holding smashes into my bare foot.

Jason flies out of bed and is at my side in an instant. "What is it, baby? What happened?" He frantically looks me over and sees the blossoming redness of my foot with the wood millimeters away. Able to put two and two together without any help from me. He scoops me up and sets me down on the armchair, where he kneels before me to inspect my injury.

"Oh, baby. Are you okay?" he rolls it this way and that way. "I don't think it's broken or anything. We'll just take it easy today to make sure. I'll run you a bath with some of those lavender salts you love. Stay here."

I couldn't move if I tried. Jason heads into the bathroom. The faucet lets loose into the large tub. My mind swims in all directions like it's chasing the water through the pipes around me. With shaking hands, I flip the baggie back over. My heart stutters when I realize I didn't imagine it.

Laying in my palm is a depiction of hellfire melting the heavens above it. Flames rush to reach the expanse of the night sky to snuff out its celestial lights. AstraMalum.

My heart pounds as I pull the edges apart. I knew with the weight what I would find, but actually seeing the white powder sends a whole new level of pain through my body.

I don't hear Jason come back into the room. My gaze is firmly on the flames' movement. They prance in elegant chaos — a fractured harmonic performance. "Baby?" his voice pierces through the fog in my mind. I meet his concerned gaze, and his eyes fall to the forbidden grail of destruction in my hand.

"Did you bring this here?" my voice sounds hollow, even to me. My breaths stutter in my chest as I await his answer.

Jason looks at me in confusion and back to my hand. "What is *this*?"

"Don't fucking play with me right now, Jason. This is not funny. Where did you get this?" I scream and throw the sachet at his chest, sending powder floating in the air between us. I hold my breath to avoid inhaling the toxic dust.

His brows knit as he lifts the bag to study it. His head shakes, "Charlie, I don't know what this is. I've never seen it before. Please tell me what's happening." He pleads, and his voice is so earnest that I can't help but immediately deflate. Of course, he didn't do this. Why would he? *How* would he? But then who...

This is crazy. I feel crazy. Maybe Jason is right. I've been working too much and getting too little rest, and my mind is paying the price. I do this time and time again. Every time my life is going well, I find a way to self-sabotage. It's like I can't function unless everything is going to shit, and I can say, "Ah ha! I knew it!".

I breathe out heavily and lean my head against the top of the chair to look up at him. "It's nothing. I'm sorry. I guess I'm just more sleep-deprived than I knew and overreacted. Waking up freezing and smashing a thousand-pound boulder

I CHOOSE YOU, CHARLOTTE

into my foot clearly affected my faculties." I smile and try to ease the tension. Jason watches me while his brain calculates the validity of my excuse and whether he wants to push for more.

He smiles and shakes his head, "It was like a two-pound twig at best. You'll be right as rain after a dip in the tub. Come on." He motions for me to stand and scoops me back up in his arms, taking me to the bath.

* * *

A loud, repetitive buzzing awakes me. I reach my arm out and tap Jason. He grunts but doesn't move. The buzzing stops, and I settle back to fall asleep.

BUZZ

Motherfucker. "Jace. Get your phone before I throw it into the fire." I sleepily threaten. His eyes finally pop open, and he scrambles for the device.

"Hello?"

He springs into a sitting position, and sleep is instantly forgotten.

"Okay, let me give it a try. Thank you for calling." He hangs up the phone and scrolls through his contacts, pressing on one. The line trills until a voicemail picks up. He ends the call and tries again, but to no avail.

"What's going on, babes?" I ask.

He gets out of bed and begins to dress. "That was the security company for the shop. The alarm is going off, and they want to know if I want to send the cops. They tried to call the foreman but didn't get through. I can't get him either, so I'll need to go check it out. The motion sensors inside haven't been tripped, just the door alarm."

I nod and start to get out of bed. "Okay, let me pee and throw on some pants, and I'll be ready to go."

"No, no. It's the middle of the night, and I won't be gone long. Get some rest, and I'll eat you for breakfast when I get back. How's that sound?" he speaks the words against my lips before kissing me. How can I say no to that?

"Sounds like I've got a great incentive to go back to sleep." I chuckle and lay back on my still-warm pillow. Jason tucks the blanket back up to my chin and presses a kiss to my forehead.

"I love you. Sweet dreams." He says.

"I love you most. Careful babes." I respond with a yawn.

"Always." He chuckles and closes the door behind him.

* * *

The bed dips behind me, and I blearily reach back for Jason. His arms coil around my middle, and I begin to drift back to sleep.

His fingers lightly tap along my belly and work their way lower. He slides beneath my panties and traces circles around my slick lips until he finally gives my clit some much-needed attention.

"Is everything okay?" My question comes out on a moan as he thrusts a finger inside me. My eyes still haven't opened against the darkness of the room.

"Mm, couldn't be better." A deep voice growls as he painfully thrusts another finger inside of me.

The breath is stolen from my lungs as my eyes spring open. Darkness, everywhere. It's *still* dark. I take a stuttered inhale through my nose. No fresh rain. No cedar wood. Oh my God.

My body trembles uncontrollably as a sharp pinch hits the tender flesh of my neck. The world spins and begins to fade around me.

"We're going to have so much fun."

Chapter 42

January 2017

Jason

I tuck the Glock 20 back into place in my truck console and pull out my phone to call the security company. I let them know all is well, and I've re-armed the system.

It must've been a glitch or something. The front door was still locked and didn't seem to be tampered with. I cleared the whole shop and found nothing amiss.

My foreman, Jerry, still hasn't responded to my many calls or texts. Not that I expect him to be at my beck and call or anything, but if you've received numerous calls from your boss and the alarm company in the middle of the night... it's probably important. It also would've saved me an hour's drive each way.

Pulling back into the small, sleepy town, I decide to bring my girl a treat for having to bail on her. The little bakery we passed on the way in has its open sign illuminated, and I can taste the chocolate croissant on my tongue already.

"Morning! Oh, how exciting it is to see a new face in town. And what a handsome face. Are you single?" A very chipper, very elderly woman rushes out. Her hands are covered in flour, which she dusts off on her black apron.

I chuckle, "Ma'am, I'm flattered, but I don't think I could handle you. You seem like a firecracker." I wink, and she laughs heartily. Too long. It wasn't that funny.

"You silly boy. My Hank is the one and only love of my life, but my son, Dexter, would eat you up." She proclaims with stars in her eyes.

Why the fuck would she just assume I'm gay? I briefly look over my attire: black joggers, Chuck Ts, a plain black tee shirt, and a leather jacket. What about me screams, "I like dudes"?

"My apologies to Dexter, but no, I am definitely not single. As a matter of fact, my girl is going to be so happy when I bring her that delicious looking cheese Danish."

The bakery lady packs up a large box of mouthwatering treats for me to take to Charlie. Hopefully, she's still in bed, and I can slip under the covers to see if the Boston cream is as satisfying as the tiramisu.

Creeping up the stairs to the cabin, I balance the bakery box in one hand while I unlock the door with the other.

The large wooden door creaks as I enter, and I shush at it. Charlie is a fucking beast in the morning if she's not woken up in the right way. Coffee, food, or dick.

The firelight carves just enough of a path that I make it to the kitchenette without face-planting. I take a large bite of a jelly donut and strip back down to boxers before taking the Boston cream to the bed.

Very quietly, I crawl onto the bed and pull the covers up so I can slither in between Charlie's legs.

Uh. My hands tap all across the empty sheet. Confused, I look around the darkened room. No Charlie. Did I miss the

270

bathroom light being on? Maybe she went in the dark so she didn't wake up too much.

I sit in silence for a few minutes, hearing nothing but the crackle of the fire. Did she fall asleep on the toilet or something?

Deciding that we may as well lose the mystery at some point and shit in front of each other, I head toward the bathroom.

Which is empty. I flick on every light switch I can find and check the cabin from top to bottom. She's not here.

A black haze coats my vision as I frantically fling open the door and step onto the porch. Looking left and right, there's nothing. No lights. No extra tracks. No Charlie.

I run back in and immediately see her phone on top of her nightstand. My gaze jumps to the armchair, where her coat is still draped. Checking the pockets, I verify her wallet is indeed still there.

"Charlotte?" I yell into the empty cabin. Not surprisingly, there's no response. What the fuck do I do? Where would she go? We are miles from other humans. She has no car. No cell. No coat... I jerk my head toward the right of the door. Her shoes sit exactly where she took them off earlier tonight.

Take a breath, Jason. Think.

Think.

Think.

Is anything disturbed?

I take a slower walk through the cabin, with a keen eye for any differences than I remember from earlier.

Bathroom is clear. Window secure.

Kitchenette has two glasses from our after-dinner drink.

Chair and coffee table by the fire seem to be in the same position. Logs are still neatly stacked.

Nightstands and bed seem to be as I left them, minus the girl in it.

The wicker chair beneath the large window in the front of the cabin... seems a little off. When we first got here and opened the curtains, I had to move it to the right so it wasn't directly in front of the crank to open the window.

Now, it's back in the center.

No.

Shakily, I take delicate steps around the open living area. My eyes jump from place to place, searching for the answers like they will magically appear.

Wait. Something is not right by the fireplace. I think back to earlier tonight. Charlie found a weird plastic bag. She threw it at me, and it landed on the floor beneath the hearth.

It's not there.

She seemed upset by it. Why was it significant?

I rush to her phone. *3825.*

There have been no new texts, calls, or social media posts. After pulling up Savvy's contact info, I press call.

"Bitch. It is 5 am. I am very pregnant, and I have a toddler that will be up within an hour. Why are you calling me?"

"Savannah." I bark out, and silence fills the line.

"What's wrong?" she asks in a panic.

"Charlotte is missing."

* * *

Pacing our bedroom floor, I run over the last forty-eight hours. Tracking every movement, every conversation. I can't think of anything that would explain this.

The police came to the cabin and took my statement. They

looked around inside and out and found nothing unusual. I drove around the small town aimlessly before popping into the few businesses and showing her picture around. No one had seen her.

The owner of the resort checked in with the few occupied cabins, but they hadn't seen her either.

I traced our path over and over until the cops very sternly suggested I head home and wait by the phone. On the drive back to River View, I called everyone I could think of. Not a single person had seen or heard from her.

So here I am, driving myself fucking crazy trying to make puzzle pieces without edges fit into each other. I can't just sit here and wait for news. Or even worse, never hear anything at all. It's like she just vanished. Leaving no clues behind except for a slightly moved chair and a missing plastic bag.

Emily and Savannah have busied themselves in the kitchen. Stress baking, I suppose. The sweet smell of vanilla that permeates the air makes me want to fucking puke. I don't want that scent anywhere near me until it's wafting off of Charlie's skin.

My phone buzzes with an incoming call. My heart falls to my ass as I scramble to grab it out of my pocket. **"JACOBS"**

I press the phone to my ear. "Tell me good news."

"Nothing yet. But we're taxiing now. I'll be on the ground in River View at 1800."

"I'll be there. And Jacobs?"

"Yeah, man?"

"I hope you left your morals in Texas." I say with conviction.

"Whatever you need. I got you."

273

Chapter 43

Charlotte

Light. I feel so light.
  And tingly.
  Light and tingly.
  "Shhh, not yet."

Chapter 44

February 2017

Jason

It's been six fucking days.

I don't need any more fucking reminders of the likelihood of recovery versus rescue at this point.

She's alive. I know it. I will find her.

Jacobs has been working around the clock with me since he arrived. We are calling in every favor we have. Using some not-so-legal channels to check traffic cams, doing background checks on the locals in that town, and getting in touch with a black hat he knows from God knows where.

Where are you, baby?

"Donovan. We've got a possible lead. My guy combed through the traffic cams, and one vehicle showed up and left several times in the 24 hours prior to Charlotte's disappearance. It was seen heading south and was able to be tracked until about 8 miles outside of River View."

"Who's the owner?" I ask, coming to a stop in front of him. Jacobs checks the information on his phone, scrolling and scrolling until I want to snatch it out of his hands and see the

275

information for myself.

"It comes back as owned by a Linda Espinoza."

"Okay, and what do we know about Linda?" I ask, but Jacobs shakes his head and interrupts.

"Ah shit, it was reported as stolen eight days ago. Fuck!"

The small flame of hope is doused with an icy reality. What if we don't find her? Fuck. What if we find her, but it's too late?

A hand clamps onto my shoulder. I don't have the energy to shrug him off. "Don't go there, man. We'll find her. I won't stop until we do. I've got you."

I look at my best friend and the dam breaks. I let loose the tears that have been held back by outrage and determination. I'm tired. So tired. I can't keep doing this. I have to find her. I have to know she's okay.

Jacobs stops me from collapsing to the floor when my knees give out. I latch onto him and sob while he holds me steady.

Savvy reaches out and rubs my back. "Come on, Gothic Boy. You know our girl is stubborn as fuck. She'll come home. Don't give up—" Her words are sure and steady, but her voice cracks and shows the terror beneath. "—Please. Don't give up. She will come home." I'm pretty sure she's trying to reassure herself more than convince me.

Emily packs up some of the baked goods she and Savvy made and lets us know that she's taking them over to Mary and Grayson.

Charlie's dad has been here every waking moment since I called him five and a half days ago. I finally convinced him to go get a shower and some shut-eye. That he wouldn't be useful if he were exhausted and delirious. I'm well aware of my hypocrisy. I've slept for maybe five hours since she was abducted.

I refuse to call it a disappearance. She didn't just vanish into thin air. Someone took her. And when I find the person who dared to touch what's mine... I will end them.

* * *

The icy water pelts down over my body as my mind races. Seeing a million scenarios and yet seeing absolutely nothing, all at once. My hands flap relentlessly at my sides. I clench my fists over and over, trying to regain control.

A knock startles me out of my head. "Yeah?" I shout.

"I've got some info. Get your ass out here." Jacobs shouts from the other side of the door.

I immediately shut the water off and wrap a towel around my waist before rushing into the bedroom.

Jacobs, Savvy, and Jensen stand around the open laptop on the bed. Jacobs gestures at a mugshot on the screen.

"We dug a little deeper, and it turns out Linda has a son."

"Okay... and?" I draw out my question.

Jacobs picks up the laptop and thrusts it at me. I begin to scroll through the very long rap sheet. Drugs. Guns. Assault. Robbery. Rape.

"And he has a connection to Charlie."

Chapter 45

February 2017

Charlotte

Light and tingly.

The familiar sensation rolls through my body. A smile kicks up on my face. With great effort, I blink my eyes open, but nothing comes into focus.

"There she is." A rough, deep voice calls out. Seeming to be a million miles away.

My mouth opens and closes as I fight through the fields of cotton taking up residence on my tongue.

A loud whirling sound tickles my ears from somewhere on my right. My head lolls in the direction of the noise, and I blink against the dark figure standing in front of the daylighted window.

His voice prickles a sliver of recognition at the back of my brain, but I can't call the details forth. My mind is too hazy. I pull my head back to its original position and blink slowly at the ceiling until the large water stain becomes more defined.

Where am I?

Nothing smells familiar here. Nothing feels familiar... or

really feels like anything at all. My body is entirely numb, as is my mind.

Something is not right.

Shuffling feet get closer, and slowly, I turn back to the figure. It's big. And angry. He leans down and places his left hand against the bed beside my head. I blink as rapidly as my lazy eyelids will go until the blurry edges begin to gain focus.

What the fuck?

"Bennie?"

"Hi, Astra. Miss me?" He grins before pulling back his right hand in a fist, and blackness takes me once more.

* * *

Jason

This is not fucking good. None of the scenarios that ran wild in my mind were good. But this... this is an unhinged man with nothing to lose. Who just so happens to have an axe to grind with my girlfriend.

Bennie Espinoza. 32. Was a resident of River View Correctional Facility until a few months ago. According to the black hat, he was the right hand of Caleb "Priest" Kirkpatrick. While Priest was gunned down at his sentencing, Bennie had taken a plea deal for his culpability of the drug running and rape of not only Charlotte but countless others.

Spending nine years behind bars gives someone plenty of time to hatch a revenge plan. Fuck. We need to find her. Now.

"What were his usual haunts before he got locked up? Known associates?" I ask Jacobs, who nods as he types into his phone.

"Already on it. Standby." He assures.

I'm in the car before the ink dries on the paper that Jacobs handed me. Stop number one? Patrick "Rick" Biltmore.

I pull up to the shithole mobile home and storm up the stairs. My fist bangs on the rickety metal screen door. When no one answers immediately, I hit it another three times.

"Cool your tits, I'm fucking coming! And if it's the cops, I don't consent to searches!" A scratchy female voice shouts, volume increasing as she nears the door. She shoves the screen door open, narrowly missing my face.

She looks me up and down, calculating what my visit might involve. The lascivious mask that falls over her face, coupled with the very risque attire, gives me an idea of her profession.

"Well, hey there. What can I do you for?" She purrs, spiraling into a coughing fit at the end of her question.

I can't keep the sneer off of my face or out of my voice. "Rick." Is all I say. Her eyes widen momentarily before she knits her brows at me.

"What about him?"

"Where is he?" I growl.

She laughs and puts a cigarette to her lips. "Same place he's been for the last... hmm... five or maybe six years."

I wait for her to expand upon her statement. She takes her sweet ass time lighting the cigarette and taking a large drag. She blows the smoke directly in my face and smiles with yellowing teeth. "River View Meadows."

Fuck.

I spin around without a word and get back in my truck. I slam my fist against the steering wheel as I peel out of the gravel trailer park.

Well, I can't question a fucking dead man. So, I'll skip the visit to River View's cemetery.

Irritation flows off of me in waves, and I reach for the paper to see where my next stop is. Hoping like hell I'll get the chance to take this aggression out on someone.

Stop number two: Erick Poole.

I roll my tires at the entrance of a pretentious condo building, not giving a single fuck that it ruins the upper-class aesthetic of the joint. I park on top of the once very lush and carefully decorated garden.

The doorman eyes me carefully. "You Donovan?" he asks.

I nod. He lets me pass and calls out the number I need. Fucking Jacobs. That man has scary good connections. He must've given this dude a heads-up.

Unit 7.

Not your lucky day today, fucker.

I slam my palm against the door three times before clacking sounds against tile on the other side. The door opens, and a strikingly beautiful, tall brunette stands, giving me a welcoming smile. "Yes? Can I help you?"

This could get messy.

I paste on a warm smile, "Hey, I'm so sorry to bother you. Is Erick in by chance?" I ask, sweet as pie like we are good ol' buddies.

She shakes her left wrist until the face of her watch is visible. "Oh, uh, he should be home any minute now. And you are?"

I don't recognize this chick at all. Chances are she didn't go to school with us. So I should be safe with that excuse. "My apologies," I hold my hand out for her to shake. "My name is Jason. I went to school with Erick. I'm recently back in town and wanted to catch up. I'm eager to pick his brain."

She laughs and shakes my hand. "Well, hello, Jason. I'm

Whitney, Erick's wife. Please come in. He should be walking up in just a moment."

I nod and thank her as I enter the bastard's apartment. Whitney, the great hostess she is, offers me a beverage and shows me to the couch to wait for her hubby.

Five minutes later, the front door slams shut. Random banging noises allude to Erick putting his things away. "Babe! I hope you're wearing that sexy black thing I like. I've had a shit day, and I need you on your knees ASAP." The prick shouts, and Whitney scrambles to meet him while shooting me an embarrassed, apologetic look.

"Honey, an old friend of yours stopped by to say hello." She tells him as they round the corner together. His brows shutter in irritation. This is definitely not his lucky day.

"Who—" Erick's words are cut off as he locks eyes with me. There's no real recognition, not that it surprises me much. We didn't run in the same circles and had no business with each other.

Whitney strolls right past him, looking back at him over her shoulder. "Jason! He said you guys went to school together. That is just so cool that you could reconnect like this!" She gushes, and Erick looks back at me and down to my lap. All color leaves his face.

"Hey buddy, come on in. Have a seat." I smile like this is just a normal day and keep my tone light. He audibly gulps and takes a shaky step forward.

Whitney looks at him, puzzled, and then turns to me. The smile slowly slides off her face when she sees the glinting metal of the Glock 20 resting against my thigh. "You too, sweetheart."

Wordlessly, she collapses on the couch beside her husband.

Who finally grows some balls to open his useless mouth. "What do you want? Money?"

I roll my eyes. Rich assholes are all the same. Always thinking someone wants their money. We could play pockets right now, and guaranteed, I'd win.

"Charlotte Johnson."

I didn't think his face could drain any further, but it does. "W-what about her?"

"Where is she?" I keep my tone light. Not wanting to spook the wife as much as possible. Shit will get bloody if he fucks me around, but for her sake, I hope he plays ball.

"Why would I know that? I haven't seen Charlotte in years." He seems truly confused. Okay, maybe he doesn't know where she is. But... "Bennie Espinoza."

There's that audible gulp again.

So, he does know something about Bennie Boy. How fortunate for his kneecaps.

Chapter 46

February 2017

Charlotte

Fuck. Fuck. Fuck!

My head feels like I tripped and fell face-first into a wood-chipper. I wince as my eyes open. The room is dark, signifying it's nighttime, and I've clearly been unconscious for at least a few hours.

"Welcome back." Bennie laughs and kicks my foot. I try to pull it back, but it doesn't move. Leaning as forward as I can, I look down to see a rope attached to each ankle leading off the bed. A tug of my wrist reveals the same fate as they intertwine above my head.

"Why are you doing this, Bennie?" I ask, trying desperately to keep the panic out of my voice.

He laughs again, with no trace of humor, and stomps his way beside me. His large hand grabs my cheeks and squeezes painfully. His putrid breath fans across my face as he leans close to my mouth. "I lost nine years of my life because of you. Time for you to pay—" His other hand grips my vagina unbearably tight, and I wince. "Maybe I'll take this pussy for a few rides before we take you out. Since I went away for raping you, I might as well get my money's worth."

Did he say *we*? "Don't do this. Let me go." I steady my voice and demand. He wants to see me weak and broken. I won't. I can't.

"No can do, babe. This has been a long time in the making, and I'm getting so much more out of keeping you here."

I need to try to figure out where I am so I can make some kind of escape plan. I won't just lay here and take what's coming next. My eyes trace around the dingy room. A motel room, maybe? The window has a ladder attached to it, like a fire escape. Maybe an apartment building?

What do I remember? The cabin. Jason. Oh my god. Did he do something to Jason? How long ago was that? I've clearly been unconscious for some time, going by my sore limbs and stench. "How long have I been here?"

Bennie shrugs a shoulder and walks toward the end of the bed, reaching out and griping the rope attached to my right ankle. He yanks it sharply, causing me to hiss in pain. "Oh, about a week now."

A week. A fucking week?! Fuck. Fuck!

Keep him talking, Charlie. If he's talking, he's not raping and murdering... I hope. "What's the plan here, Bennie?"

His hand glides along the braided rope before setting it down and doing the same with my left ankle. "That's the fun part. It's a surprise!"

Ringing sounds out, and Bennie lets go of the rope to pull his phone out. Maybe I could kick it out of his hand and shout at whoever it is that I need help. "Yo, Boss."

I wiggle my foot, and I am nowhere near being able to reach him. I slam my head as far into the mattress as I can get, internally cursing up a storm.

"She's awake. I gave her the last dose about five hours ago."

Dose? Dose of what?

"Hurry up, I'm ready to get the party started. Hell, we might start without you."

No. No. No.

Bennie rounds the other side of the bed, strokes his finger up my calf, along my thigh, and slides under my shirt. He pinches my nipple between his fingers and twists forcefully. I bite my cheek to keep from crying out, and blood floods my mouth.

"An hour. Got it."

Bennie tosses his phone to the floor behind him and strips off his hoodie. Bile rises up my throat seeing the familiar tattooed arms that have caused me so much pain. "Bennie..." His name comes out in a whisper. He doesn't hear me. He doesn't care. He roughly yanks my pants and underwear down. The tension pulls my legs tightly against the ropes, holding them in place.

"Now, if memory serves me correctly, there was a special spot that forced the sweetest cries out of you. Let's see if we can find it, hm?" His right hand walks up my body until it cups the side of my head. His thumb settles in the little divot between my jaw and the bump behind my ear. His left hand reaches down and forces its way between my legs. Thrusting several fingers inside me at the same time, his thumb presses against that divot.

A blood-curdling scream rips out of my throat, and tears immediately leak out of the corner of my eyes. "There it is." His thumb strokes the painful pressure point while he slows the thrusts of his fingers. "How many times do you think we can do it before you pass out?" He presses against me in time with forceful thrusts; another scream is ripped from my body.

"That's two."

This went on for what seemed like hours. I never did pass out, but I did wish I was dead after a while. I'm pretty sure the only reason he stopped was due to his hand cramping up. My battered vagina burns, and it feels like my insides have been prodded with a hot poker.

Bennie cuts a line and sneers at me before doing a bump. He cuts another line and holds the metal tray up to my face. I shake my head and turn away. "Nose or vein. If you make me choose, it'll be the one that makes you bleed."

Goddamnit. How did I get back here? I've worked so fucking hard. I've clawed my way out of hell once. I don't know if I can do it again. That is, if I even survive the night. It sure doesn't look like it.

He's going to force me no matter what. May as well be as numb as I can be for whatever is to come once this "Boss" gets here.

"I hate you." I growl and lean down. My hand can't quite reach my nose, so he loosens the rope on my right wrist a little. When I don't move fast enough, he slams my head into the tray. Stars dance along my vision. I pull back and do the bump as fast as I can.

The effects are immediate. It takes hold deep inside, like a missing piece of me has finally returned. Euphoria taints my senses, and my eyes flutter and become unfocused.

"We're just getting started, Astra. By the time I'm done with you, hate will be the nicest thing you can say about me."

Softly, almost carefully, he releases my right hand and cradles it in his. I know I should react, pull away, punch him, flip him the bird. *Something.* But the effects of the drugs are muddying my synapses, causing misfires to ricochet around my cranium.

His finger traces my pointer finger. "This is what you used to identify him. Priest?" Before I can wrap my mind around his words, he bends my finger backward until a resounding *crack* fills the air, and yet another scream tears out of me.

My heart beats dangerously fast as pain takes over every other sense. Blinking away the tears, I roll my head to the right to see my finger bent back in a scarily unnatural position.

Bennie growls and grabs my face in a bruising grip. "You're lucky I don't cut out your fucking traitorous tongue, bitch." He shoves me back and wipes his tear and sweat-soaked hand off on the side of his pants. "Actually, don't count that out quite yet."

My breathing becomes stuttered, pain surrounds me, and I want to die. I close my eyes and try to find that place. That place that lets me escape the physical plane. A loud slam jolts me out of the descent to my mental salvation.

"Show time." Bennie says with a wicked grin across his gaunt, stubbled face.

I can't move. My body is shutting down on me. He places his hand on top of my head and twists my gaze to the door.

Moments later, it swings inward, and what little sanity I was clinging to washes straight down the drain.

"Hey, Charlie. Long time, no see."

Chapter 47

February 2017

Jason

"An abandoned warehouse on 12th. That's what he said." I shout into the truck with Jacobs on Bluetooth as I haul ass to the place Poole told me about.

If his story is to be believed, he lets Bennie stay there out of fear and a little guilt. The Poole family owns the warehouse, which has been unoccupied for many years. Making it the perfect fucking place to stash a kidnap victim. *Fuck*! I growl and slam my fist against the dashboard.

"Keep a calm head, Donovan. Wait for us. Do not go in there alone. Do you hear me?" I end the call without responding.

Nothing is going to keep me away from Charlotte. Nothing.

Reaching into the console while keeping my eyes trained on the road, I feel for the chunk of metal that fits perfectly in my hand.

The warehouse comes into view, and I smash on the gas until I pull up to the entrance. I thrust the gear into park and jump out, running to the entrance. Just before I enter, I drop the magazine. *Fifteen rounds.* I shove it back in place and pull the slide back. *One in the chamber.*

I'm coming, baby.

* * *

Charlotte

I don't understand. My eyes squint at the small figure in the doorway. It can't be. Why would it be? "Rebecca?"

Rebecca Crowe. My one-time college friend, who went batshit crazy and fucking drugged me for unknown reasons. The girl who made me believe she was my friend. Got close to me, and I let her in. Just to have her turn around and stab me in the back. She took my sobriety from me once. Now, she's doing it again.

Rebecca twirls while holding her hands out, "In the flesh."

"Why?" my voice breaks with the question. Why does this girl hate me so much? What the hell did I ever do to her? I tried to be her friend. I opened up. I defended her when people were talking shit and making up rumors. Well, I guess the rumors were technically true. But I didn't know that at the time, and I still took up for her.

She claps her hands excitedly. "Oh yay, storytime! Gather around everyone." She motions her hands for everyone to come closer, though I can't because I'm high as fuck and am strapped to a goddamn bed.

Bennie chuckles as he takes the only seat beside the bed and flicks my broken finger just for funsies. I gasp in pain but clench my teeth tightly to keep my face stoic. They don't get my pain.

"Because of you, I lost the love of my life." She accuses

while looking at me like I'm the dirt beneath her shoe.

"What? I don't understand." How the fuck did I do that? The only person I ever met that she was involved with was the cheating douche-canoe from my psych class. And I certainly had no interest in him.

Rebecca reaches into her bag to grab a thick, black object. Crackling sounds roll off of it as lightning zaps between two prongs on the top. She lets go of the trigger, and the stun gun goes silent once more. She walks closer to me and presses the prongs against the exposed flesh of my thigh.

"Charlotte Johnson. Little Miss Perfect. She's got the body, the friends, the grades, and you think you can have the man too?" she scoffs and depresses the trigger, sending a burning electrical jolt across my leg and in all directions. The howl flies out of me without permission.

"Zachy was *mine*. You sunk your whore claws in him, but *I* was carrying his baby."

Zachy... Zach? My Zach? What? No. "Y-you? You were the girl in the video?"

"Of course I was, you twit. He wanted me, not you. But still, you managed to ruin everything."

This isn't right. I unlock the box that's been tucked safely away in the dark corners of my mind. I mentally roll the tape on when I watched the video.

"Mmm, fuck darlin'. So good. You're always so good when you take my cock."

"Mmm, better than anything... Little Bit... Love... Favorite..."

Slurring. He was drunk. He was always drunk. But... was that all?

"Little Bit..."

The girl in the video had blonde hair. Rebecca is a brunette.

291

The wigs in her dorm room.

Did he...?

"Love..."

"You fucking bitch. He thought you were me!" I spit at her. Anger turns her sunken cheeks a deep shade of red, and she slams the stun gun on my hip. She leans forward in my face and screams while pressing the trigger. "He just needed a little incentive, but I knew if he would just fuck me once, he'd be mine forever!"

Tears pour out of my eyes, the pain throughout my body is unbearable, and the effects of the AstraMalum are long gone. Replaced by adrenaline and fear.

Oh God. She chose that time specifically to fuck him without protection. "He's the one who knocked you up." It's not a question. The timing makes sense, and she's a sneaky vindictive cunt.

"That was the plan. But stupid fucking Hunter had to open his big ass mouth and tell Zachy the truth. I miscalculated my cycle by a few days, and Hunter was the baby's father."

My head shakes slowly as I parse through this information explosion. "You *raped* him. You piece of absolute garbage. You fucking raped him!" I scream, and she slams the gun against my bare stomach. Sharp jolts light up my insides, and blood fills my mouth.

I spit a mouthful of blood in her face and smile when her smug grin falls to seething disbelief. "I'm going to kill you." I promise.

Rebecca nods to Bennie, "You're up, big guy. Time to let her know what a real rape feels like since she feels like such an expert on the subject. And I—" Rebecca drops the stun gun, but my momentary relief immediately floods away when she picks up a tray. The very tray that still stars in my nightmares from time to time.

A vial.

A long rubber tourniquet.

A very intense-looking needle.

"No. Rebecca, stop. Don't do this." Fuck not begging, this bitch is crazy enough to kill me. She is clearly fucking delusional. She mocks my words back at me while pushing the needle tip into the vial. She turns it upside down and fills *the entire thing* with liquid.

The hard thumping in my ears whomps to a deafening level. I've been so distracted with fuckface number one that I forgot about fuckface number two.

Bennie takes a switchblade out from his pocket, slices each rope at my ankles in a clean sweep, and rips the wad of leggings and underwear fully off of my legs. I kick my legs out the moment they are free, but the freedom is short-lived when he cups both of my kneecaps and presses down painfully.

"If you kick me again, I'm going to stab this perfect flesh right here—" He traces the blade tip along the patch of skin just above my kneecap, digging in just enough to draw a thin line of blood.

My head snaps upward as Rebecca thumps her middle fingernail against the syringe. I tuck my arms as close to my head as I can get. A sad attempt at hiding my veins from her. She laughs, "Oh, Charlie. This isn't going in your arm. I'm going to do what Priest failed to, and it's going right here—" her finger glides across my carotid.

"You ready, big guy?" she asks him. My gaze bounces back and forth between the two threats.

"I've always wondered what it would be like to come and go

293

at the same time. Too bad I have no intention of making this pleasurable for you whatsoever."

God, please kill me now. Give me a heart attack. A brain aneurysm. A fucking stroke. Just don't let them do this to me.

Please.

Please.

Please.

And I scream.

Chapter 48

February 2017

Jason

A symphony of pain pierces through the air as I smash my shoulder into the entrance door over and over until it splinters off of the hinges. It's an old storage warehouse with an upstairs office converted into a studio apartment.

There's only one set of stairs, and I take them two at a time. A drumline of terror hits its height inside my chest. I have no idea what I'm walking into. I have no backup. I have no plan.

All I know is I'm not leaving this building without Charlotte.

In for a penny, in for a pound. If that pound has to be in flesh, then so be it.

"Did you know blood is one of the best lubes? Yeah. It's so slick and warm. And as long as it's fresh, it stays wet—" The sound of skin hitting skin crawls out from behind the closed door, followed by a soul-crushing whimper. "Oh yeah, just like that. You see how well it glides along my cock?" A dark chuckle rumbles. "Well, considering both of your eyes are pretty much swollen shut, I guess not."

I move my body as fast as possible. An older-style wooden

door is the only thing between me and the horrors on the other side. Slowly, I reach out to the round, brass door knob. Locked.

Thank fuck I wore the combat boots today. I move back a couple of steps and raise my foot before bringing it down as hard as I can on the door. It immediately gives way and swings inward.

Several gasps and shouts sound around me, but all I see is the huge man on his knees in between Charlie's legs. She's naked from the waist down, and his hard dick is coated in blood as he lines it up with her entrance.

No thoughts enter my brain. Just reaction. I launch myself at the fucker. We roll over the bed onto the floor, and though I have the advantage of surprise and being fully clothed, this guy has at least 50 lbs of muscle on me.

We land with an oomph as the air is punched out of me, but I don't stop swinging at him. Hitting any part of his body I can reach. I hook a fist into his ribs as he moves to straddle me.

If he pins me to this floor, it's fucking game over. I rock my body violently, trying to throw him off. He links his hands together and brings them up high over his head before landing a breath-stealing blow to my chest.

It takes me a moment to realize the stringy wheeze sound is coming from me. He gives me no time to recover, pressing his knee into my stomach and grinding something painful into my back.

My back... The Glock.

He rains fury down on my face with punch after punch. I can't protect my face and reach for the gun at the same time. If I can't get it, he will kill me.

"No!" A high-pitched wail calls out. *Baby.*

The giant fucker on top of me starts laughing. "Hey bro,

how's her head game these days? Owee back in the day, give her a little powder, and her body opened up like a damn flower. Ready and willing, whenever and for whoever."

Another fist hits my face, and black spots dance around my vision. His ugly mug blurs in and out of focus.

"You know, one night we had a line, a fucking line of assholes waiting for their turn. We made some good money off that whore."

My trembling fingers finally reach the metal beneath my back. *Punch.* I'm not sure if my eyes close or I've just lost my sight. *Punch.* Just a little further.

"Stay still bitch!" A new, nasally voice screeches. Giving me the momentary distraction I need. As this man looks over at the scene beside us, I have milliseconds to grip my gun and pull it out.

I'd love to give him a big speech and taunt him with his mortality, but nothing is more important than Charlotte right now. This fucker will just have to go into the afterlife thinking his dick is much bigger than it actually is. And since it's been unimpressively pressed against my stomach since we landed on the floor, I'm certain he's been laughed at more than once.

A grin spreads across my battered face, and he looks down at me in disgust. "What the fuck are you smiling about?"

BANG.

* * *

Charlotte

Bennie is going to kill Jason. His fists land blow after blow, coming away bloody. A fire ignites in my throat and crawls its way to the surface. "No!"

Rebecca grabs a handful of my hair and rips my head backward. My legs flail and kick out. The movement wiggles my body rapidly back and forth.

I've got to get that fucking syringe away from her.

My right hand is completely numb from my broken finger and being tied up for so long, but I yank on the binds anyway.

Grunts and violent punctuations fill the small room. So loud that I can hear them over the blood flowing through my ears. *He's going to kill him. I have to help him.*

With renewed gusto, I fight against my restraints and rock my body sporadically. Rebecca's grip loosens momentarily. I hear the tink of glass against metal. She set the syringe down to deal with my unruliness.

"Stay still bitch!" She screams at me and digs her nails into the top of my head. I push past the pain and latch onto her wrist with my non-broken finger hand. She scrambles to grab the syringe.

Holding it above me, poised and ready for murder. Her eyes are completely empty. This girl is a psychopath. She feels nothing about my murder. Somehow, in her narrative, I'm the villain.

Why didn't I see it? I thought she was a little weird and clingy, but I never imagined her to be capable of something like this. She single-handedly blew apart my entire life. She raped my boyfriend. She framed me for cheating. She fucking drugged me repeatedly.

No. Fucking hell no.

BANG.

The gunshot startles Rebecca, but not me. I use her temporary derailment to grab the syringe out of her hand.

"Baby?" Jason calls out, his voice gurgling, no doubt from blood.

I see the moment in her eyes when she realizes Jason is the victor, and she's now outnumbered. Panic falls over her for a split second, followed by rage and determination.

Rebecca grips my broken finger and twists it. I bellow in pain, but as she reaches over me to grab the syringe, I fist it and slam it to the nearest part of her body and depress the plunger.

She staggers backward, a razor-sharp wail dispersing out of every lunatic cell in her body. Jason uses the edge of the bed to pull himself up. A soft cry leaves my lips at the sight of him.

His face resembles ground beef. Blood pours from unknown sources around the upper half of his body. His movements are jagged and unsteady, but he crawls his way to me anyway.

"Ah!"

We both turn in time to see Rebecca crash backward into the only chair in the room. A squelching thud is heard as her head slams into the edge of the marble-top table.

I wait for her to get up and come after us. To scratch and claw her way back. To shout all the reasons I deserve everything that's happened to me and have ruined *her* life.

But that doesn't happen. She doesn't get up. She doesn't move as a rapidly growing pool of blood encases her mousy brown hair. A bubble of laughter works its way up my throat as I take in the large syringe sticking out of her eye.

"Cunt." I mumble as I watch my former friend leave this world. Good fucking riddance. Goddamn wacko.

Jason stands over me, his bloodshot steel gaze raking over my body, cataloging my injuries.

A small smile pulls up the part of my mouth that isn't too

swollen to move. "You came for me." I whisper in awe and can't stop the burning tears from flowing.

He hobbles close to me, his hands hovering. He wants to touch me but doesn't know where is a safe place that wouldn't cause pain. I know. I feel the exact same way about him.

"I will always come for you, Sweets." He coughs, and a little blood spurts out of his mouth.

"Even now, when we almost died, you make sex jokes." I attempt to shake my head, but now that the adrenaline and shock are slowing, I realize how much damage there might be.

Jason leans forward, and our sore noses brush, but it's the closest we can get to intimacy at the moment, so that makes it perfect. "Gotta keep you on your toes, baby... and later, your back." He tries to wink and fails miserably.

A crash from somewhere in the building sets my spidey senses on overdrive as terror takes hold. "That'll be the cavalry. A little late, but at least they came."

Jason moves to stagger toward the door, and I reach my damaged hand out to him. "Wait." He turns and meets my stare.

I almost lost him. Not for the first time. He nearly lost me. Not for the first time. If I've learned anything in the last twenty-eight years, it's that life waits for no one. It's a roller coaster ride with no maintenance, poised to go off the rails at any moment. All we can do is hold the fuck on and try to find some happiness along the way.

He is my happiness. He is my reason. He is my person.

"Marry me?" My question weaves its way through the stillness of the moment.

I can't keep holding myself back out of fear. Sometimes

marriages don't work out, and that sucks, but women have been able to ask for a no-fault divorce since 1969. I refuse to let fear of the unknown rule my actions any longer.

I have an amazing man who not only says how much he loves me but fucking shows me, day in and day out. He walks the walk. He doesn't try to change me or treat me like I'm a fragile artifact to be displayed and admired but never handled. He sees me. He's always seen me. And he's still here. After everything. All my faults, all my shitty choices, my bitchy attitude. He sails through all of it with love and acceptance shining in his eyes. Eyes that I want to see in our baby one day. Eyes that I want to wake up to for the rest of my life.

"Marry me." I alter my question to a demand. He doesn't get the choice. I'm laying my claim permanently. I've licked him; he's mine. I don't make the rules.

"I thought you'd never ask." He attempts a smile as he accepts my proposal. God, I hope we come up with a better story to tell when people ask us about our origin. It's fucked six ways from Sunday.

"Did you guys just get engaged surrounded by carnage and death?" Jacobs huffs out a laugh. And not for the first time; I wonder just how much bad shit he's seen to always be so unfazed by everything.

"Fucking A right." I retort but keep my eyes pierced into my fiance. My fucking fiance. I'm going to marry this man. Holy shit. I can't wait to tell Savvy about this.

Chapter 49

February 2017

Charlotte

Oblique fracture to the right pointer finger. Orbital rim fracture to the left eye. Lacerations to both wrists and ankles. Several burns from a high-voltage transfer. Multiple superficial cuts and bruises throughout the body. Vaginal trauma. A chipped tooth and a fucking partridge in a pear tree.

I'm really over waking up in hospital beds. But at least this time, I know the person who tried to kill me is no longer a threat. I know this time, there will not be someone pressuring me for information while dangling my freedom in front of me. No, this time, I wake with hope and eagerness for the future.

Most of my trauma is internal and not physical, so the doctor wants to keep me for one to two days, and then he'll release me to lick my wounds at home.

My rugged caveman got the shit rocked out of his face piece but don't worry; the doctor assured me he will be fine as hell again... eventually.

They already discharged Jason after patching up his cuts, giving him some pain relief and an ice pack. Lucky fucker.

I, on the other hand, have refused pain relief for obvious reasons. When I was first admitted, they ran all the standard tests. Drugs, rape... all the fun stuff. I tested positive for an older version of AstraMalum, cocaine, and a high-powered sedative.

"Knock, knock," my nurse says with all the chipperness one should not possess this early in the morning.

"For God's sake, Betty, we've been over this. Saying 'knock, knock' does not negate the need for the action. What if I was flicking the bean in here?" I sassily reply.

"Oh shush, grumpy pants. I come baring gifts!" I lunge, as much as I can, for the proffered caffeinated gold in her hand. She holds it just out of reach and winks. "You think you would be the first patient to be caught masturbating? Ha!"

My good eye rolls as I snatch the coffee cup and take a sip, letting out a moan as the elixir of the woken slides down my throat.

"I also brought you a visitor. Well, two technically."

I'm about to ask her why she's being so cagey when she steps out and wheels my best friend inside. She spins Savvy to face me and brings the wheelchair as close to my side as it can get, locks the wheels in place, and waves as she exits.

"Always trying to steal my thunder, aren't you, Savs? A girl can't even get kidnapped, drugged, nearly raped, and murdered without you jumping in to hog the spotlight."

"Ah, yes. It was all part of my master plan. Pre-eclampsia and I are tight like that. We staged a coup. High blood pressure, dangerous O2 levels, and an emergency c-section. All to upstage you." She mock whispers with one hand cupping her mouth like she's telling a secret and the other hand cradling my newest nephew.

We chat and exchange battle stories from our recent tousles with staying in the land of the living. She wasn't surprised at all that I asked Jason to marry me. Even now, in the light of day and sobriety, I stand by my proposal. How could she know that was going to happen? I didn't even know. Maybe she does know me better than I know myself sometimes.

After a while, Nurse Betty returns to take Savvy and un-named baby Channing back to their room. I order some super bland meatloaf but scarf the shit out of it as if it were a steak and lobster dinner. With a full belly and a light heart, I drift off.

When I wake, it's to my fiance sitting beside me with one hand in mine and the other scrolling his phone. I watch him in silence. Taking in his presence and staving off the memories of almost losing him.

"I'm here, baby." He says in response to my internal meltdown that he's somehow attuned to.

"I know." And I do.

I clear my throat and shake off the sudden onslaught of nerves at what I need to tell him. "Jace? So there's something I want to do. Well, need would be a better word. I guess I don't *need to*; it's not like I'll die if I don't. It's just a feeling that I won't be okay until I do. Does that make sense?"

Jason chuckles and sets his phone off to the side. "No. It doesn't. You're babbling, Sweets. Spit it out. What's up?"

I blow out a long breath and say what's been on my mind since finding out the truth. "I want to write a letter to Zach." There. I said it. It's out there in the universe.

I don't really know what I was expecting his response to be. Anger? Irritation? Jealousy? All of those crossed my mind. The one thing I didn't give any thought to... was acceptance.

Jason nods his head in agreement. "I think that's a great idea, baby. I'll give you some privacy and grab an envelope and some stamps. Be back soon." He presses a kiss to my forehead while I am still staring at him, stunned. Okay... well, that was... okay.

Zach,

You didn't know it, but I once told myself that the first letter I wrote to you would be the last. Don't worry, you're not crazy. I never sent it. It was a therapy thing. ANYWAYS...

I'm not really sure what my goal with this letter is other than absolving any residual guilt or bad blood between us.

I'll spare you the gory details—and trust me, they are gory—but I know the truth of what happened in college.

I want you to know two things:

1. *It wasn't your fault*
2. *I'm sorry*

I should've known by the look in your eyes that day at my dorm, the pure agony across your face, and the emptiness in your soul. You hated yourself. You may still.

We can't change the past; what's done is done, but I needed you to know that I forgive you. I forgive you for breaking my heart, for moving on, and for the horrific words you said to me at the reunion.

I see it now—the hurt, the pain, the self-loathing. I've been where you are, Zach; you know that. You don't deserve to stay in that place of destruction and recklessness. You are worthy of good. Hell, great even.

Please stop punishing yourself. Get some help. Lay off the booze. Stop sticking your dick in anything willing. And for God's sake, get a haircut, you hippy.

I've said it to myself, but now, I say it to you: I wish nothing but the best for you. I hope you're happy. And if you're not happy, I hope you allow yourself to get there.

You and I were always meant to cross paths. I truly believe that. I'll never regret you. You will always be a great love of my life.

Thank you, Zach. Thank you for all the love you've given me, for caring, for listening, and for wrapping your arms around me that day in the woods so long ago.

You changed my life. You gave me a reason to stick around when all I saw were exit signs.

Be good to yourself. Find your peace.

Love, Charlie— Forever your Little Bit.

* * *

Settling back home feels oddly okay. Like I didn't just spend a week being held against my will and didn't participate in the possible murder of who I thought was a friend. I really hope I'm not so fucked up and jaded that human life is meaningless to me... nah, just kidding. There haven't been two more deserving people of life's final fuck you.

I will lose no sleep over their deaths. But unfortunately, I will, and have lost sleep over their actions.

I don't like to play the "what if" game, but sometimes, I can't help it. What if I never went to AU? I wouldn't have met

Rebecca and put Zach in her sights. What if Priest was never gunned down in front of us? Zach might not have started a long-term drinking problem. But the one that stings the most... what if Zach and I stayed together?

Don't get me wrong, that ship has sailed, crashed into an iceberg, and currently resides at the bottom of the Mariana Trench. But what if? What would that have looked like? Would he have been drafted into the NFL and made me his trophy wife?

In the words of a wise TV Doctor: "If ifs and buts were candy and nuts, we'd all have a merry Christmas."

Writing that letter lifted a heavy mental weight, one that I thought I had rid myself of years ago. Keeping with our honesty policy, I offered Jason the letter to read. He declined, saying it was private and he trusted me. But it was more than that for me. I know that he knows I love him. He also knows I loved Zach. But I wanted him to know how that love has evolved.

I don't know if Zach will respond to my letter. I hope he gets it. I have no idea where he lives now, so I sent it to his mother's house. I'm not sure if I want him to respond or even what good it would do. But I don't get to decide what helps someone heal. If he needs additional closure, I won't rob him of that.

I know Jason still worries about me. We banter and tease, but I see him watching me sometimes. I worry, too. Sometimes, the bad days come out of nowhere, fast and hard. But I'm stronger now than I have been in the past. I've accepted the things that have led me to this point in my life. I've surrounded myself with a family of my choosing. I always try to take the next right step.

Which brings me to the request I made earlier today. My only minute, sliver, or even hint of remorse around Rebecca's death is the welfare of her child. Did she even have one? I wasn't around to know if she took the pregnancy to term or if she was ever pregnant at all.

I asked Jason to look into where that child is now and if it does indeed exist. Did I just contribute to taking a loving mother away from her baby? That would be a hard pill to swallow— no pun intended.

I've spent most of my life walking in the dark, alone. Always alone. But what I couldn't see at the time was that I had made it that way. The darkness couldn't be helped, but having company could have. I chose to shut out anyone who could've been dragged down with me. I became an island. An unstable, unreliable, sinking island.

I can't change my past, but maybe someone else can learn from my mistakes. That's why I do what I do. I see myself reflected in the kids' faces every day. The addiction. The mental struggles. The rage. The loneliness. The hopelessness. The self-hate. They need to know there's a better way. That someone does care and will be there every step of the way. Someone who sees them, understands them, and cares. Not just care for the short time they are in the facility or transitional house, but forever. Like Emily, every one of these kids leaves with my card and the knowledge that they can reach out any time.

So, north to the future, then. I never thought I'd say this, but it looks like I need to start planning my wedding.

Chapter 50

May 4th, 2018- 1 Day Before Wedding

Jason

The smell of green soap permeates the air and the steady hum of hundreds of needles dipped in ink traces meaning into my skin. Decorating my temple always brings a sense of calm over me.

I once sent Charlie several sketches. She thought they were just random doodles. That couldn't have been farther from the truth. Each one was carefully designed with the knowledge that one day, I would bring them to life on the tapestry of my skin.

I started with her lips on the left side of my neck and the Valkyrie with her initials on my thigh. And over the last few years, I've added a full back piece. The Celtic cross with the Latin phrase "Ad Astra Per Aspera" *Through suffering to the stars,* takes up a majority of the real estate on my back, running down my spine. On the left side of my chest is a regal set of angel wings with a crown and a trinity symbol resting safely beneath the cocoon of feathers.

My choice for today is one that I started designing long ago

309

but only recently finished. Charlie hasn't seen this drawing, and I didn't want her to until tomorrow. Was it the smartest plan to get a pretty large tattoo over my ribs down my left side the day before my wedding? Probably not. But this was the only option if I wanted it to be a surprise.

When the artist finishes cleaning me up, I head to the full-length mirror to check it out. A large pocketwatch covered in a frame of traditional-style roses lays across a backdrop of stars, most notably the Big Dipper. The time on the clock is set to 5:05— May 5th. Our wedding date.

Everyone has asked all the typical pre-wedding questions:

Am I sure? Yes.

Am I ready? Yes.

Any reservations? Not a single one.

Am I happy? Absofuckinglutely.

Charlotte asked for a small, intimate wedding. What my girl wants, she gets. Although, I was really relieved to hear her say that. I don't want to see a bunch of acquaintances or people I don't give a shit about on such a momentous occasion. I want our people there. That's all that matters.

Unlike other little girls, my girl never imagined her wedding. She didn't play dress up or have themes picked out before she was barely old enough to understand the concept. She didn't think she'd ever get married.

But I did. Charlotte thinks the first time we met was the first time I saw her. That's not necessarily true. About two weeks before that, my parents had a huge fight, and I couldn't take it anymore, so I stormed out and started walking aimlessly around town. It was pretty late, so there weren't many cars and next to no people walking.

I ended up at this small hill in the center of town; it's what everyone refers to as the "sled hill." So I sat there on the hill, wondering why the fuck my parents don't get divorced already. Why would people sign up to be fucking miserable forever? I started sketching some random patterns, just letting my creativity flow without a plan. It's what I do to calm down.

There was no wind that night. The air was so still that any little noise was amplified in a sound wave straight up to me. As I was shading, I heard the sweetest, off-key rendition of a Staind song. Something about being right here waiting. A small blonde bopped her way through the park, singing her heart out to no one. The pain in her voice was palpable, and I felt it deep in my gut. I almost went to her, but a car pulled up with a very loud girl shouting about some guy named Charles.

I remember wondering if anyone saw the pain she put behind the lyrics or if they simply stopped at the pretty face on the surface.

Imagine my surprise when a couple of weeks later, fate throws me right back in her orbit. Only this time, I would go after her.

And I'll continue to go after her for the rest of our lives.

* * *

Jacobs sulks in the corner while Asher, Cal, and Jensen set up the poker table. He's been married for years, and still, he's pouting because I refuse to go to a strip club. Jenna would rip his balls off if he dared. I have a sneaking suspicion that he wouldn't have actually gone but just wanted to be invited so he could play the hero and turn it down.

"How's it feel to be the last one to get locked down?" Asher asks as he passes out the poker chips.

I take a small pull from my beer bottle. "Feels no different than it did 14 years ago. I've got the girl I love. Nothing's changed, except now I've convinced her to take my last name."

The guys chuckle and nod. I'm not shy about how I feel about my wife—fuck, I like the sound of that. None of us are. I think that's why we get along so well. Ash and Cal immediately felt like brothers. We shared a possessive spirit that at first had us on a razor's edge with each other until we discovered that we were well and truly whipped by our women.

Jensen was a harder sell. Logically I know that one kiss and a distance of twelve years doesn't mean shit. They have been professional, friendly, and not sexual for infinitely longer than a short-lived crush.

He's a good dude, though. And he's kept the only secret I've harbored from Charlotte in many years.

When I turned twenty-five, I gained full access to my trust fund. That wasn't really a secret. Charlie just never cared about money. It means shit to her, which makes me love her all the more. But, also makes her very stubborn when it comes to asking or accepting help.

That leads us to the secret. I'm the anonymous investor for Ellie's House. I put up the funds, but I made sure every scrap of paperwork was in her name. She owns all assets outright. She would've never taken it from me if I had simply offered. So I take this to my grave—well, mine and Jensen's. I may have threatened him with just a little death if he broke our covenant.

"Are you worried that the ex might show up and object?" Cal teases.

My hand flaps on the table, and I glare at him. "Well, I fucking wasn't!" I grab a handful of popcorn and toss it at his face. "Dick."

In all honesty, I'm not concerned about that at all. Not that he couldn't show up, I guess he could. It wouldn't make a difference, though. Charlotte is mine. We were each other's firsts, and we'll be each other's lasts.

Our story could never end any other way.

Chapter 51

May 5th, 2018- Wedding Day

Charlotte

As I watch the strands lift and fall over and over, I can't help but reflect on how we got here. I'm getting married today. *Married. Me.*

I met my future husband at a very dark and impressionable time in my life, in both of our lives. We were two broken souls on a course for a crash collision— and crash we did. Spectacularly.

Our beginning was so beautiful, poetic even. Our middle sucked ass. But our ending? It's going to be glorious.

I've grown up with this man in every sense of the word. We've experienced things that put couples at a fork in the road. You can grow together, or you can grow apart. We fought to keep things going, and we'll continue to fight for us every day for the rest of our lives.

He's seen every dark part of my soul. The tainted edges. The violent middle. The gluttonous filling. All of me. And still, he chooses me— and I, him.

I never heard back from Zach, but that's okay. I've let that part of my life go. I had to in order to fully move on and give Jason my whole, damaged heart. I got the closure I needed from that chapter in my life, and I hope he does, too.

The guys were joking the other day about whether any exes would show up at our ceremony. There's a snowball's chance in hell that happens. But even if it did, nothing would change our minds. We were always meant to end up here together.

A stray tear breaks loose before I can stop it. I wish my mom were here. She's missed nearly every milestone in my life. She would've loved Jason. Amelia Johnson always had a keen sense of character. She could sniff out a pure heart like a bloodhound.

She would've been the most amazing grandma. When our newest family member arrives, they will know all about Grandma Ellie.

Sadly, I have still not been able to conceive naturally. My body just isn't having it. It took me a long time to make peace and realize this opens another window of opportunity. The Emilys of the world need a safe, loving, and permanent home—one where they don't live in fear and feel love and affection bone deep. Jason and I agree; we'd love to adopt.

Speaking of Emily, the beautiful, kind-hearted sister of my choosing has offered to be a surrogate for us should we want to pursue avenues of biological children as well. I love her for that. Maybe one day. But for now, I want to give all my time and attention to our first child. Because they will be ours in every sense of the word. As I've learned over and over in my life, blood does not equal family.

Ari blots my tears away with a tissue. "Aw, Charlie. Are these happy tears or sad tears?" she asks while covering the tear track with more powder.

A small smile curves up my lips. "Both. I was thinking about my mom." I'm not quite ready to share our family expansion plans with my friends. Not because I think they'd judge or criticize, but because I want to make sure everything is ready to go before bringing more people into it.

The door rips open, and Savvy bursts through. Our eyes meet in the mirror, and she nods her head vigorously as she begins rummaging through her purse. "I knew it. I'm prepared."

A huff of laughter comes out before I can ask. "You knew what, Savs?"

"That you were going to pull a Runaway Bride moment. I parked the car at the front of the line of cars. I packed a smoke bomb to create a distraction so we could make a clean getaway. Here—" she throws a bundle of clothes at me. "Tear off that godawful dress and put these on. Better for running."

I roll my eyes and throw the bundle at her face. She bursts out laughing and collapses in the camping chair beside me. Wind rolls across the canvas of the tent we're in. "Jesus Savs. First, there is not going to be any running anywhere. And second, this is your fucking dress, and I know you love the damn thing. So, shut your cake hole."

"Oh my *God*, how good do cake holes sound right now?" Savvy groans, and Ari and I shoot each other a look.

"Savannah Nova Mitchell-Channing." I snap out at my best friend. My *glowing* best friend.

"Yes?" she asks flippantly, studying her nails. Purposefully avoiding eye contact with both of us.

"Is your eggo preggo?" I ask and quirk a brow at her when she finally looks up at me.

A sheepish look, unnaturally takes its place on her face. "Today is about you. We can talk about me tomorrow."

"Like hell! We will talk about it now. Am I about to become an aunt for the fourth time?" I demandingly ask, injecting faux anger to tamp down my excitement. I love being an aunt. Her two and Ari's kids are the joys of my life. Also, it's my way to get back at Savvy for all the shit she's done over the years.

She punched me in the tit? I give her kids chocolate for breakfast.

She ripped my favorite sweater in the sixth grade? I give the kids permanent markers.

She laid her head on my future husband's lap fourteen years ago? I give the kids noisy toys that need a screwdriver to remove the battery. And then hide said screwdriver.

Savvy nods. Ari and I both squeal and launch ourselves at her in a weird group bear hug. "Shh! You heifers know these tents have paper-thin walls. Ash doesn't know yet. I just found out a few days ago, and I wanted to do something special to tell him. Like maybe spray paint it on his new car or something."

We all laugh. "He really hit the jackpot with you, Savs. It takes a special person to put up with your shit. My hat is off to Asher for taking it on."

"Ladies, are we ready?" Mary pops her head into the tent. She graciously took on the position of wedding coordinator. She knows me well, and I think she did a fabulous job keeping things quaint and breathtaking.

My hands glide down the front of my borrowed wedding dress. The white lace tickles my fingertips as I reach the baby blue sash around my waist. I give it a sharp tug, making sure it doesn't fly off when I step out. Ari bends down to verify the laces on my brand-new, all-white Chuck Ts are tight. Savvy fluffs my hair and adjusts the chain on my mother's grandmother's necklace.

Savvy hands me a small bouquet of Eggplant Calla Lillies with an elegant spotting of Forget-Me-Nots. She swats my ass and nods at Mary, who pulls the tent door open for us to exit. We file out with Savvy behind me and Ari behind her.

The breeze flutters across my face, and I close my eyes, inhale the crisp air, and smile.

I'm getting married today.

* * *

Jason

The moment she steps out, Charlotte steals my breath away. Her long, blonde hair flows around her face. Errant strands float among the slight breeze. Her ivory gown hugs every curve that I've become intimately acquainted with over our years together.

A metal instrumental version of *I Choose You By Sara Bareilles* begins as she makes her way down the aisle to me. I hold back the tears that prick the back of my eyes as we make eye contact. She blows a kiss to me, and I shoot her a wink. She saunters her way toward me with her best friends trailing her.

Our nieces and nephews stand on each side of the aisle and toss handfuls of leaves at their feet as they pass. I can't help but imagine our little one standing beside them one day.

We kept things small and intimate, just wanting our inner circle present for the official joining of our lives. On my side sits my mom, Alex, and his boyfriend, Jacobs and Jenna, Lowkowski and her husband. On Charlie's side are Mary, Ash, Cal, Jensen, and his wife, Emily, Reggie, Sariah, and Willow. But front and center sits an empty chair decorated with a picture, hot pink glitter, and sparklers in honor of Ellie.

Grayson stands at my side, ready to officiate the ceremony. I was pretty shocked that Charlie asked him to do that. They've mended their relationship over the years, but even if you try to glue a broken plate back together, the cracks are still visible.

Charlie reaches the end of the aisle and hugs Savvy and Ari before they take their seats. She pauses at the empty chair, whispering words to her mom as she lays the bouquet down on the seat. She presses a kiss to her fingertips and places them against the photo of Ellie.

Her eyes shine when they meet mine again. I hold my hand out for her, holding back my own emotions that threaten to burst through. She clasps her hand in mine and stands beside me.

Grayson reads from the paper we picked up at the courthouse—the one with the cookie-cutter vows since we "agreed" not to write our own. I rub my thumbs against her hands, our eyes never leaving each other as we agree to all the promises.

Grayson clears his throat, "The groom has a few vows of his own he'd like to share today. Jason?" Charlie's head snaps from her dad to me, and I grin at her while pulling a folded piece of paper out of my pocket.

"Don't worry, Sweets, I'll keep it brief. I've always believed in actions over lip service, so yes, I promise all of these things. I vow myself to you, now and always. But more than words, I vow to show you every day, to walk the walk, to validate your choice in me. I will love you long after your beloved stars burn out. I'll love you harder than the pull of a black hole. Eternity isn't long enough, but for as long as forever lasts, you will be a part of me."

I carefully unfold the paper and hand it to her. Tears collapse from her lashes as she takes in the drawing. "Jace..." She whispers.

"Forever, baby."

Chapter 52

May 5th, 2018 – Wedding Day

Charlotte

The paper sits heavily in my hands. The weight of its words twist and wind around my heart, permanently etching themselves in the very core of my being.

Caw.

Caw.

Caw.

The sound draws my attention to my bench, where a harbinger of darkness and endings perches. His onyx eyes bore into me, and I smile back at him.

The thing about ravens is that they don't only symbolize death and finality like I once believed. They also symbolize the duality of existence: good and bad, light and dark, beginning and end.

He may have been a witness to some of the darkest days behind me, but he came back to show me the light. No longer do I crave to walk the edge of the cliff and peer down at destruction.

I'll always bear the scars of my past, but they don't decide my future.

"Charlie-bear? Did you have anything you wanted to add?" Dad asks, pulling my focus away from the guardian of my dreams.

"Well, since we had agreed *not* to do this, I have nothing prepared. So, I'll just say: Ditto, my love."

We exchange rings. Jason accidentally sticks it on my middle finger for a brief moment before realizing his mistake. The nerves are getting the best of him. Everyone chuckles, and Dad brings things to a close. "By the power vested in me by some weirdo with a porn stache at the courthouse, I now pronounce you husband and wife! Jason, you may now *respectfully* kiss your new bride."

My husband smirks at my dad and gives him a look, saying, "*Yeah, okay.*" He steps forward and slides both hands along the sides of my face, locking his fingers through my hair. His eyes search mine, and I grip his wrists. "I love you, Charlotte."

"I love you, babes. Now, put those lips on me, and it had better be the furthest thing from respectful. Sorry, Dad! Close your eyes."

Jason does not disappoint. His mouth crashes into mine, an exchanging of silent vows with each movement of lips. Sealing his promises with flicks of his tongue against mine. Cheers and hollers erupt around us.

All too soon, he pulls back and rests his forehead against mine. "Come, wife. We have our whole lives to get to."

I place my hand in his as I look across the expanse of Sky Ridge. For as long as I can recall, this place has been a source of solace for me. I've retreated here when I needed to lick my wounds. I've carved my pain into my table. I've screamed. I've cried. I've lusted. All from the one place that's always felt right to me.

Now, it has even greater significance. I've married my best friend here. We've taken all the pain, hurt, and devastation and intertwined it with love, joy, and hope, creating the ties that will bind us together forever.

"We're married, bitches!" I scream to the air and walk with my husband to our truck. I guess we needed a getaway vehicle after all.

I clutch the paper he handed me and gaze down at it one more time. A vibrant smile takes over my face, and I look at my soul's mate. Fuck, I love this man.

A sharp gust of wind swirls around us. Ribbons of air wrap around the paper and carry it off into the open horizon, where promises and truths live eternally.

Never did I think that punching some douche in the face would lead to this moment. But I would knock Chad out over and over for eternity if it always brought me to him. My love. My twin flame. My Jason.

The dark boy with the secret notebook who saw me...heard me...chose me.

The End.

I SEE YOU
I HEAR YOU
I CHOOSE YOU

Epilogue

Present Day 2024

Charlotte

"Charlotte, you are a saint! Thank you for filling in on such short notice."

I smile at Susan, the office manager of Aurora North, the adult treatment facility. "Of course, I'm happy to help. How many residents were lined up for Kathleen?" Kathleen is the lead therapist of this facility. She's extremely reliable and dedicated to her work, but apparently, her appendix had other plans today. We've filled in for each other as needed over the years for vacations, sickness, school plays... that sort of thing.

Susan shuffles through a pile of papers on her desk before pulling one out. "We were able to reschedule everyone who has a standing appointment. The only ones we couldn't change are the mandatory court-appointed slots."

"Sounds good. How many of those do we have?" As long as I'm out of here by 6:15 pm, I'll make it to the airport on time. I'm so fucking proud of Reggie for making his dreams come true. His very first movie premiere, and he wants to bring me!

"Just one! He should be here any second. I have his file here somewhere, just a moment." Susan ducks behind her desk and flips through more papers, drawers, and her briefcase. I

325

leave her to it and enter Kathleen's office.

The contrast between the two spaces is staggering. Susan is a whirlwind of disorganized chaos, while Kathleen is the polar opposite—organized, minimalist, and attentive.

I take a seat behind the desk, and finally, Susan scurries into the room. A bead of sweat dots her brow, and she hands me the file with a small smile of embarrassment. I flip the file open, and a piece of paper shoots out of it and drifts under the desk. But there should be way more information in this folder.

"Susan? I don't think this is the right folder. There's nothing but one paper in it. Can you check again, please?" I shout to her while standing to search for my own rogue parchment.

Maybe there's something on Kathleen's desk I can check. "What's the resident's name?" I ask, eyeing the paper that has slid partially under the filing cabinet. *Of course, it has.*

"Matthews? Michaels? Uh... no. Maybe Mathers?" she huffs, continuing her search through the chaos of her desk.

"Morris." A deep southern drawl crawls up my spine, and I freeze. In an unfortunate position, with my ass in the air as I reach for the paper. My fingers brush against it. I close my eyes and pull it closer to me. When I open them and look down, I find it's not a paper at all. It's a mug shot. "Well. Ain't this somethin'? I'd recognize that juicy peach anywhere. Hey, Little Bit."

My fingers curl around the picture of a man with sandy blonde hair and bloodshot emerald eyes. I take a deep breath before slapping on a professional mask and standing. Looking at my ex-boyfriend for the first time in thirteen years, I barely recognize him. His looks haven't changed too much, but his spirit has.

Like I've always been able to, I see the lifelessness behind his charming smile. "Zach." I say and gesture toward the chair opposite Kathleen's desk. He makes a show of following my direction, and I choke down the curse that wants to come out at him being a prick.

Susan runs in with the correct folder, mutters her apologies, and closes the door behind her. She then makes her way back to her desk, which is an abyss.

I take a moment to flip through his file, familiarizing myself with his history while also taking a much-needed moment to gather my thoughts.

Three DUIs.

Six arrests in fifteen years. Mostly for public intoxication. A few for public indecency.

"Do you know why you're here, Mr. Morris?" I ask, proud that my voice comes out steady and unbothered.

He snickers at my professional greeting. "Well, Miss Johnson, I reckon it's because I put that fuckin' Honda through someone's fence... again."

He thinks this is funny? He could've killed someone. The complete lack of remorse is unbelievable. "You are here for me to determine appropriate action. Will you be admitted to Aurora North, complete the rehabilitation program, and become a functioning member of society? Or will you be going to prison?" I eye him critically and raise a brow. "That is up to me. And it's *Mrs.* Donovan." I lift my left hand and let my wedding ring hang between us.

Zach simply stares at me, his face an expressionless mask. *What happened to you?*

"I was never good enough for you. You wanna know what happened to me? I accepted that. I let you go. And I've been chasin' death ever since." He sighs, pressing his palm to his eyes.

I don't know what to say.

"What happened to your wife?" I finally ask.

A bark of laughter escapes him. "Mel? Well, it seems like she didn't care for the countless women I fucked, but she stuck around for the money. Until my Papaw cut me off. When she realized her comfy lifestyle was well and truly down the shitter, she bailed."

"I'm sorry, Zach." I whisper. And I mean it. I had hoped he was living a great life. Filled with happiness, babies, football, and video games. All the things he loved and saw for himself. Minus me.

"You really mean that, don't you?" he asks in wonderment.

I nod. "I do. I meant what I said in my letter. I never wanted this for you."

"Letter?" His face pulls back, and he looks at me with confusion and knitted brows.

I cock my head to the side. "Did you not get it?"

Zach shakes his head slowly back and forth like he's combing through the alcohol-hazed memories to verify.

"Oh." I say, deflated.

"What did you say?" His voice comes out small, young, timid.

I lean back in the office chair and blink at the ceiling. It's not that I don't know the words. I do. But I wrote them thinking he was happy. I don't want it to seem like I'm rubbing my life in his face. Especially knowing how rough it's been. He doesn't need a full recap. Just the important parts.

"I know you didn't cheat on me. I know Rebecca drugged you and assaulted you. Rape. She raped you. I wrote that I wanted you to know it wasn't your fault. And that I forgive you for everything, up to and including your evisceration of me at the reunion."

"Men don't get raped, sweetheart. Clearly, my dick was into it." He retorts, but there's no heat behind it. It's like he feels like he has to keep this hardened front up. But he doesn't. Not with me.

I stand and round the desk, inserting myself between him and it. "Listen to me. What she did to you is assault. You were not able to consent. You thought she was me. That's rape, Zach."

His brows slowly fall and scrunch together. "But... I was hard..."

I probably shouldn't but I feel a need to broach the physical connection between us, I place my hand in his. He immediately latches on and squeezes while looking at me like I have the guillotine rope in my hands and will take him out at any moment.

"It's a physical response, Zach. That means nothing. You did nothing wrong, do you hear me? That was not your fault."

Tears well in his eyes, and my heart fractures. I know what it feels like to accept these things as truth for yourself. It's soul-crushing. But we get through it. We move forward. "I'm so sorry, Charlie." His voice cracks on my name, and we reach for each other at the same time. I cradle his head against my stomach while he latches his arms around my legs.

"I'm sorry. For everything. For what you've been through. None of this would've happened if I had stayed away from you in high school. I ruined your life. I'm so fucking sorry, Zach." I sob, and he clutches the bottom of my sweater tightly.

"I'm gonna find her and fuckin' kill her." He forces out, and my heart sinks again. This could go a couple of different ways. We did what we had to do to keep ourselves alive and safe from that lunatic, but I've killed someone. No matter what, that's bound to change his perspective of me.

"You don't have to worry about her. Ever again." Is all I say. He nods against my legs. I hope he really does just let any vendetta he may have go. She's no longer a threat to anybody. The kid wasn't Zach's, and Rebecca had signed away all parental rights at the birth to the dad.

After a few long moments, he pulls away first and wipes the remnants of tears away. I go back to my chair, and we just watch each other for a minute. "I don't want this for you. Will you let me help you? Rehab or prison, Zach? Which will it be?"

Zach runs a hand through his hair and lets out a long breath. "Rehab, Little Bit... I'll take rehab."

Afterword

Wow. I can't believe we've finished Charlotte's journey. It's been a hell of a ride full of ups, downs, and craziness.

Thank you so much for taking a chance on my stories. I appreciate all the readers and indie authors who have cheered me on from the start.

A huge thank you to Brandi, Jennifer, LeAnn, Mikayla, Nicole, and Rachel for being a part of my Alpha and Beta teams. You ladies have been such a huge help, and I've enjoyed getting to know you all over the last year. Also, shout out to all the ARC readers! Thank you for volunteering your time and giving honest feedback.

I'd also like to thank *my Jason*. We've had a hell of a journey for the last 20 years, filled with some of the same ups, downs, and craziness of Charlotte's world. But I wouldn't have wanted to do life with anyone but you. You are worth it all, and I'd do it again without question. Thank you for always being an unwavering support to any and everything I set out to do. I love you.

NOW, for the Zach girlies. I get it. But it was always going to end this way. As much as we love Zach, he wasn't ready to be a partner. Their chemistry and connection were undeniable, but he's got a lot of work to do on himself. Good news, though! You can watch his journey in his own story: If I Were A Better Man.

I hope everyone is fortunate enough to be loved the way Charlotte is, not just by a partner but also by the family around you. Never settle for things or people who don't enrich and bring peace to your life. Blood doesn't always equal good for you. Sometimes you have to make your own family. But the beauty of being part of a found family is no one is there out of obligation; it's all love and support.

If you've connected to Charlotte's story on a deep level, I'm sorry and thank you. I'm sorry that you've experienced pain, loss, or devastation—maybe all of them. Thank you for staying.

From personal experience, I know how, all too often, mental health struggles can invoke feelings of isolation and despair.

I'm glad you're here.

Suicide Prevention Hotline or Call 988 for additional resources.

If you are struggling with your mental health, you don't have to face your pain alone. Help is available, and there is a path forward, no matter how impossible things may seem right now. Your story is still being written, and there are brighter chapters ahead. Stay.

Join my Facebook reader group for all things Charlotte and upcoming projects. Members get first dibs on ARCs. I post teasers and give exclusive looks at my WIPs and new covers! See you there!

I See You Coralee-Reader Group

For signed paperbacks, visit my website

www.cltaylorbooks.com/store

Follow me on socials for Bookish content
  Tiktok @coraleetaylorauthor
  Instagram @coraleetaylorauthor

More By Coralee Taylor

Ties That Bind Series

1. I See You, Charlotte
2. I Hear You, Charlotte
3. I Choose You, Charlotte

Fated Hearts of River View Series (Standalones)

1. If I Were A Better Man- Zach's Story
2. Supernova- Savvy's Story
3. The Stars Over Norsville- Ari's Story

Milton Keynes UK
Ingram Content Group UK Ltd.
UKHW030955181124
451360UK00006B/628